AFTER WARD

ALSO BY JENNIFER MATHIEU

The Truth About Alice
Devoted

AFTERWARD

JENNIFER MATHIEU

ROARING BROOK PRESS · NEW YORK

Text copyright © 2016 by Jennifer Mathieu
Published by Roaring Brook Press
Roaring Brook Press is a division of Holtzbrinck Publishing Holdings Limited
Partnership
175 Fifth Avenue, New York, New York 10010
fiercereads.com

Library of Congress Cataloging-in-Publication Data

Names: Mathieu, Jennifer, author.
Title: Afterward : a novel / Jennifer Mathieu.
Description: First edition. | New York : Roaring Brook Press, 2016. |
    Summary: When eleven-year-old Dylan Anderson is kidnapped,
    his subsequent rescue leads to the discovery of Ethan Jorgensen,
    who had disappeared four years earlier, and now Dylan's sister
    Caroline befriends Ethan and wants to learn the truth about her
    autistic brother's captivity.
Identifiers: LCCN 2016004764 | ISBN 9781626722385 (hardback)
Subjects: | CYAC: Kidnapping—Fiction. | Missing children—Fiction. |
    Friendship—Fiction. | Brothers and sisters—Fiction. |
    Autism—Fiction. | Memory—Fiction.
Classification: LCC PZ7.M4274 Af 2016 | DDC [Fic]—dc23
LC record available at https://lccn.loc.gov/2016004764

Our books may be purchased in bulk for promotional, educational, or
business use. Please contact your local bookseller or the Macmillan
Corporate and Premium Sales Department at (800) 221-7945 ext. 5442
or by e-mail at MacmillanSpecialMarkets@macmillan.com.

First edition 2016
Book design by Elizabeth H. Clark
Printed in the United States of America
1 3 5 7 9 10 8 6 4 2

For Michaela Joy Garecht
and all those who have yet to come home

dearmichaela.com

CAROLINE — BEFORE

MY MOTHER TAKES THE VASE FROM THE BOOKSHELF AND HURLS IT, smashing it to bits by my father's bare feet. My father doesn't even step back as the tiny pink and white pieces of ceramic skid past him on the hardwood floor. He just stands there, staring.

"Dylan! Dylan, where are you!" My mother shrieks my brother's name and collapses into the mess she's just made.

I've never heard my mother yell like this. Like the yell has crawled from the base of her feet and up her spine and forced itself out of her mouth. Like it's coming from some other planet. Her screams are especially scary because they're so different from the calm and collected way she behaved just moments ago when the police arrived. They came to say they don't know anything new. That they don't have the slightest idea where Dylan might be.

My mother nodded numbly, but as soon as she shut the door after them, she started to scream.

My father crouches down next to her on the floor, but when he tries to put his arms around her, she shrugs him off and spreads herself flat, kicking the pieces of broken vase out behind her with her feet and sending them spinning wildly out in front of her with her hands.

My grandmother and aunt run in from the kitchen, and as the anxious huddle around my mother grows, I slip down the hallway toward my bedroom, even though I don't understand how my body is managing to move at all.

Since my little brother disappeared four days ago, I'm actually not sure how we've all managed to stay alive much less move. My mother isn't eating, and my father isn't sleeping. I've done a little bit of both, but barely. Now I make it inside my bedroom and shut the door, then crawl into my unmade bed. I'm still dressed in my Violent Femmes T-shirt and butterfly-patterned pajama pants that I've been wearing since Saturday. I've got on the same underpants from that day, too, if you want to know the truth. My parents haven't changed clothes either, or brushed their teeth or combed their hair. It's like we've been frozen in that moment when we first realized Dylan was missing. And I mean scary, terrible missing. Not lost in the woods missing, which is bad enough. But taken missing. Kidnapped missing.

Burying my head under my pillow, I decide to count to one

hundred and tell myself that by the time I'm finished, we'll have found Dylan alive.

"One . . . two . . . three . . ." I whisper.

With my whole heart I will the police to call our house or ring our doorbell with good news.

"Four . . . five . . . six."

I imagine some nice lady ordering a pizza and seeing the neon yellow MISSING flyer with Dylan's picture pasted on the pizza box—the one where he's wearing his sweet toothy grin and his favorite cartoon space alien T-shirt—and then I imagine her looking out the window and spotting Dylan standing in her front yard, just waiting to be found.

"Seven . . . eight . . . nine."

I fantasize that one of the many made up, hair sprayed, honey-voiced television news reporters who've been interviewing my pale, barefooted parents in our family room over and over these past few days runs another story, a story where the right person realizes the right thing and makes the right phone call and my brother, my sweet little brother, comes home safe.

"Ten . . . eleven . . . twelve."

I make it to one hundred, but nothing happens.

ETHAN — BEFORE

ALL IT TAKES IS SOMEONE WHO ISN'T MARTY OPENING THE DOOR OF
the apartment. In the end, it's as simple as that.

Simple. Yeah.

It's not one police officer who shows up but four or five.
They have their guns up like on television and in the movies, and the little kid whose name I don't know and who is sitting next to me on the couch watching me play video games wets himself when they bust in. It's the third time he's pissed himself since Marty brought him here, and the first two times Marty swore and I scrubbed out the kid's pants in the kitchen sink and the kid just walked around making circles with his feet and whimpering.

But this time when he wets himself, I don't move to help him. I don't move at all. Because now the police are here, and they're shouting and asking us who we are, and the little kid is wet and crying and he gets up and runs to the door, and one officer takes him outside and for a split second I'm jealous. Because I don't know if I'm going to get to go, too. And I sit there, my game console still in my hands, the bleeps of the video game speeding up. They're going as fast as my heart is pounding. Suddenly, the electronic beats explode into a sad tune and I die on the screen, but my real heart—the heart inside of me—it's still pumping. I glance at the television and I look at the officers and I don't know what's up or what's down, what's real or what's not.

But my heart is beating, so I've got to be alive.

"What's your name, son?" says one officer. She's a girl. A woman, I mean, with dark hair pulled back into a tight ponytail. There hasn't been a woman in this apartment in all the time I've been here.

I'm trying to catch my breath. I'm trying to speak. Without even realizing I'm doing it, my eyes go to the closet in the corner of the room. The one with the Master Lock on the outside. My tongue fills up my mouth, and I can't answer.

"Son?" she says. Her voice gets a little softer, and I look at her again.

The other officers are racing around the apartment, opening doors, yelling at each other.

"What's your name, sweetheart?"

It's the way she says *sweetheart*. That's what works.

"I'm Ethan," I tell her.

May 25, 2016
HOUSTON, TEXAS.

An 11-year-old boy who disappeared from the town of Dove Lake, Texas, was found alive Wednesday in a Houston apartment complex almost 100 miles away from where he had been abducted, along with a 15-year-old boy kidnapped from the same area in 2012, authorities said.

The boys were found in the Houston apartment of Martin Gulliver, 43, who died of a self-inflicted gunshot when authorities attempted to arrest him at his workplace, Sheriff Joseph Garcia said.

The boys appeared physically unharmed. Dylan Anderson, 11, who has autism, was reunited with his parents and older sister on Wednesday evening. He had been last seen walking in his neighborhood on Saturday afternoon.

An area woman witnessed Dylan walking past her house alone, which she found unusual as she had never seen him outside of his house unsupervised. She told authorities that a few moments later she spotted a black pickup with severe damage to the rear bumper speeding away from the area.

Searchers from Dove Lake and surrounding communities searched on foot and horseback through the night and during the weekend. A break in the case came when Houston authorities were serving a warrant at the apartment complex on an unrelated case and discovered a pickup that matched the description of the vehicle seen near the scene of Dylan's disappearance. A check of the vehicle tags connected the vehicle to Gulliver's apartment.

Garcia says officers were shocked when they entered the apartment and discovered Ethan Jorgenson, 15, who had disappeared from Dove Lake in May of 2012. He had been heading to a friend's house and never arrived.

Ethan was reunited with his parents, Phillip and Megan Jorgenson, on Wednesday evening. In the four years Ethan had been missing, his parents had emptied retirement accounts to hire private investigators in an effort to find their son. Psychics hired by the couple told them their son was most likely dead. Ethan's disappearance served as a cautionary tale in the small community where residents often left doors unlocked and let children play unsupervised in nearby creeks and wooded areas.

"We lost our small town innocence the day Ethan disappeared," said Beth Murphy, a resident who helped organize annual vigils held during the four years Ethan was missing.

After authorities found the boys, police approached Gulliver at his workplace, Gina's Italian Kitchen, where Gulliver had worked as a cook since 2008. According to Garcia, when Gulliver saw the officers approaching, he exited on foot through the back of the restaurant and shot himself with a concealed weapon he had been carrying. He was pronounced dead at Houston's Ben Taub Hospital.

Despite owning a vehicle, Gulliver often walked or took the bus for his shifts at the restaurant, and fellow employees say he rarely missed work. They were unaware of Ethan Jorgenson's presence and believed Gulliver lived alone.

According to Garcia, authorities in Houston and Dove Lake are working together to establish the motive behind the kidnappings. One law enforcement source who wished to remain unidentified said Gulliver lived in Dove Lake briefly as a teenager and may have returned to the town because he was familiar with the area but would not be recognized.

"It's highly unusual for there to be two abductions from the same area by the same perpetrator," said Garcia. "There are a lot of unanswered questions right now. But the most important thing is two boys are back home safe with their families tonight."

Abel Hernandez, 54, who lives at the apartment

complex where the boys were found, said Gulliver was a polite but quiet man who kept to himself. Hernandez said he and other residents assumed Ethan was Gulliver's son, and that the two were regularly seen outside the apartment. According to neighbors, Ethan went by the name Ethan Gulliver. Hernandez said Ethan never appeared frightened of Gulliver and seemed to come and go as he pleased.

"One time I asked him how school was going, and he told me he was going to school online," said Hernandez. "He didn't seem like a kid who'd been kidnapped."

At a brief news conference held Wednesday evening in Dove Lake, both families thanked law enforcement for helping to find their sons.

"We are so grateful to have Ethan back, I can't even express it in words," said a tearful Megan Jorgenson. "We've finally managed to wake up from our nightmare."

Dylan's parents, Andrew and Mindy, were equally thankful as was Dylan's sister, Caroline, 16.

"I want to hold my little brother tight and never let him go," she said to reporters.

ETHAN — 92 DAYS AFTERWARD

THESE ARE THE SOUNDS FROM HOME THAT I HADN'T REALIZED I remembered until I came home after four years and heard them again:

- The yip-yip-yip of Missy the Chihuahua next door
- The clunk-plunk of the ice maker
- My dad's car pulling into the driveway and the thud of the driver's side door shutting, and then exactly eight beats later his keys in the front door
- The sigh my mother makes after she takes her first sip from her nightly cup of Earl Grey decaffeinated tea— how it starts really loud and then gets smaller and smaller like it's running downhill or something
- The theme song to *All Things Considered* on the kitchen radio

- The screech of the garbage truck brakes on Monday
  mornings

All those sounds kept happening while I was gone. The
refrigerator kept making ice. Missy kept barking. The garbage
truck kept stopping. And I wasn't here to hear them.

. . . .

It's been three months since I've come home, and I keep
remembering sounds. And smells. All summer long they've
been coming back to me. As soon as I remember them I
realize I never really forgot them. Maybe I just kept them
somewhere deep inside me that Marty couldn't get to. Which
makes me glad, I guess. But it makes me depressed, too.
Because I realize how much I missed those sounds. Even the
Chihuahua.

These are the smells from home that I hadn't realized I
remembered until I came home after four years and I smelled
them again:

- Fabuloso floor cleaner in lavender that Gloria uses to
  clean our floors
- Yankee Candles in Honeydew Melon and Kitchen
  Spice—my mom orders them in bulk online
- The Irish Spring soap my dad uses in the shower

- The stink of my old gym shoes, which were still in my room four years later even though they didn't fit me anymore, and which still managed to smell like my middle school locker room
- Clean sheets on my bed. I don't even know what Gloria uses to wash them, and I don't care. Clean sheets. I can't tell you how much I fucking appreciate those now.
- Venison-and-pork sausage grilling on the stove top—my dad's favorite on Saturday mornings

Damn, now that I think about it, I could make a whole list of tastes I'd forgotten/secretly remembered.

I've wondered about asking Dr. Greenberg about all of these smells and sounds, but I'm not sure how I'm supposed to phrase the question. Like, is it normal to think about sounds and smells so much, Dr. Greenberg? Do all the other guys that you treat who were kidnapped when they were eleven and a half and then were found after four years also think about sounds and smells? I mean, it's not like there are a lot of us who fit this description. He's probably as clueless as me about to how to deal with me. We've been meeting twice a week for three months now and basically all we talk about is the weather and how I'm sleeping. He always wants to know how I'm sleeping.

My answer is always, "Not so good." Which is why I'm

on one medicine to help me fall asleep and one medicine to help me stay asleep.

Neither one helps me sleep with the lights off, so I have to sleep with them on.

The nights are the worst.

. . . .

These are the sounds from when Marty had me that I don't realize I've kept somewhere deep inside me until I hear something that reminds me of them:

- That clicking sound a doorknob makes when you shut it
- The squeaks a mattress makes sometimes
- Heavy bass in hip-hop music
- Microwave beeps
- Cigarette lighters clicking

And these are the smells:

- Cigarette smoke
- McDonald's
- Italian carryout heated up too many times
- Palmolive dish soap
- Red wine

Maybe next time I go see Dr. Greenberg I can ask him about the smells and the sounds. But probably I won't. Probably I'll do what I usually do, which is sit and nod at what he's saying while on the inside I'm wondering all these weird things that I can't say out loud to this Dr. Greenberg guy who I barely know. Probably I'll do what I usually do, which is look out the window at this huge pecan tree growing outside of Dr. Greenberg's office and think about how for the four years I was gone it was there, growing and getting to be this pecan tree. Doing its pecan tree thing. Waking up every morning under the sun and becoming a little bit bigger each day. Not worried about anything.

CAROLINE—96 DAYS AFTERWARD

ALL DAY LONG MY MOM HAS BEEN AFTER ME TO HAUL THE STACKS of old newspapers and magazines that have been breeding in the garage out to the garbage can at the back of the house. When the sun starts to set, I finally get around to it. As I struggle to lift the lid and dump the junk, I notice one of the yellowing papers has a big picture of Dylan under the front page headline. It was taken the day he was rescued. I stare at the picture of him standing between me and my parents, clutching my mother's arm, and I can't believe it's been just over three months since Dylan came home and we were on the front page of almost every major paper in Texas.

I mean, never once in my soul-sucking, mind-numbing, small-town Texas life did I think that one day I would be standing in front of CNN anchor Gloria Conway in all her hair sprayed, stiletto-wearing glory as she asked me what any rational person would qualify as The Stupidest Questions in the World.

How does it feel to have your little brother back?
How did you keep it together these last few days?
Have you felt like a support for your parents as they've dealt with this unimaginable situation?

Gloria fired questions at me while I was standing in the Dove Lake High School gymnasium, the only place the local police could think to put all the reporters and cameras because it was the one space in town that would hold all of them. Blinking as the camera flashes went off. Stuck in the very same spot where my best friend Emma Saunders and I regularly lied to that rat-faced Coach Underhill about having cramps so we wouldn't have to complete the volleyball unit. There I stood, clutching my baby brother's hand as he rocked back and forth and pushed his face into my mom's armpit. My parents cried, and I thanked the God I wasn't sure I believed in for bringing Dylan home to us. I even answered all of Gloria Conway's stupid questions as a sign of thanks to some higher power.

And I said a silent prayer, too, that she didn't ask the questions that I didn't want to answer.

Why was Dylan outside unsupervised?

Who normally would have been keeping an eye on Dylan at that time?

How are you planning to help Dylan recover from this traumatic event, given his special needs?

The reporters, some of them from as far away as England, were pretty interested in us, but Ethan Jorgenson got most of the attention. To be gone four years and found just over an hour away? And to have apparently had the chance to leave and not have left? That's what everyone was talking about under their breaths.

The police kept our two families mostly separated in the aftermath. I didn't see Ethan during the interviews at the police station. Or the examinations at the hospital. I'm not sure why. But we were all hustled into the gym together for the news conferences, and I caught a glimpse of him through the crowd of reporters. Tall. Dark hair. A bunch of piercings in his left ear. Not bad looking, to tell you the truth, but skinnier than I remembered him. Maybe that bastard who took him and Dylan didn't feed him much, I don't know. He looked so different, but of course that makes sense since he'd been gone for so long, and a lot happens to you between eleven and fifteen. I mean, at eleven I could wear clothes from the boy's department, but by fifteen my boobs were as big as my mother's.

Ethan had been a year behind me in school, but Dove Lake is tiny enough that it was easy to recall how he always played basketball at recess during elementary school and whacked away at the drums in the school band. I still remember his lopsided smile staring out at us from the MISSING posters taped to the front doors of the Tom Thumb and the Walgreens and the Wal-Mart and the Dairy Queen and the waiting room at his dad's office. Dr. Jorgenson is my dentist just like he's the dentist for every kid in town because he's the *only* dentist in town, and for years, even after everyone was pretty much sure that Ethan Jorgenson was a skeleton at the bottom of a lake somewhere, even after all the other flyers had been taken down because it was just too sad to keep them up, Ethan's smile stared at me from the bulletin board in the waiting room when I went in for a cleaning every six months. And when Dr. Jorgenson would come in during my checkups and nod and examine my teeth and ask me about how school was going, I would think about Ethan Jorgenson and his crooked smile and I'd feel so sorry for Dr. Jorgenson. I don't know how he even managed to get up each day, much less stare into the mouths of squirming preschoolers and pimply teenagers who probably reminded him of his son every second of every hour. He and Mrs. Jorgenson didn't have any other kids. They just had Ethan.

And then one awful day they didn't anymore.

Ethan and his parents got booked on the Carlotta King

show a few days after he and Dylan were found. The reporters were done asking my family questions, but the Carlotta King interview aired nationally on a Wednesday night, and there were promos running for it every hour on the hour in the days leading up to it. My parents didn't want to watch it. *Let's leave well enough alone. Dylan is back. He's safe. He's unharmed. We don't need to watch that, Caroline. We don't need to get ourselves all worked up.*

But of course I recorded it and after everyone was asleep—well, after Dylan fell asleep crying in my mother's arms and my mother passed out on the floor next to his bed because it was the only way he'd drift off and my father acted the whole time like nothing was going on by shutting himself inside his bedroom, after all of that—I crept into the family room and watched it. I watched as Carlotta King tilted her head, furrowed her brow, and parted her lip-glossed pink lips just so before asking another probing question. She had this way about her, Carlotta King did, of making you feel like you were just sitting at the bus stop with her having a chat. It seemed like talking to her would be like talking to your favorite teacher from elementary school, the one who gave generous hugs and smiled sweetly when you accidentally called her Mom. No wonder Carlotta King scored all the big deal interviews with politicians who'd cheated on their wives and celebrities who'd gotten arrested drunk driving.

Phillip and Megan, you moved here to Dove Lake from Austin when Ethan was a preschooler in the hopes that you'd be raising your son in a safe, almost idyllic environment. Small Town, USA. And then this tragedy happens. How do you settle that in your minds?

Ethan, this question is delicate, but can you tell me how you got through these past four years? What was your day-to-day life like?

So what's next for the Jorgenson family? Will you be continuing with the foundation you've started? You've done such wonderful work for the families of other missing kids across this country.

I texted Emma, **This is so freaking weird.**

No shit she wrote back. She had watched the interview earlier, and she wanted to know what I was thinking as I watched it. But pretty soon I was ignoring her texts, totally immersed in listening to my dentist and his wife and their son—a kid I used to pass by in the cafeteria at Dove Lake Primary—talk to the entire country about what had happened to them. They looked pretty put together considering. Ethan's piercings had disappeared from his ear. Dr. Jorgenson was wearing a tie and a blazer, and Mrs. Jorgenson had on a swanky plum suit she must have found in the city or at least online. No store in Dove Lake would carry something so pricey.

They talked like they'd gone over the questions ahead of time, and maybe they had. Ethan's answers were short, and he kept glancing at his parents in between. I felt sorry for him, but a lot of people were saying the Jorgensons were doing this to get the media off their backs. One Carlotta King interview and then hopefully everyone would leave them alone.

I waited for Carlotta King to ask Ethan why he didn't try to run away, especially since reporters were finding out he'd been seen biking and hanging out outside the apartment complex in Houston all by himself while that bastard was at work. Some reports even said he'd made friends with other kids in the neighborhood. But she didn't ask those questions.

I waited for her to ask about Dylan, too. About how that bastard had managed to kidnap him from practically in front of our house. About what had happened to him while he'd been gone. But she never said a word about us. I guess she figured like everybody else that my little brother was only gone a few nights. That was nothing compared to what Ethan had been through. Never mind that on the evening I was watching Carlotta King and Ethan Jorgenson and his parents, I heard my little brother waking up in his bedroom down the hall, shrieking at the top of his lungs so loud that I couldn't begin to make out the words my mother was using to try to calm him down.

It's been three months since that interview aired. Three months since I saw Ethan Jorgenson in the Dove Lake High School gym. Three months since Dylan came home. And he still wakes up screaming, and my mother still sleeps on his bedroom floor a lot of the time, and my dad still comes home later and later. As for me, I hide in the shadows of my house, my mind unable to stop wondering and worrying about what happened to my baby brother when he was taken from us.

ETHAN—105 DAYS AFTERWARD

WHEN MY MOM DRIVES ME TO DR.GREENBERG'S, WE HAVE TO TRAVEL the same highway Marty used when he first took me, and this makes me anxious as hell. It takes an hour on the interstate to get to Dr. Greenberg's. There aren't any therapists for me in Dove Lake or even in the next town or two over. So twice a week I get in the front seat of my mom's Volvo and she lets me pick out something to listen to (usually nothing, sometimes Green Day). We start the drive to Dr. Greenberg's, and I fight the urge not to puke because I feel so bad. At first I thought about asking my mom if there was another way, but I know that if there is, it involves taking a million back roads and would take two hours instead of just one. So mostly I just squeeze my hands into fists and rub my thumbs over my knuckles until we get there. I imagine my thumbs are little mountain climbers and my knuckles are the mountains.

Up down and up down and up down and up down . . .

I used this trick when I was with Marty. It helps calm me down. Sometimes.

At first I didn't have to worry about all of this because Dr. Greenberg came to us, back when the media was still all crazy and reporters were literally camping out in our front yard. Dad's old college friend who lives in New York and is some big brain doctor or something recommended Dr. Greenberg and put us in touch and everything. Mom said he had a national reputation and lots of experience helping patients dealing with severe trauma. Those are the words she used. *Severe trauma.* Which made me feel more like someone with a broken leg than a kid who'd been kidnapped, but okay.

When Dr. Greenberg first visited us, my initial thought was *this guy looks really weird.* I wasn't sure how old he was, but he looked like a grandpa. He had a huge white beard and these bushy eyebrows that were so out of control I couldn't even figure out how he managed to see. He basically looked like a skinny Santa Claus. He came out every single day and met with me alone, and with my parents alone, and with me and my parents together, and then with my parents' therapist— this guy they started seeing while I was gone. That therapist met with my parents alone, and with Dr. Greenberg alone, and with my parents and Dr. Greenberg together, and then we were all sitting together and through all of it I offered one-word answers and grunts, basically feeling like curling up and disappearing or at least going to sleep. But of course I couldn't sleep. So Dr. Greenberg prescribed these sleeping pills and something called an SSRI and something for anxiety plus this other stuff my mom keeps track of. She keeps the bottles in her bedroom, and she has her phone all set up to ding when she needs a reminder to give me my pills.

But that was in the beginning. I'm still on the pills, but about a month ago Dr. Greenberg said I could start coming to his office twice a week instead of him coming to us so much.

"Mom," I said to my mom when she told me this, "I really don't think I need to go. I'm fine." Part of this was because of the drive I didn't want to do. And part of it was because the idea of having to talk about any of this made me want to disappear or melt or vaporize or something. I mean, if I'd spent all the time with Dr. Greenberg in my house not talking, I didn't see how that was going to change by sitting in his office.

"Sweetheart, this is an important part of your recovery. Your dad and I are still seeing Dr. Sugar." Yeah, their therapist is called Dr. Sugar. Which is weird because my dad is a dentist, but I guess they like him a lot.

"I know you're still seeing Dr. Sugar," I said. "That's good. But . . ."

Then I looked at my mom's face and her teary eyes. I can't say no to my mom. I can't say no to my dad either. Not after everything I've put them through. Those first few days back my mom kept following me from room to room. She hugged me every five seconds and she still kind of does, which was okay at first, but lately her hugs make me push my shoulders up to my ears and hold my breath for a second, and then I feel bad again. When I first got back and I went to the bathroom, she would wait outside the door. And when I went to sleep, she slept on the floor next to my bed until my dad talked her out of it. Those first few nights I would wake up a million times and blink and try to figure out where I was, and then I would see her on the air mattress on the floor and I would be happy and then sad because I was such a messed up person.

The bottom line is, I can't do anything else to hurt her. I can't put my parents through anything else. So I didn't really fight going to Dr. Greenberg's when my mom said I had to keep going. I just said, "Okay, I'll go. It's fine."

And that's how I'm here, zipping along the freeway, trying to distract myself by reading the exit signs and people's bumper stickers and running my thumbs up and down over my knuckles and trying not to throw up.

"Get on the floor. This is a gun on your neck."

Just read the signs. Just focus on your hands.

"Sorry, buddy. You were in the wrong place at the wrong time."

No, no, no, it's not him. He's gone now, Ethan.

"Don't cry. I don't like crying."

I cough because sometimes that helps stop the feeling that I'm going to hurl.

"Are you okay, Ethan?" my mother asks, glancing at me.

"Yeah, I'm okay." I cough again.

Finally we get to Dr. Greenberg's, and once the car stops I start to feel a little better. Dr. Greenberg has an office in his house on the north side of Houston. It's a big, old-fashioned two-story house with a porch that goes all the way around. Sometimes his dog, Groovy, is on the porch taking a nap. Yeah, as if it wasn't weird enough that my therapist looks like a skinny Santa, he has a dog named Groovy. I wonder if my dad's college roommate really knew what he was talking about when he said this guy is some world-famous expert in severe trauma.

"Hello there!" Dr. Greenberg says as he comes out the front door to meet us on the porch. Like we're coming over for Thanksgiving dinner or something.

"Hello, Dr. Greenberg," my mother says, smiling. When she smiles she looks younger. One of the first things I noticed when I came back was how much older my mom looked. Like way more than just four years had gone by.

"Ethan, how are you?" he asks, grinning at me like he just can't wait to sit in a chair opposite me while I stare out the window of his office and give one-word answers. "How was the drive up here?"

"Fine," I say, nodding, and we head inside for our session.

CAROLINE—109 DAYS AFTERWARD

THE TRUTH IS THAT JACKSON FAMILY FARM IS NOT OWNED BY THE Jackson family but by the Saldana family. Only Enrique Saldana, my boss, told me once that "Saldana doesn't sound as good as Jackson." When I asked him what he meant, he said, "Saldana sounds too Mexican." I reminded him that not only had he been born here, which made him as American as me, but that the people who drive the hour or so out here from the city don't care if the farm they take their snotty kids to is run by Mexicans. I mean, they all drive hybrid cars with stickers for Democrats on them. But Enrique says he doesn't want to take a chance. If anyone asks to speak to one of the Jacksons in charge, we have to tell them to talk to Enrique, and he says he's just the manager.

Jackson Family Farm is one of those places where city families come to have a country experience without actually having to live in the country. These people show up dressed in overalls that they bought especially for the occasion, and their kids have names like Asher and Henry and Amelia and Josephine. They spend their time posing by the corn maze (in the fall) and the strawberry patch (in the summer), and then they pay way too much for homemade jerky and summer sausage, and by the time they leave they've posted pictures of their day all over the Internet. I sound rude, but I don't mean to be. This is just how these people are. To be honest, I'm thankful for them because they're the reason I can earn my own money in a town without a lot of part-time jobs, so I don't have to bug my parents for extra cash I know they don't have.

Enrique hired me last summer, just before tenth grade. I tried to get Emma to get a job here with me, but she said the thought of being around that much hay made her break out in hives. Among my many duties, I run the cash register, hand out the white plastic buckets for collecting strawberries, and point out where we keep the porta-potties. The name of the porta-potty company is Doodie Calls. That always gets a laugh from the guests, but once you've seen the name fifty million times, it isn't even funny anymore. It's just another part of working at Jackson (actually Saldana) Family Farm.

There are two other Dove Lake High kids who work here. One is Milagro Saldana, Enrique's daughter, who's a freshman and super quiet.

The other is Jason McGinty. He's a junior, like me.

Jason McGinty is a lazy stoner and not the sharpest tool in the shed, but what I like about him the most is that when he kisses me he makes me feel like a head without a body. Actually, to be honest, just lips without even a head. And sometimes, if I'm lucky, he brings a joint to work and we go smoke by the back fence line after hours.

Which is how I find myself on Saturday night, sitting on the split rail fence, trying not to cough from inhaling too deep.

"Oh, hell, I know you need to cough, so cough," Jason says. Which of course makes me only want to not cough even more. He smirks at me, and I give up.

The burning sensation passes, and I wait for the pleasant feeling of being high to begin. The pot Jason gets is pretty good, but I never ask him where he gets it. It's just one of the many things we don't discuss. Usually we just come back here and get high and fool around.

But tonight Jason feels like talking. And as soon as he starts, I wish he hadn't.

"So, is shit basically back to normal with your brother? You haven't brought him around lately."

I used to bring Dylan to the farm when I wasn't working. I mean, before everything happened. Enrique let him spend hours touching all the grooves on the wheels of the tractor that doesn't work but that the city kids climb on to get their pictures taken. But I haven't brought Dylan by in months, and now Jason McGinty wants to talk about it.

"Everything's fine," I say, reaching out my fingers for the joint so he knows I want another hit. Jason is holding in a big swallow of pot and air, and even in the last remaining bits of daylight I can see his face turning just a little red. Finally, he exhales.

"Yeah, but isn't it also, like, a little weird? Like, when you think about what might have happened to him while he was with that dude?"

Oh, Jesus, Jason McGinty. Not now.

"Yeah, I guess," I answer. I squeeze my eyes shut and think about this morning when my mother was trying to give Dylan a bath. I think about his high-pitched shrieks and the thud of his feet kicking the sides of the tub and the splashing of water and my mother starting to cry. I think about my dad getting into his truck to go on a job that suddenly, magically appeared out of nowhere.

A swimmy fuzziness starts to come over me, which is good, but my heart is beating fast, which sometimes happens when I smoke. I don't like that part so much.

"And Ethan," Jason keeps going, like I'm not even there on the fence next to him, like he's talking to himself, "I still don't get it. The neighbors saw that dude hanging out alone all the time, and he never tried to leave? Or call his parents? That makes zero sense. Shit, even if he liked it there for some

[31]

weird reason, you would have thought he would have at least called the cops for your brother."

My heart is pumping so fast I start thinking back to the drug movies they made us watch in Human Growth and Development last year and I wonder whether any of them showed 16-year-old girls dying from pot heart attacks. Pot sometimes makes Jason chatty, and normally I don't mind getting high with him and talking shit about people we know before we start making out. But now I'm so jittery I slide off the fence and start walking parallel to it, away from Jason toward the back of the property.

"Hey, what's up?" Jason's behind me. For a second I think he's concerned about me. Then I realize I have the joint in my hands.

"Here," I say, turning around to give the joint back to him. He scratches under his neck and looks at me, and his eyes look beady and tired all of a sudden in the darkening sky.

"What's going on?" he says, and suddenly his free hand is around the small of my back and he's tipping his face into mine. He asks me this question in a soft, worried voice. I think he's sincere, too. But the trouble with Jason McGinty is that he only gets sweet and gentle when he's high.

"I don't ever want you to talk about my brother again, okay?" I say, and my words are a whisper. They sound like they're coming from far away, like they're floating down from the black walnut trees above us.

"Okay, fine," he says, confused. "It's cool. I'm sorry. I was just asking if he was okay."

"Okay," I answer. "But seriously. Don't bring him up again. Okay?"

"Okay," he says, his voice turning even softer, which makes him sound more appealing somehow. "I'm really sorry. I didn't mean to make you mad." I don't know where the joint is because now both his hands are around me, holding me around my waist. I press a cheek into his chest, which feels like a warm, safe wall I can hide behind. I listen for his heart. Maybe it's beating slower than mine. Maybe if I listen to his long enough, mine will slow down, too.

But I never do find out if his heart is beating fast or slow because now Jason is kissing my neck and the back of my ear. And like I said, he's a really good kisser. He delivers these tiny, goosebumps-inducing kisses and nibbles all over that make my hair follicles go electric.

He doesn't look like the type of guy that could kiss like this, but he is.

It's nice being high and kissing Jason McGinty. And that's all I'm trying to think about when he takes my hand and pulls me down to the ground underneath the trees and the moon and the dark Texas sky. That's all I'm trying to think about as I stretch out on my back and give in.

ETHAN—132 DAYS AFTERWARD

TODAY I WOKE UP AND HEADED DOWNSTAIRS TO FIND MY PARENTS waiting for me in the kitchen with a pancake breakfast. My mom made a smiley face on the pancakes with chocolate chips and whipped cream, and there's a bowl of fresh fruit and a big glass of orange juice to go along with everything.

"Happy birthday, Ethan!" they shout. My mom has her hands clasped together under her chin, and my dad is standing there with his hands on his hips, nodding. They look so eager. So happy.

"Hey, thanks," I say, trying on a smile. I'm not hungry, but I sit down at the breakfast table anyway and start taking a few bites of the pancakes.

"I remember how much you liked these," my mom says, reaching out to pet my arm. I tense up and close my eyes briefly until she stops.

"This is really nice," I say. I feel like they're watching me eat, so I try to chew with some enthusiasm. But I'm pretty tired. I slept really bad last night, waking up every hour with my heart racing and feeling sick to my stomach, too.

It's October fourth. My birthday. I'm sixteen. And I haven't celebrated my birthday since I turned eleven. I shove another mouthful of pancakes down my throat and remember that day. How Jesse and Eric and all the guys came over to play video games, and my mom made us tacos and Jesse told us about how he'd spied with his dad's binoculars on his babysitter who lived next door to him and how he'd seen her with her top off and everything.

I never told Marty when my birthday was, and he never asked. It was hard for me to know the days when I was there, and even now when I think back there are blanks—long stretches where I can't remember anything. I can't figure out if the not remembering makes me anxious or relieved or both. But I do know that just thinking about Marty makes my breathing tighten up.

Don't think about it, Ethan. Don't think about him. He isn't here. He isn't even alive anymore.

I run my thumbs over my knuckles a few times and then shove another mouthful of pancakes into my mouth and make myself chew. They taste like dirt and air and nothing. My parents are still watching me. My mom is still grinning so hard I think she might break her cheeks. Her eyes are tearing up, too.

"Buddy, when you're done there, we have something for you in the garage," my dad tells me.

"Great," I say, shoveling another bite in my mouth and wondering how much I have to eat before I can say I've had enough. This would at least be easier if they were eating, too. But ever since I've been back they just seem to like watching me do stuff. Even boring stuff like eating.

Finally, after a few more bites I tell my parents I'm full, and they lead me out the back door to the detached garage at the end of our long driveway. We never park our cars in the garage. We just keep them in the driveway, so mostly the garage is a building full of my dad's tools and random Tupperware crates full of Christmas decorations and other junk. When I first got back I saw a whole stack of posters with my eleven-year-old face on them and the word MISSING stamped across them in big red letters, but pretty soon after I got home they disappeared. I don't know where they went.

This morning my dad uses the clicker to open up the garage door, and sitting there in the middle of the garage is a brand new drum kit.

My eyebrows pop up. My mouth drops open.

It's not just any kit. It's a Ludwig. Deep blue with Zildjian cymbals.

Shit.

"Wait, is this for me?" I ask.

"Yes, it's for you!" my mother cries, and she claps her hands.

I want to touch it, but it's like I can't move my feet. I can't believe what I'm looking at. I mean, it's a Ludwig. A fucking Ludwig!

"Wow," I say, and I finally manage to move forward and touch the cymbals just a bit. They feel so solid in my hands. So sure of themselves.

"Play us something!" my dad booms, and suddenly my stomach crumbles a little.

"Oh, he doesn't have to," my mom says super fast in this high, singsong voice, and she looks at my dad with a *You should know better than to ask that, honey* look like I'm not even there. Like I'm still eleven and wouldn't get the meaning.

"Oh, yeah, there's no rush," my dad says, shaking his head like he was being silly to ask me to play this instrument that they had to have dropped serious cash to get.

I let my fingers circle the cymbals again. "What happened to my old drums?" I ask, thinking of the cherry red Pearl set that used to live in here. I'd messed with it a couple of times since coming back, just to see if I could still play. At Marty's I only played drums in my mind. He doesn't like rock music or punk. I mean, he didn't.

Stop, stop, he's dead and he's not here.

"The old drums are in the attic," my mom says, and her voice is cracking. "Is that okay? We can get them out for you. It's no problem. It's just that we thought this one would be so much nicer." She does that silly, high voice again, and it sounds forced enough to annoy me, and as soon as it does, I feel bad.

"No, it's okay," I say. I'm glad the Pearl kit is gone. I like that this one is new. Brand new. "I love this," I say. "Thank you."

And I look at my parents and I want to start crying all of a sudden, but I don't. I just stand there, uncertain, and then my mom walks over and pulls me to her, and she smells like pancakes and soap and that perfume she keeps on her dresser—Shalimar. She kisses me on the temple. Once. Twice. Over and over again. This time it doesn't bug me as much as it did when she petted me at breakfast, but I still find myself holding my breath.

"Oh, Ethan, it feels so good to tell you happy birthday," she says. "Happy, happy, happy, happy birthday!" She's crying now, which she does three to four times a day. Which is a few times less than when I first got home. Sometimes they're sad tears and sometimes they're happy tears, but I think lately the happy tears have been winning out.

My dad is standing there in his tie and jacket, all dressed to leave for the office. He's not crying but he is nodding and smiling, like he could stand there all day and watch my mom hug me.

Finally I pull away because I know my mom will never pull away first, and my dad says he has to get going, but what about driving into the city tonight for a fancy birthday dinner? I think about making that drive on I-10, and my heart starts to pick up speed a little.

"Maybe we could just stay home," I say. "Maybe we could make our own pizzas." The idea just comes to me. It's something we used to do when I was little. Before. Until I say it I realize I hadn't remembered it in a long time.

"Oh, that's nice," my mom says, nodding, dabbing at her red eyes with her fingertips. "We'll go to the store today and get everything."

"Sounds good," dad says, nodding.

Finally my dad gets going to work, and my mom goes inside to make a shopping list for the pizza stuff. I tell her I'm going to mess around on the drum kit. I know she's going to watch me through the kitchen window, checking on me every five seconds. She can't help herself. She has a real hard time letting me out of her sight even though I'm sixteen now. Even though I figure the odds of anything awful happening to me again are a million to one.

Then again, the odds of the first awful thing happening to me—of Marty taking me—were a million to one, too. And it happened anyway.

Maybe my mother doesn't believe in luck or chance anymore. She just needs to be sure.

I'm biting my lip so hard I can taste blood. I wince and shake my head a little, and then without thinking about it too much I grab the sticks and sit down at the Ludwig and adjust the stool so I'm at the right height.

Like I said, I messed around on the Pearl kit a little when I first got back, but I haven't really played the drums in over four years.

Four years.

A quarter of my life. Twenty-five percent of it lost.

I rub my thumbs up and down the wooden drumsticks. I nurse my bit lip a little with my tongue. I close my eyes . . .

And suddenly I'm drumming. I can't tell if I'm any good even though I'm pretty sure my fills are for shit, and I wonder what my old band teacher, Mr. Case, would say if he were listening to me play right now. But all that really matters is I'm drumming. I'm drumming and I'm a drummer and I'm drumming. I hear Green Day songs in my head and I'm pretending I'm Tré Cool, and I give the kick drum a couple of smacks and whomps and wallops. I keep at it until I feel sweat starting to bead up under my hairline and my shoulders start to ache. And for the first time since I've been home, my mind blanks out but it's not a bad thing. Not like the blanks from before, from when I was gone. These blanks feel good, actually. Almost peaceful. And, yeah, I probably need to build up my stamina, and maybe I'm good, and maybe I'm not.

But that Ludwig, man. I'm telling you, it sounded fucking awesome.

CAROLINE—140 DAYS AFTERWARD

ONE OF THE GOOD THINGS ABOUT BEING THE NORMAL ONE IS THAT I can get away with my room being an absolute shit show, and no one seems to bother me about it too much. Like right now I have what most geologists would define as a mountain of dirty laundry in the corner of my room, and my bookshelf is covered in empty cans of Coke Zero and stacks of old BUST magazines my cousin in Chicago mailed me, and my floor is decorated in spiral notebooks full of homework I might or might not do, depending.

My closet is a train wreck, too. The other day in some pathetic attempt to make room for the dirty clothes I might someday get around to washing, I tried to empty it out. I still had my sixth grade All School Spelling Bee trophy in there, which shows you how long it's been since I cleaned out my closet. It also goes to show you how much I've changed since the sixth grade.

I shoved the trophy back on the shelf along with my favorite black Converse high tops and the teeniest, tiniest little bag of weed I bought from Jason McGinty, and then I covered it all up with some random T-shirt and a bunch of junk.

I really didn't have to cover the weed because no one goes in my closet but me. Like I said, there are perks to being the normal one. The one who met her milestones and didn't have meltdowns in public places. The one who didn't have to be carted around to a million doctors from birth only to have them all give the same diagnosis. Autism. Low functioning. Cause unknown. Therapy available but sorry, your insurance doesn't cover it. And anyway, the closest therapist is over a hundred miles away.

I remember when my parents told me I was going to have a little brother. I was five and in Ms. Sweeny's kindergarten class at Dove Lake Primary, and when my parents sat me down in the kitchen and my mom put my chubby little girl hand on her belly to try and explain, I immediately pulled away, ran to my room, and came racing back carrying Slumber Party Barbie, my favorite.

"What is this for?" my mother asked, confused.

"For my new baby brother," I said. "I want to share."

It's one of those stories that gets told over and over again at family reunions and everything. One of those cute things kids say or do. A little anecdote to prove how precious I am.

Or, rather, I was.

There are no stories like that about me anymore.

When Dylan was born I loved that I got to hold him (as long as I was sitting on the couch with my mom or dad next to me), and I loved how his baby heels were so soft and smooth, and his skin smelled better than my fruit-scented markers. He was my baby brother. Mine.

But it didn't take long before my parents noticed something was wrong. Mostly my mom noticed it. I was too tiny to put it all together, but I remember my parents sending me to my room when they talked about him. I remember my mom hovering around while he was in the crib or in his high chair. I remember her long conversations with her sister in Chicago and her crying as she talked in soft whispers. And as he got older, I remember being dragged around to doctors' appointments, stuck in waiting rooms on vinyl couches, doodling in old *Highlights* or *Ranger Rick* magazines while we waited for another doctor who was running late.

Later on, I took my homework to those doctors' appointments, especially when we had to drive all the way into the city to go to them. I'd show my mom the stickers my teachers gave me, like the one with the funny parrot on it that said, "Awk! Good job, matey!"

"That's so nice, honey," my mom would say, her eyes on

Dylan as she tried to get him to stop sucking on his fingers or making some strange noise over and over again.

It would be a lie if I told you Dylan didn't frustrate me sometimes. He did. He does. But Dylan and me, we have our own thing going. Or at least we used to before everything that happened to him in May. I could get him to laugh when I made him his breakfast. I would put his favorite blue plastic bowl on my head (it's the only bowl he'll eat out of, so we have, like, ten of them), and then I would say, "Where's Dylan's blue bowl? Where'd it go?" And he would do this high-pitched laugh that's totally his and smack the kitchen table with both fists.

And I could distract him. When he threw fits in the middle of the Wal-Mart because he wasn't allowed to climb inside the shopping cart or he decided he didn't like the feel of his new socks, I could distract him by whistling. Mostly David Bowie's "Space Oddity" but sometimes that "Dock of the Bay" song my grandfather likes a lot. If I whistled loud enough and long enough, he would sometimes calm down. And if people in the Wal-Mart stared at us, I gave them the business right back with a dirty look.

It felt good knowing Dylan depended on me. Which only makes what happened that morning he wandered outside worse.

In the months he's been back, my whistling doesn't help. Bowls on my head don't help. Nothing seems to be helping

Dylan. He still wakes up shrieking. He still wakes up crying. There are moments when he doesn't want my mom or me to touch him even though we were some of the only people who could touch him before, and this makes life hard because Dylan still needs help with basically everything from washing to dressing to eating.

And he's really scared to go outside, even though it's October now and the Texas summer is finally over and the weather is actually nice and cool. This means my mom has to practically drag him to the car to get him to go to school, where he spends his time in a special classroom for other kids like him. He used to like going there, but not anymore.

You would think my mom would want to take him to the doctor. Now, more than ever. But after that first checkup at the hospital, it's like my mom wants to act like everything is going to be okay if she just says it over and over enough. *("Let's just get Dylan back in his regular routine. Let's not make anything about this bigger than it is. He was barely gone from us.")* It pisses me off the way she seems to want to pretend nothing happened. And my dad spends so much time taking extra calls for the exterminating company he works for, he's not around enough to give an opinion. He spends most of his days in people's attics chasing rats, which is a probably a heck of a lot more satisfying than taking care of a kid who'll never get better. Who'll never change.

But Dylan is changing. For the worse. Like tonight. To-night was crazy awful. We were eating dinner and my dad got up suddenly to go to the refrigerator to get something. Probably another can of whatever cheap beer was on special at the Tom Thumb.

Slam!

Dylan's blue bowl was on the floor, spaghetti everywhere. Then he scooted into the corner of the kitchen like some sort of hurt animal, crouching into a little ball, and he wet his pants, a little yellow pool forming underneath him on the floor.

"Jesus," my dad said, closing his eyes, standing by the fridge, still holding his beer.

"Dylan, honey!" my mom yelped, running over to him.

The rest of my spaghetti became as appealing to me as a bowl of worms. I stopped eating and made my way over to my screwed up baby brother.

"Hey, Dill. Hey, Dill Pickle." That's my nickname for him. Sometimes it works.

But not tonight. He just cried and sat in his own pee. Then he sucked on his fingers and said, "Damn, damn, piece of cake. Damn."

My eyes met my mom's over Dylan's head. Sometimes Dylan parrots back stuff he hears on television and from other people, but it never makes much sense. This piece of cake thing was new, though, something he'd only started re-peating since he was taken. When I'd asked my mom early on what she thought it meant, she'd just sighed and said he probably picked up the swear word from my dad. Like any-thing connected to the kidnapping, she'd only wanted to ig-nore it.

"Damn, damn, piece of cake!" Dylan yelled.

My dad sighed really loud.

"I need some air for a sec," he said, and he headed onto the back porch with his beer. My mother acted like it was nothing. She's always cutting Dad slack over Dylan. She says he has it harder than any of us because he always thought he would have a son he could talk about sports with and take hunting.

After we got Dylan all cleaned up—and not without a struggle—my mom took him into her room and let him lie down on her and my dad's bed and watch the same DVR'd episode of *Jeopardy!* that he watches like a hundred times a day. We all have it memorized by now.

The categories are . . . Potent potables, By the numbers, 19th Century France. . . .

It's a Daily Double!

I'll wager two thousand, Alex.

My mom headed into the kitchen to clean up, and I thought to myself that if I were a better daughter, I would probably go and help. But I couldn't bring myself to do it. And anyway, why doesn't my dad ever help? He doesn't even help with Dylan very much. That's always on me more than him.

So I just scowled to myself and shuffled into my disaster of a room, where I've been hiding out since, surrounded by my mess of a life.

I love my room, but I hate it, too. I love it because it's my escape, but I hate it because it's where I was hanging out the morning Dylan was taken. I hate that I can't remember exactly what I was doing when it happened, which proves to me how epically selfish I must have been that day if I couldn't even figure out what was so important that I couldn't watch my baby brother for five minutes while my mom took a shower. I was probably just messing around on my phone or texting Emma about how far I'd gone with Jason McGinty.

I should have been keeping an eye on Dylan. My mom told me to. She asked me to keep an eye on him, and I didn't.

He got taken, and it was all my fault.

The thought makes me sick like it always does. I go into my closet to find that teeny, tiny bag of weed I got from Jason. If I smoke with the door shut and a sock under it and blow the smoke out of the window, my parents will never know. If they even bother to check up on me.

But one pin joint later and I don't feel better. Only fuzzy

and sweaty and my heart is beating too fast again. Maybe I should stop smoking pot.

Dylan. Dill Pickle. Sweet little baby brother, what happened to you? What did that bastard do to you?

Shit. I hate it when my brain goes to this place. Months later and I still can't stop wondering.

I get up off the floor and shut the window, then crawl up into my bed. I take a breath and close my eyes, trying to ground myself.

I can feel a ball of tears dying to expand inside my throat, but I've gotten good at stopping myself from tearing up when I don't want to.

I'm not the best student anymore, but I've always been a good big sister. That's the one thing I've always managed to pull off. And now I'm not that. Not even close. In fact, I'm probably the worst big sister in the entire world.

Through our paper thin walls I can hear my mother walking Dylan to his bedroom to go to bed.

"Damn, damn, piece of cake," he repeats, over and over.

Maybe it's Jason McGinty's weed or my own desperate, clawing attempt to try to do something to help Dylan, but I get an idea. The beginning of one, anyway. Something hazy and weird and probably screwed up.

As the idea swims through my skull, I hear loud noises between my mother and Dylan as she tries to settle him down for bed. I feel the weight of the idea sink on me along with the painful awareness that I'm the only one in my family who seems to want to face the fact that something awful happened to Dylan. From down the hall I hear another one of Dylan's shrieks. I close my eyes and try to wish away whatever demons keep coming for my sweet baby brother.

ETHAN—146 DAYS AFTERWARD

SINCE I'VE BEEN BACK, I'VE MOSTLY ONLY BEEN AROUND MY parents, the therapists, and my mom's parents who came to visit me right after I got back. The only person I've seen a lot who is around my age is Jesse. We've hung out like six or seven times in the past few months, and each time he's stayed a little bit longer than the last, and this has made me happy. I guess he's the one friend from before who decided all the television news cameras and the interview with Carlotta King and the weirdness in general weren't going to keep him from spending time with me. He didn't just come over right away, though. His mom called my mom first. I know because about a week after I came back, I overheard my mother on the phone in her bedroom with her door almost all the way shut. She didn't know it, but I'd seen the name Lisa Taylor on the caller ID, and I knew it was Jesse's mom calling our house. My parents never let me answer the house phone in case it's a reporter who has managed to get our number, and that's fine by me. I don't want to answer it.

I'd stood outside my parents' bedroom door that morning after my mom picked up the phone. And I'd listened in on what she was telling Jesse's mother.

"I think it would be good for Jesse and Ethan to see each other. My gut is telling me it would be good for his healing process. But let me call Ethan's therapist and get back to you on specifics, all right?"

I acted like I didn't know anything, and then a few days later my mom asked me if I would like to see Jesse. I wasn't sure what to say. Part of me wanted to see him. Just to be around someone my own age again. The last time I'd been around any other teenagers was with Bennie and Narciso. After Marty finally let me outside, I ran into them when I was taking out the garbage, and I guess you could say we became friends. We played video games, mostly. Sometimes we skateboarded around the apartment complex or smoked a little weed or walked over to Taco Bell. Bennie and Narciso were one of the few not-so-messed up things in the most messed up part of my life.

Part of me was scared to see Jesse. That it would just be really weird, and neither one of us would know what to say. But I knew it would make my parents happy to see me being normal, having a friend. I thought it might make me feel happy, too. So I said, *Yes. Jesse can come over.* And a few days later, he did.

He looked so different. He was almost a foot taller than me, and the Afro that used to jump out a good few inches from his skull was cut super short. He looked like he'd been lifting weights or working out or something. Basically, he looked like he could beat up my dad.

"Hey, man," he said when my mom and I opened the front door. He gave me a big, toothy smile, and for a second he was eleven-year-old Jesse again.

"Hey, man," I said back. And after a couple of awkward seconds he reached out to me and I reached out to him and we gave each other a hug. Quick and one-armed and with a pat on the back. I used to give hugs like that to Bennie and Narciso.

That first time he visited, Jesse and I mostly played video games while my mom came in to check on us every five seconds. She even made us those Totino's Pizza Rolls like she did when we were in fifth grade, and after we ate them, he told me he had to get going.

"I work at that frozen yogurt place next to the Tom Thumb," he told me. "Got my license last week, and I'm saving up for a used car."

"That's cool," I said, still trying to put together the idea that Jesse Taylor is old enough to drive a car. It was like he was some grown-up, and I was a kid. Then it hit me that I was old enough to drive a car, too, and for a second something came over me so strong and so heavy I'd wished he had never come over at all and that I could go upstairs and hide or scream in my room.

But mostly it was okay to have him over, and he showed up every couple weeks to play video games. Then today, like two weeks after my sixteenth birthday, he shows up with some Mountain Dew, our favorite soda. Or at least it was when we were kids.

"Happy late birthday," he says to me, holding up the six-pack.

"Hey," I say, and I smile as big a smile as Jesse's.

What I've liked the most about hanging out with Jesse is that we haven't really had to talk to each other. A few times I've asked him how tenth grade is and what some of the friends we'd had in common are up to, and he's asked me about starting online school and having a tutor, but mostly we just get swallowed up by the enormous couch in the family room and play video games. We've hung out enough that my mom has stopped hovering around us and standing in the kitchen like she's making lunch when she's obviously trying to overhear whatever we're saying. Because basically we're not saying anything to each other except for talking about the game we're playing. We just zone out. I like it.

I'm good at the video games. It's maybe the one thing I did with Marty that I didn't hate. And it's all I did, some days.

While he was at work and after he let me out of the closet, I was able to move around inside the apartment. I played game after game like I was willing myself to disappear inside one of them.

Once I got home, I wondered if I would want to still play, but it turned out I did. And I was still good at the games, too. Like today, after Jesse and I drink two Mountain Dews each, I end up kicking his ass at Halo.

"Give up?" I ask, smirking at Jesse.

Jesse rolls his eyes. "Yeah. Let's take a break."

I go to the kitchen to get us each another soda, but when I get back Jesse seems different. More serious. He's just looking at the wall behind the television and not saying anything.

"What's up?" I ask. He's never done this before. Just sitting there staring at the wall.

"Man, I've wanted to tell you something," he starts. "I wanted to say it to you those first few times I came over. But I couldn't bring myself to do it."

There's a big empty space. A huge silence. My heart starts beating a little faster.

"What?"

Jesse takes a big breath and bends forward, putting his head into his hands so I can't see his face. Then to his feet he says, "I wanted to tell you I'm sorry."

"Sorry for what?" I ask him, but I can feel my throat go dry.

He sits back up and looks at me, and then away like he can't. Then he says, "I wish I'd never asked you to come over that day."

I don't want it to happen, but Jesse's words pull me back to that hot Sunday in May. No homework since school was almost out. The pool not open just yet. Nothing to do.

"Mom, can I bike over to Jesse's? Please?"

Gravel road. Sun beating down on me. I'm five minutes from Jesse's place.

"Get on the floor. This is a gun on your neck."

Numb and sweating. Sure what was happening was a dream.

"Sorry, buddy. You were in the wrong place at the wrong time."

Realizing it wasn't a dream. Realizing it was real life. My life.

"Don't cry. I don't like crying."

An empty pack of Marlboro Lights on the floorboard. Gum wrappers. Streaks of mud.

I shake my head, like I can shake out the thoughts. I blink a couple of times. My heart is racing really hard now, and I cough a few times to keep the nausea back.

Jesse takes a big breath and still doesn't look at me. But he says again, "The number of times I fucking hated myself for calling you up and asking you to come over to my house. Dude, you can't even know."

I don't know what to say. I think if I say anything I could

puke. I run my thumbs up and down my knuckles, over and over again.

"I just . . . ," Jesse tries again, shifting in the uncomfortable silence. "I mean . . . shit. Maybe I shouldn't have even brought this up."

I want him to leave right now, and this makes me feel like an asshole. In the same way I feel like an asshole when my mom hugs me, and I desperately want her to let me go. In the same way I feel like an asshole when my dad delivers one of his little pep talks about how great I'm doing, and I want to go in my room and shut the door and sleep until he goes away.

How come I'm an asshole to people who care about me?

There's more silence, and I still wish he would go away, but finally I manage a soft, "Don't worry about it, man." But I can't look at him when I say it.

"Yeah?" I hear Jesse answer, and when I do glance over at him he's finally looking at me, trying to make eye contact. His body relaxes a little. It must be nice to feel so much better about something so easily.

"Yeah," I say. "Seriously, man. I don't think about it like that. Really."

And in a way this is true. For all the years I was with Marty, my mind blocked out that day in May. But since I've come back—since I've been in the same bedroom and the same kitchen and the same town as before—I have thought about

Jesse asking me over all those years before. About him calling our house phone from his new cell phone and me being jealous that he could call me from his own number. Being pissed for a second that his parents got him his own phone and my parents told me I needed to wait until I turned twelve to get one.

What if I had missed his phone call?

What if I had gone outside to shoot hoops and my mom had gone into the bathroom at just that moment and neither of us had heard the phone ring?

What if I had decided it was too hot to bike over? That I wanted to stay home instead?

Maybe I'd be in tenth grade at Dove Lake High instead of sitting at home with a tutor doing school online, completely screwed up and sleeping with the lights on.

Maybe.

Jesse is fiddling with his controller now, and I wonder if he wants to play some more. But I don't feel like playing. I just want to be by myself. Or better, disappear. Then my mom walks in and starts asking us if we want a snack.

"Actually Mrs. Jorgenson, I got to get going," Jesse says, standing up.

"All right," my mom answers, and she's reading my face, trying to make sure I'm okay. She's constantly checking in with me. Every millisecond of every second, she's scanning my eyes and my nose and my mouth to make sure I'm not about to lose it or something. Sometimes I feel like a science experiment.

I try to hold it together, nodding. My mom and I walk Jesse to the door.

"I'll try to stop by next week," he says.

"Cool," I say. But I think he might never come over again, and this makes me relieved and depressed at the exact same time.

"Cool," Jesse says, and he makes his way over to his mom's Camry and drives off, giving me a little wave as he pulls out. No guy hug this time.

"Did you have fun?" my mom asks after I shut the front door, her eyebrows popping up.

"Yeah, sure," I say. I might as well tell her what I know she wants to hear.

"What do you think you want for dinner?" she asks me, her eyebrows still up like two umbrellas.

"Anything's good. Maybe mac and cheese." I just need to get out of here. I need to breathe a little.

"Okay, mac and cheese it is," she says, smiling.

She heads back toward the kitchen but I say, "I'm going out to the garage. To practice."

"Oh, that's great, Ethan," my mom says, and yeah, when she looks back at me, she tears up. Again.

Outside, I take a deep inhale as I watch the garage door roll back like I'm the winner on some game show and here is my prize. A Ludwig in deep blue. I gaze at my drums and slide onto the stool, taking the smooth sticks into my hands. And I start playing, wailing away until I'm sure my arms are about to fly off. Until my mind is nothing but machine gun beats.

CAROLINE—148 DAYS AFTERWARD

BECAUSE IT'S DOVE LAKE. BECAUSE IT'S ONLY A COUPLE OF THOUSAND people who call this place home. Because Emma and I even drove past it a few times in the days after Ethan and Dylan were found to gawk at the news trucks hanging around. (Emma wanted to do it because it was something exciting that was happening in a place where nothing exciting ever did, but to me, it just felt creepy.) But because of all of these reasons, I know exactly where to find the house where Ethan Jorgenson lives. It's one of those big, beautiful homes with a wraparound front porch and a landscaped garden and a giant backyard that gently nestles up against Dove Lake Creek. It's an older neighborhood, but most of the homes only look old on the outside and are probably totally new and Pottery Barnish on the inside—not that I've ever been inside any of them. The people who live here are mostly people with money who came here to get away from city life. Some of them don't even live here year-round. They just come and spend the weekends and long breaks.

Must be nice.

As I bike down Ethan's street, I catch glimpses of the cute Halloween decorations in the gardens and yards of these big fancy houses. Clusters of pumpkins by front doors and gauzy fake spiders' webs pulled over bushes and hedges. Emma and I would always trick-or-treat in this neighborhood when we were little because the people who lived here gave out the best candy—whole Snickers (not just the mini size), Ring Pops, and jumbo-sized bags of M&Ms. Dr. Jorgenson didn't give out candy on account of being a dentist, but he and Mrs. Jorgenson would answer the door and give out glow-in-the-dark spider stickers and temporary tattoos of ghosts and witches.

I remember during those years when Ethan was missing and we would come and ring the doorbell. They would appear, the two of them, Mrs. Jorgenson's face searching ours as we stood on their porch, our bags outstretched and open. I remember her distracted half smile as her eyes skimmed over us, taking us in one by one. As if she almost expected Ethan to show up on her front doorstep dressed as Sponge-Bob SquarePants or Captain America.

After two years I stopped trick-or-treating there. It was too sad.

But here I am on my ten-speed in the driveway. My eyes search the house, wondering if I could just go up and ring the doorbell and ask this guy—this poor kid who suffered what was probably some sick, crazy shit for four years—what went down with my brother so maybe I can get an idea of how to help him. Assuming he can even be helped.

Then I hear the drumming coming from around back, from the detached garage.

Whoever it is, it's pretty good. I mean, it's no Keith Moon, but still. Decent.

I drop my bike on the front yard and head around toward the source of the noise. And there he is in the flesh. Ethan Jorgenson. Carlotta King interview subject. Nationally known crime victim. Small town cautionary tale.

He's wailing away on a Ludwig. Deep blue. That set must have cost more than one of my dad's weekly paychecks.

He doesn't see me at first. His eyes are closed, and he's playing along to some song making its way out of some fancy wireless speakers near his feet. I listen for a few seconds. It's some crappy song by Green Day. God, I hate that band so much. Not only are they ancient, the lead singer's facial expressions always look like he's about to have a seizure or something. But Ethan is drumming like he's in some perfect mental place. He's wearing a light blue polo and dark jeans and a soft smile. He looks weirdly old to me. I think it's because even though I saw him briefly in the gym during those news conferences and, of course, on the Carlotta King show, in my head he's still the same middle schooler staring at me from those MISSING posters in his dad's waiting room. That eleven-year-old boy wearing some Abercrombie shirt and trying to seem cool.

I wait until he's done and he opens his eyes. When he sees me he gasps out loud.

Way to go, Caroline. Great plan sneaking up on a kidnapping victim.

"Can I . . . are you . . . ," he stands up, his expression confused.

"Hey," I say, holding my hands up in an I-bring-you-no-harm-take-me-to-your-leader pose. "I'm sorry if I scared you. I'm, um . . . I'm Caroline Anderson? I'm the older sister of . . . Dylan? Um . . ."

The lunacy of this plan hits me hard. This entire idea seemed much better inside my head when I was stoned.

I hear a back door slamming and turn around to see Mrs. Jorgenson heading over to us across the backyard. She's wearing some super classy summer getup. Like, who wears khaki shorts with a belt? She must not buy her clothes at the Fallas Paredes or the Wal-Mart like the rest of us, that's for sure.

"Hi!" she shouts way too loudly. "Well, look at who I've spotted!" Like I'm a rare bird or something.

"Hi, Mrs. Jorgenson," I say.

[65]

"Hello, Caroline!" Her smile is really big and wide, and I can see the tops of her gums.

At the mention of my name, Ethan's face seems to register who I am. He sits back down at his Ludwig really slowly, and I can feel his eyes first on me and then on his mom and then on me again. But he's gripping his drumsticks so tight his knuckles are white, and suddenly I feel like the biggest jerk on the planet for even being here.

"So . . . ," Mrs. Jorgenson says, still bright as the Texas sun, "how is your family? How is Dylan doing?" Her face does this weird cross of maniacally upbeat and super concerned, and I'm surprised her eyes don't cross.

"He's . . . okay," I say. "We're just . . . getting back to normal."

"Of course," Mrs. Jorgenson says, nodding vigorously. "It takes time. Lots of time. That's what our therapists have been saying. Time, time, time." She smiles again. Too big. She's nervous I'm here. She doesn't want to be rude, but I'm making her anxious. With every word she scoots microscopically closer toward Ethan. I try to cut the tension.

"Is that a real Ludwig?" I ask Ethan even though I know it is.

Ethan frowns a little, and his eyes go all wide. He peeks down at his drums like he needs to check.

"Uh . . . yeah?"

"Wow," I say. "It's totally gorgeous."

Mrs. Jorgenson is watching us. Watching me. Deciding what to do.

"Thanks," Ethan says. "I just got it. For my birthday."

"Hey, happy birthday," I say.

"Thanks," Ethan offers again. He glances at his mother. Silence.

"I don't drum myself," I say, and now I think I sound like the nervous one, just talking spastically, filling the air up with my words. "I play guitar," I tell him. "It's this cheap little Fender Squier. I mean, it's not fancy like this Ludwig or anything. But it's still kind of cool, I guess."

Ethan is staring at me. When I mention my guitar, he breaks into this goofy, lopsided grin for the briefest of seconds. It's the same grin that stared at me from the MISSING posters. He's got a touch of stubble around it now, but it's the same grin. The same goofiness.

"Well," Mrs. Jorgenson says. "Can I . . . would you . . ." She crosses her arms. She uncrosses them. "Would you two like some lemonade?"

"Oh," I answer, "I . . . well . . . ," but Ethan gives her a half nod and I hear myself mumbling, "Sure, that would be nice."

As Mrs. Jorgenson crosses the backyard toward the door, she looks at us over her shoulder three times.

"So," I say, leaning back, sliding my hands into the back pockets of my shorts. "This is a pretty cool gift."

"Yeah," Ethan says, rubbing his thumb over a drumstick.

Now that Mrs. Jorgenson isn't here, I should try to start in on my plan. But how? Just wander in here and ask this trauma victim why my little brother keeps repeating the words *damn, damn piece of cake* all the time? And why he can't even go outside our house anymore?

It's not like Ethan and I were friends before he was taken. He was a year behind me in school. You don't live in a town like Dove Lake and not coexist constantly, like you're all a bunch of marbles in the same pinball game, bouncing off of and into one another all day long, most of you looking for a way out. But we don't really know each other.

I normally hate it when people don't just say what they're really thinking, but just because we've lived here together for most of our childhoods doesn't mean I can come right out and just ask him about what happened. No, I need to "engage" with him. At Jackson Family Farm, Enrique is always telling me to engage with customers. Build rapport. At the farm I do it so maybe I can get the lady from the city to buy one more jar of Meemaw's Kuntry Kitchen Preserves. With Ethan I need to do it to figure out just what happened to my sweet baby brother. Just what that bastard did to him.

"So," I start, "what were you playing?" I know it was Green Day, but I'm just trying to get him to relax. Maybe I'm trying to relax, too.

"Green Day," he says.

"Oh," I answer. "Have you ever listened to The White Stripes?"

Before he can answer, Mrs. Jorgenson is back out with two glasses of lemonade in these cut crystal glasses that are fancier than anything my family owns. These have to be the two fastest poured glasses of lemonade in the history of the world. Ice cubes clink together as she hands me mine.

"Thanks," I say, taking a swallow.

Mrs. Jorgenson stands there, smiling frantically. I end up drinking all my lemonade as she stands there watching, and then I hand her back the glass. She takes it and clutches it tight. Ethan just takes a sip of his drink and places it carefully on the garage floor next to his feet.

"So . . . ," says Mrs. Jorgenson. I know she wants me to leave.

"I was just, you know, talking to Ethan about music," I say.

Ethan isn't looking at either one of us. Just down at his drums. But then I hear him ask sort of quietly, "Which White Stripes album is the best?"

"Oh," I answer, all in a rush, "*White Blood Cells*. Their third album. It's really good."

Ethan nods and glances back at me, then at his mom, then at his drums again.

"So . . . ," Mrs. Jorgenson says again. "Well."

"The White Stripes are just drums and guitar," I keep going, and Ethan is actually looking at me now, peering out of the sides of his eyes. "I mean, you wouldn't think that would be that great, but it really is. It's awesome." Even though I just gulped down all that lemonade, my mouth is super dry.

"I'm sure Ethan will give them a listen," Mrs. Jorgenson says, and she puts one hand on my shoulder. Her touch is firm and means business. Her nails are a perfect pale pink.

I don't know if I've built any rapport. Mostly, I think I've come across as a really hyper fan of The White Stripes. This is not going at all like I'd planned. Then again, I didn't really have a good plan in the first place.

"I guess I should be going," I say, disappointed but trying not to show it. "It was nice talking to you, Ethan."

Ethan nods at me, then looks away. He's gripping his drumsticks again.

"Nice to talk to you, too," he murmurs.

"Maybe I'll see you around," I manage, but nobody answers me. I hop on my bike and as I glide toward the end of the driveway and turn onto Ethan's street, I listen for his drumming to start up again, but there's nothing but silence, and I feel so bad about this that my stomach twists a little out of guilt.

ETHAN—149 DAYS AFTERWARD

I NORMALLY MEET WITH DR.GREENBERG ON FRIDAYS ANYWAY, BUT IF I didn't have an appointment today I think my mom sure would have scheduled one for me anyway. Because of what happened with that girl Caroline coming over yesterday. I know my mom wasn't crazy about Caroline showing up randomly because after Caroline left, my mom asked me like five hundred times if I was okay. Then after I started playing video games, she took her phone and went into the living room and started talking in this hushed voice, I think to my dad or to her therapist or maybe even to Dr. Greenberg.

Anyway, I have an appointment this morning already, so now here I am, having survived the nightmarish drive into the city. I sit, swallowed up by this big, overstuffed beige couch, glancing first at Dr. Greenberg sitting across from me in his office chair and then out the window at the pecan tree, wishing I could be that ordinary.

I know I said Dr. Greenberg looks like a skinny Santa Claus, but if you dressed him in more worn-out clothes instead of in the khaki slacks and plain button-down shirts he usually wears, he could also pass for one of those guys who stands at freeway off-ramps holding a sign that says HOME-LESS VET ANYTHING HELPS. Plus, Groovy usually joins us in sessions. Groovy is this big golden retriever with liquid-brown eyes like a human's, almost. The first time he came into Dr. Greenberg's office while I was in there, he leaped up onto the couch that I sit on during appointments like some sort of dog superhero. Then he curled up next to me and did this dog sigh of total contentment.

I thought it was weird at first, but I got used to it. When I walk into the office for today's session, Groovy follows me in and sits down right next to me, and I spend the next ten minutes scratching behind his ears and giving Dr. Greenberg the shortest answers I can come up with, wondering how much more time until our session is up.

"Groovy likes you," says Dr. Greenberg, giving me a soft half smile.

"I like Groovy," I answer.

Silence.

I wonder how much my parents are paying Dr. Greenberg. If he's so famous, probably a lot. Which sort of makes me feel guilty since in the five months I've been seeing him I just answer his questions as simply as I can, and we make basic conversation about the weather or what we ate for breakfast. I mean, I'm not rude or anything. He's a nice enough guy. I'm just not sure why I keep coming here if we don't even really talk about everything that happened.

Not that I'm dying to talk about any of it.

"You don't have any pets, do you?" asks Dr. Greenberg.

"No," I answer. "My mom doesn't like animals in the house." I bet if I asked for a dog now, though, I would get one. I could get five, probably. I feel so guilty over that realization that I'm pretty sure I'll never ask for a dog ever. Probably not even a goldfish.

And suddenly a memory comes at me. The image of that stray tabby Marty let me feed sometimes. The one I found hanging out around the apartment complex. The one I found after he finally started letting me go outside and breathe fresh air. The picture shoots through me like a needle through fabric. Quick and sharp and exact.

No, don't think about it.

I squeeze my eyes tight.

"Ethan, you with me?"

I blink a few times, and my left hand moves to pet Groovy's soft, silky head. It steadies me a little.

"Yeah, I'm with you," I answer.

My eyes scan the back wall of the office. I'm trying to get

my bearings. After all these months of sitting in this room in Dr. Greenberg's house, the room that he's turned into his office, I've memorized the diplomas with the names Harvard and Columbia on them. Along with the diplomas there's a framed black-and-white photograph of a younger looking Dr. Greenberg with a darker beard marching in a street, surrounded by other guys with crazy beards and girls with long, messy hair. I've always wondered about it.

"What's that picture of?" I ask, motioning at the image. If I can take up time asking questions, the session will go by faster. And I won't have to talk about myself.

Dr. Greenberg twists around in his seat and smiles fondly.

"Oh, that's me protesting the war in Vietnam," he says. "Back when I was a student. I was arrested shortly after that picture was taken."

"And they let you become a therapist?" I ask. There's a mug shot of my therapist somewhere in a police station. I swear to God, this guy gets weirder every time.

"Ha!" Dr. Greenberg says. "That's terrific. Yes. They let me become a therapist. That's not the only time I was arrested, just so you know. I used to be very active in the no nukes movement in the eighties."

"No nukes?"

"Nuclear weapons. I protested against them, too."

"Oh," I say. People don't talk about countries firing nuclear weapons much anymore. It's just terrorists blowing shit up or people shooting up schools that freaks every-body out.

Dr. Greenberg picks at something in his beard with his enormous, old guy fingers. He probably gets a lot of food stuck in there.

"You still playing the drums you got for your birthday?" he asks.

"Yeah," I say. "I am."

"You like practicing on them?"

"Yeah, I enjoy it." I could say that I'm not sure if I'm any good or that it's been so long since I've really played, but the whole idea just feels too exhausting to even discuss.

"Your parents told me a girl came to see you yesterday while you were playing," he says. Dr. Greenberg has explained to me that while our sessions are private, he talks to my parents about the "general course of my treatment." Whatever that means. So it's no surprise to me that he knows about Caroline. Although I guess I was hoping he wouldn't bring her up.

Almost right after he mentions her, though, he gets up and walks to his desk, where he puts his hands on the bottom of his back and stretches. His belly sticks out a little.

"Now where did I put that thing?" he mutters, like he didn't just mention Caroline. He opens one desk drawer, then another.

"What are you doing?" I ask. I wonder again how much money my parents are spending on this guy. I mean, he's nice.

But still. He's been arrested more than once, and now he's randomly digging through his desk drawers?

"I'm looking for Groovy's brush," he says, his eyes down, his hands opening and closing drawers. "Oh, here it is."

He walks over and hands me a plastic brush with a blue handle. I catch a faint whiff of the same Old Spice deodorant my dad uses.

"He loves to be brushed," he says, and then he settles back into his chair. "I mean, only if you want to."

Groovy notices the brush in my hand and flips over, squirming in excitement. His tail even wags. I'd have to be a pretty big asshole not to brush this dog right now.

So I do. I start tugging the brush through his soft, golden retriever hair. The teeth leave tiny, orderly lines in his fur.

"So this young woman . . . ?" he says. I keep brushing. Groovy stays still.

"Yeah," I say.

"She's the older sister of the other young man who was kidnapped. Right?"

I nod. I keep brushing. I feel my face getting hot.

"Okay," says Dr. Greenberg, and I think he's wondering what to say to me. I must be pretty messed up if this world-famous therapist doesn't even know what to say next.

There's a long pause, and then I just can't help it. "Did my mom seem worried?" I ask. "About me talking to Caroline?"

"Is it important to you that you not worry your parents?" he answers. Answering a question with a question. I hate that.

"Yeah, I guess so," I say. "I mean, I made them worry so much while I was . . . gone." I never know how to refer to the time that I was kidnapped. I hate saying the word *kidnapped* out loud because it makes me feel awful. But if I say my time with Marty, it makes it sound like I was there cutting school and having an okay time. I already know that's what some people think is the truth. That I was just there hanging out. I feel my heart start to pick up speed, but just then Groovy scooches over to me and rests his head on my thigh. I keep brushing him. He's starting to fall asleep.

Dr. Greenberg waits for a while and finally says, "Maybe your mother seemed a little anxious about it. I think considering how you and Caroline are connected, she's just concerned about how it might make you feel."

"Connected," I repeat, like Caroline and I are puzzle pieces or threads in a spider's web. I know what he means, of course, but I don't want to think about Caroline's little brother. My brain has gotten good at shoving memories around where I can't get to them. And the ones about Dylan are hazy and gray and untouchable and probably right where they belong.

"Do you want to share what she wanted to talk about?" Dr. Greenberg asks, interrupting my thoughts.

I shrug. "We didn't really talk about anything." I remember

Jesse's last visit, and him bringing up his guilt over the past. "She didn't, like, bring up, you know . . . ," I offer. I'm gripping Groovy's brush hard in my hands. "She plays guitar. She mostly seemed to want to talk about music."

Dr. Greenberg nods. "What if she did bring it up?" he asks.

This is the closest Dr. Greenberg and I have ever come to really talking about me in any kind of serious way. I mean the stuff that happened to me. I feel the slightest wave of nausea building in my stomach. I drag the brush over Groovy's fur and close my eyes for a moment.

"I mean . . . I know my parents want to protect me," I say. I wonder if they've told Dr. Greenberg to tell me to stop talking to Caroline. The idea bothers me. I feel guilty for making my parents worry about me so much, and I feel guilty that I get so annoyed by them worrying. I want to be able to decide who I hang out with. Not that I necessarily want to hang out with Caroline. I mean, it was kind of cool how Caroline knew so much about my drums and music, but the idea of hanging out with her makes me nervous.

How am I supposed to come talk to a therapist about my feelings when I don't really know what the hell I feel?

Dr. Greenberg gives me a half smile again. "Of course your parents want to protect you," he says. "I wonder why they might feel especially protective with regard to Caroline."

It's not phrased like a question, but it's like he expects an answer. I give Groovy one last brush and try to respond. "Maybe they're worried that talking to Caroline would bring stuff up about . . . everything," I say. "And I could get, like, hurt?"

"Drawing healthy boundaries is something that's sometimes hard for victims of trauma," Dr. Greenberg says, resting his hands on top of his belly. "I'm sorry. To translate that into normal language, what I mean is that people who have been through something like what you've been through sometimes have a hard time knowing who to trust. Knowing who to make friends with."

"Yeah," I say. I mean, what am I supposed to say to that? *No shit?*

"If you'd like, that's something we could talk about here, during our sessions," Dr. Greenberg says. "How to have good friendships. Good relationships."

"Okay," I say.

Friendships. I'm not sure I have any left. I'm not sure if Jesse is still my friend, or if I even want to be his. And I think back on Bennie and Narciso, the two guys from the apartment complex. I try to imagine what they're doing now—skateboarding, complaining about their teachers, talking about girls—and I wonder if they ever think of me.

All of a sudden, I want to stop thinking about all this. Talking about all of this. So I flip through my mind for something to say. "I liked brushing Groovy. I put him to sleep."

Dr. Greenberg smiles. "I've found he helps patients relax because he loves to relax himself."

An idea dawns on me. "Wait, did you get me to brush Groovy to make it easier to talk?"

"Well," Dr. Greenberg says, and he looks a little bashful. "The answer is yes, I admit it. Groovy has a way of knowing when people need an extra little security blanket during a session."

It should piss me off, but it doesn't. "It was nice to brush him," I say, shrugging my shoulders. I bury my hand into Groovy's fur. I don't care that he's a trained security blanket and Dr. Greenberg set it all up. It just feels good to sit next to this dog.

Dr. Greenberg takes his notepad off the end table next to his chair and scratches a few notes with a pencil he has tucked behind his ear. His hair is so wild I didn't even notice the pencil until he slid it out.

"We're getting to the end of our session," he says, glancing up at the clock I know is on the wall behind my head. "But we'll be seeing each other soon."

I nod. I wonder how long I'll be seeing him as a patient. Like I said, Dr. Greenberg is nice enough. But these sessions don't ever make me feel normal. Whatever feeling normal is supposed to mean. And there's no way that someone as screwed up as me can ever be normal again, probably. I should just accept it already.

"I know I have to get up," I say, "but I hate to wake up Groovy."

Dr. Greenberg grins. He gets up again and goes to his desk, to the glass jar that holds these biscuits Groovy likes. The clink of the lid coming off is all it takes for Groovy to bolt up off the couch and race over to Dr. Greenberg.

"He'll eat too many and get fat," he says, scratching the golden retriever on top of his head. "But I can't say no to him. Here, you can give him one, too."

I get up and take a treat from Dr. Greenberg, and Groovy bumps his wet nose against my hand in gratitude before gobbling the biscuit out of my palm.

"Good dog," I tell him. "Good dog."

"Okay, I'll walk you out," says Dr. Greenberg as he opens the door that leads into the room where my mother sits, perched on the edge of a chair wearing an anxious smile, waiting for me, her only child, to appear.

CAROLINE—157 DAYS AFTERWARD

THE WEEKEND BEFORE HALLOWEEN AT JACKSON FAMILY FARM IS LIKE the day after Thanksgiving at Walmart. Which is to say it's epic madness. Parents from the city come, desperate to capture fifty million photographs of little Sage or little Olivia surrounded by orange pumpkins or taking part in a gen-u-wine hayride or whatever. Pictures they can post online later to prove what amazing parents they are. I'm glad when Enrique puts me at a cash register instead of making me smile and give directions to families trooping out into the patch to pick what they hope will turn into a picture perfect jack-o-lantern. That way I don't have to engage as much with the Prius and organic snack crowd.

But it's hard to focus on my job when Jason McGinty is winking at me from the other side of the barn, by the barrels of overpriced jams and jellies. Jason is pretty cute with a good body. He's kind of a dumbass, I know. But still. Cute.

My phone buzzes. I manage to sneak a peek in between customers.

Let's go hide behind a hay bale and get nekkid

I glance up and find Jason laughing at me. I roll my eyes but I can't help but grin a little.

"Excuse me?"

"Oh," I say, glancing at Mr. Suburban Dad standing in front of me, his harried wife and two blond kids behind him. "I'm sorry. Let me help you check out." I glance back toward Jason, but he's not there anymore.

When the final customers are driving back to civilization in their hybrid SUVs, I get another text. This one is from Emma.

Hey girl . . . u done? Meet us in the parking lot

I don't know who the "us" is until I find Emma and Jason sitting on the edge of the bed of Jason's blue Chevy pickup. I know I shouldn't mind, but I do. I mean, we all go to school together, so yeah, it makes sense we would all hang out. And it's not like Jason's asked me to be, like, boyfriend girlfriend or whatever. But I guess I was looking forward to just hanging out with him alone tonight. And hopefully getting just the right amount of messed up and seeing what comes next.

The messed up part seems like it might still happen,

though, even if Emma's playing third wheel. The two of them are pouring some amber liquid into cans of Coke. It's Jason's go-to beverage—whiskey.

"Got you one," Jason says to me, handing me an open can. "Already doctored it myself and everything." It's a pretty sweet gesture, and this makes me wish we were alone even more.

"Thanks," I say, and Emma bumps Jason with her hip, forcing him down to one end of the truck, freeing up a space next to her. This puts her in the middle, in between Jason and me. I get prickly all over again and take a big sip of my drink.

"There's a party at my cousin's house in Healy," Emma says. "Like, some Halloween thing. If you want to drive out there."

I wrinkle my nose and sip some more. I hate going to parties where I only know two people. And plus, her cousin is this super annoying popular type who's head of the dance squad or whatever.

"We could go hang out at my place," Jason says. "My parents won't care. We could text people to come over."

"Then the guys will just sit around and play Call of Duty all night long," Emma says. "And the girls will just sit around and bitch. Fuck this town. It's so boring." She frowns the same tight frown she's had since we were in kindergarten together and became best friends after Ms. Sweeny assigned us to be shepherds instead of angels in the Christmas pageant.

"We never drive into the city," I say. "How come we never drive into the city?" I look down and realize my can feels pretty light. My face is starting to feel pleasant and numb. When Jason told me he doctored my drink, he didn't tell me he'd dumped half a bottle of whiskey in it.

"The city's too far," Jason says. "Too weird."

"Why is it weird?" I say. "It could be cool." There are some artsy hipster types from my school who go into the city sometimes. Who go hear bands play and everything. But I don't know them, and they don't know me. I hang out with Emma and Jason and that crowd, not the artsy types. It's too late now to change groups. I hate how in high school you're stuck in a group and when you realize later you probably belonged in another one, it's too late to change because you're already who you are.

Jason shrugs. "I wouldn't think you'd want to go into the city anyway after that sick fuck took your brother there and did whatever sick, fucked up shit those people do to kids."

Emma takes a sharp breath and glances at me.

"What?" I say. My pleasant numbness is gone, replaced with a hot anger that makes me want to spit. "What the hell did you just say?"

"Oh, shit," Jason says, a lopsided frown on his face. "I'm sorry, Caroline. That was . . . man, I'm sorry. I'm drunk."

"I hate when people blame the shit they say on being drunk," I tell him. "I told you never to talk about my brother again!" I feel like I'm going to start crying, which I hate even more than people blaming dumb crap they say on alcohol. I think I hate crying in front of people more than anything else.

"Jesus Christ, Jason," Emma says, sliding off the truck. "Come on, Caroline, let's go to my house." I'm grateful but almost surprised because I thought Emma wanted to party or hang out and lots of times that comes first before anything, including me.

"Man, don't leave. I'm really sorry." He's pleading a little, but he doesn't come after us as Emma and I walk off. He just sits there, holding his Coke can. I give him the finger as I march away.

"He's such a dick," I say, tossing my ten-speed into the trunk of Emma's old Toyota and getting in the car. I swallow the lump in my throat because I don't want to cry even in front of Emma.

"He's just clueless sometimes, you know?" Emma says, sliding into the driver's seat.

"No, you're supposed to say he's a dick," I say, irritated. I sip glumly from my Coke can.

"Yeah, he's a dick," Emma agrees, and we're silent until we pull up in front of the trailer where Emma lives with her mother.

"My mom's working the night shift," Emma says. "We

have the place to ourselves." She lets us into the front room where she busies herself by finding some of her mom's Marlboro Lights in a drawer in the adjoining, closet-sized kitchen. She knows I only smoke when I'm drinking and irritated.

"Jason McGinty can be so dumb," Emma says, lighting her own cigarette and sitting down next to me. "He needs to learn that mouth is only good for one thing."

I sink into the Naugahyde couch that's at least twice as old as I am. "I hate that he's such a good kisser," I tell Emma. "I hate that I'll probably kiss him again after tonight. Even after what he said."

"Please don't get mad at me, but he probably didn't mean it like it sounded," Emma says. "Even if it did come out sounding awful."

I shrug. I don't have the energy to debate Jason McGinty anymore. I don't want to spend another sentence on the situation.

Emma's mom has a couple of Shiners in her refrigerator, and after we drink those I realize I'm telling her about going by Ethan Jorgenson's house the other week.

"Seriously?" she says to me, tapping her ash into an empty bottle. "You just went over there? I can't believe you didn't tell me."

"Yeah. I think it was stupid," I say. "But I keep thinking about him."

"Is he, like, cute?" The question bugs me because it's all wrong. But that's mostly what Emma and I talk about when we talk about boys. How cute they are or aren't. Maybe that's why I didn't mention Ethan to her before.

I haven't actually considered the cute question. I mean, Ethan isn't bad looking. But he's not really my type. A little too lanky for me. Too dark-eyed and lost puppy dog for my liking. I wish it weren't true, but my type is muscular dumbass. Which explains Jason McGinty.

"He's okay," I answer. "He actually turned out to be pretty cool or whatever, but I guess I mostly went to see him to find out what he could tell me about what happened to Dylan. Since Dylan can't, you know . . . tell us. But I didn't actually ask him anything. We just talked about music for, like, five minutes until his mom made it pretty clear I needed to leave."

Emma wrinkles her nose and gives me her tight frown again. She's drunk, but I can tell she's trying to pick her words carefully, so I won't get mad at her like I did with Jason.

"Are you sure you . . . want to know? What happened to Dylan?" Emma says. "I mean . . . can't you sort of . . . guess?"

Flashes of Dylan being touched or hurt jump in front of my eyes, and I squeeze them shut like this can block out pictures I don't want to see. "Yeah," I say. "I could guess. I mean, I already have. I know it's messed up, but I guess I want to know details. Because then maybe I could help him. Like, he's scared to go outside. He freaks out at loud noises. And this

[88]

is weird, but he keeps talking about a piece of cake and he keeps cursing, which he's never done before. I don't know how this guy got him. What he said to him while he had him, you know? If I knew, maybe . . . maybe I could figure out how to help him be less scared now."

Suddenly, other images run in front of my eyes. Other sounds. From that Saturday afternoon when Dylan went missing.

Dill Pickle, give me a second, okay? Can you let me finish something? Go play somewhere else, okay?

Caroline, wasn't Dylan in here with you? Weren't you watching him?

Mindy, I think we need to call the police.

"You want another beer?" Emma asks me, eyeing me carefully.

"No," I answer, pressing my hands over my face. Things are starting to feel loopy and twisty and not so good inside. I've had too much to drink, and I'm going to pay later. I know it. "I need to stay here tonight," I say. "Is that okay?"

"You know it is," says Emma.

"Let me just text my mom."

I manage to put together some sort of coherent message about spending the night at Emma's, and I wait for my mom's response to be that I should come back or I've been gone too much lately or she needs me home or whatever, but there's no response for almost twenty minutes, and when she finally texts me back, all she writes is **That's fine.**

I consider texting her one more time to tell her Emma's house is full of crystal meth users and they want to pimp me out to support their sick habit, but I'm too scared to get another **That's fine** response in return, so I just put my phone on vibrate, stumble into Emma's room, and pass out on her bed.

ETHAN—161 DAYS AFTERWARD

THERE ARE CLUMPS OF MUD AND A FEW CIGARETTE BUTTS ON THE *closet's hardwood floor.*

There's one lightbulb on above me, and when I adjust my body to try and find a more comfortable position to sit in, the cord to turn the light on and off slides over the top of my head like it's trying to get my attention.

I can't stop worrying about what it will be like if the lightbulb goes out.

There's a navy blue winter coat with a broken zipper and a few flannel shirts lined up next to it, all hanging on wire hangers. I'm not tied up like when I first got here, but even though my arms and legs are free, there's no room for me to lay down and spread out. When I get tired I pull one of the shirts down and fold it up into a pillow and curl into a ball, crying into the shirt and wishing it didn't smell like him. Like cigarettes and sweat and everything scary and dirty and sick.

There's a bucket like the one Gloria uses to mop our floors jammed into the corner, only I'm supposed to use it for the bathroom. It's so close to me I can smell its stink.

And there's me.

And I'm eleven.

And the door to the closet won't open.

He put me in here after he hauled me out of the truck.

I've lost track of how long I've been locked in.

"Ethan! Ethan, we're right here!"

Someone has me by the shoulders, and I can hear a lady's voice, high-pitched and far away, screaming, "Don't shake him so hard! Oh, Ethan, sweetheart, wake up! Please wake up!"

Everything is swimmy and sideways. I can't breathe. I throw my hands up, my arms up. I swing them around, trying to reach out until I find something solid. Something real.

My shirt is clinging to me, covered in sweat.

"Ethan!" Voices are shouting my name over and over again.

I heave like I'm going to throw up, but nothing comes out.

"Ethan!"

Finally, I blink and my eyes start to adjust. My room. Not the closet.

That was before.

But this is now. After.

And I'm here. I'm here in my bedroom and I'm awake and I'm safe. I'm not back there.

I'm panting, but my breath is starting to slow down. I make out my dad in front of me, dressed in a white T-shirt and underwear.

What time is it?

How long have I been freaking out?

"I'm going to check your pulse, Ethan," my dad says, sitting next to me on my bed. "Can I do that?"

I nod, not ready to speak. My dad places his warm hand up near my neck, two fingers pressing in. His touch startles me, and I pull back.

"Not too hard," my mother says. "He needs to breathe." She's there, too, standing next to my dad, dressed in the black yoga pants and ratty Yale T-shirt she sleeps in sometimes, one hand nervously folding over the other, over and over again.

"Megan," my father says, his voice soft but firm. The same voice I know he uses with little kids when they're scared to have a cavity filled.

The sheets under me are damp with sweat. I'm cold all of a sudden, and my teeth start to chatter loud enough that I'm sure my dad can hear.

"Get him another blanket," my dad directs my mother. When she comes back from the hall closet with one, he tells her, "His pulse is slowing down. It's okay. The worst is over."

"He hasn't had one of these in weeks," my mother says, her brow wrinkled with concern. "We need to talk to Dr. Greenberg about adjusting his dosage."

"Maybe," my dad answers, wrapping me up in the soft green comforter that used to be on the bed in the guest room before my mother redecorated it. He looks me in the eyes and pushes a smile out. One of his signature this-will-only-hurt-for-a-moment-don't-worry smiles. He uses those with the kids who have cavities, too.

"I want to call Dr. Greenberg right now," says my mother. "My phone is charging in the kitchen. Let me go get it." If she's not already crying I can tell from the crack in her voice that she's pretty close to it.

"It's the middle of the night, Megan," my father says.

She turns in the doorway and glares at my dad. "I know it's the goddamn middle of the night!" she snaps.

I blink and exhale, my breath shaky. "Stop," I manage. "Just . . . stop. Don't yell. I'm okay now."

Now my mother's crying for real. Big, glossy tears pouring down her face. Sobbing coming from deep in her chest.

"Megan," my dad says under his breath. "Megan, honey . . ."

"Oh, Ethan, I'm sorry," my mother says, crossing the bedroom floor in her quick, tiny steps and reaching out for me. "Oh, sweetheart. My sweet, sweet little boy."

She hugs me like she might crush me, and I shrug my

shoulders at her touch. She senses it and backs up. I press my hands onto my face because I don't want to see her hurt expression. But I really don't want her to touch me right now. I want to disintegrate into a million little pieces and float through the atmosphere. I want to rocket up past the moon and disappear somewhere into the outer bands of the Milky Way.

I want to be somewhere where I don't feel anything.

I think I am a seriously fucked up person. And I will probably never be normal. Even if I want to be.

. . . .

When I wake up the next morning, it's so late it's almost lunchtime. I fell asleep last night only after I took one of the pills Dr. Greenberg prescribed for my anxiety.

When I go downstairs, my mom tells me she's called my tutor to cancel school, telling her I'm not feeling 100 percent. To be honest, I don't mind Mrs. Leander coming over and tutoring me. She's some retired teacher who's probably, like, seventy years old, but she's pretty good at teaching me, and she doesn't treat me like I'm some weirdo but just like I'm any other kid. One time I overheard her telling my mom that my "natural intelligence" will help me overcome the fact that I didn't go to school for four years. So I couldn't help but like her a little more after that.

But a day off from school means a day I can practice my drums. I know as soon as I head out there to play and my mom has some privacy that she's going to call her best friend who still lives in Austin and her sister in California and anyone else. I'm sure this morning before I woke up she called Dr. Greenberg and probably her own therapist, Dr. Sugar. That's what my mom loves to do. Talk. About everything. Constantly. Especially me. I guess she can't help it, but I hate how sometimes she makes me feel like I'm a problem that can be fixed with one of her to-do lists. I think I probably can't be fixed at all.

I feel like a shithead for being so mean to my mom inside my head. She had to have been hurt because I wouldn't hug her back last night. But sometimes I just can't stand to be touched, especially by her. Sometimes it's okay. But sometimes it just really isn't.

After I force myself to eat a sandwich, I head outside to my Ludwig and pick up my sticks and start drumming. My shoulders don't ache as much as they did when I first started playing again, and I think I don't even suck too much.

I love playing the drums.

I play all afternoon, and my mom brings me a snack in the garage—a soda and some potato chips on one of our nice plates. Mom doesn't like to use paper plates, even when we eat outside.

"Sweetie," she says, setting down the chips and drink,

"Dr. Sugar is fitting me in a little earlier today than normal. Can you be ready to leave soon?"

"Mom, I can stay by myself while you're at Dr. Sugar's. Even Dr. Greenberg said."

"Oh, Ethan, I don't know. You had a rough night and everything." She frowns a little and turns and looks toward the front of our house, like she can spot the next bad guy coming down the street. Since I came back she and dad have had this thing that I need to be with one of them at all times. Even though I'm sixteen. Even though Dr. Greenberg told me that I should be able to stay by myself in my house if I'm comfortable with that, and he told mom that, too, after one of our sessions.

There's part of me that wants to tell mom that guys like Marty don't want sixteen-year-old boys. That I'm too old for her to worry about that anymore. But I don't think it's the kind of thing that's going to make her feel better.

"Mom, I'm going to be fine. I've got my phone. You can text me anytime."

She crosses her arms in front of her and glances back at the street. She takes a deep breath. I can imagine her thinking this is something she'll need to talk about with Dr. Sugar. How she can allow her teenage son to be by himself.

"Okay," she finally says, "but I want you to put your phone on the ground where you can see it when I text you. You'll never hear it with all this drumming," she says.

"I promise," I say, sliding my phone out of my pocket and putting it on the ground next to my drum kit, well within my line of vision.

"I'll be home a little before dinner," she says. Dr. Sugar isn't as far away as Dr. Greenberg, but my mom still has to get on the freeway to get there. Another reason to be glad I'm not going.

She texts me three times on her way to her appointment, and each time I have to stop drumming and text back something like Mom I'm fine you should focus on driving okay? And then when she finally gets to her appointment, I text her Have a good session. Hopefully Dr. Sugar will keep her from texting me at least for the hour that she's talking to him, so I can actually finish drumming through one song.

I'm picking up my sticks when I see her, pedaling up my driveway on her ten-speed.

Caroline.

It's been like two weeks since that first time she showed up. I'd almost started to feel like maybe she'd never really been at my house at all. And now here she appears, like a magic trick.

"Hey," she says, gliding up. Her long hair is tied back in a ponytail, and there's a backpack slung over her shoulders. She glances at me and then toward the back door.

"Hey," I say.

"You saw me coming, huh?" she asks. "I'm glad I didn't scare you this time."

Well, maybe she didn't scare me, but I wouldn't exactly call this an expected visit. Only I don't say that. I just shift a little on my drum stool. Why is she here again?

"So, have you checked out The White Stripes yet?" She slides off her bike but she stands next to it, holding the handles. Gripping the handles, actually. She can't live too far from here if she biked, but I know she doesn't live in this neighborhood. Her dad's an exterminator and her mom doesn't work, I don't think. At least that's what my mom told me.

"Yeah, I checked them out," I say. "They were pretty good." It's the truth. They were pretty good, but they weren't as mind blowing as I thought they would be.

"Pretty good?" She rolls her eyes, which is kind of rude, to be honest.

"Okay," I say because I'm not sure what else to say. I pick up my phone to check, but no texts from mom. Then I look back at Caroline. My mind flashes on something Dr. Greenberg said. About trauma victims not knowing how to have healthy boundaries.

She glances at the back door again when she sees me pick up my phone. "Is your mom coming out or something?" Her cheeks are two red splotches, and she seems to be breathing a little faster than she should be, even if she did just ride a bike.

Is Caroline nervous? I feel like I should be the nervous

one, but right now I'm just sitting here confused as to why this girl keeps showing up at my house.

"My mom isn't here," I tell her, putting my phone into my pocket.

"Oh," she says, and you'd think this would calm her down a little, but it doesn't. Now she's tapping her foot. On her feet are pink sneakers covered in mud.

"So . . . ," I say. "Why are you here again? Just to ask me if I listened to The White Stripes?" That came out wrong. I sounded rude and I don't mean to be, but I'm not sure how else to figure out what she wants. And something in me wants to know. Wants to make sure she's real, not just messing with me.

Caroline is rocking back and forth on her pink sneakered feet now, full of anxious energy. She opens her mouth like she's going to say something and then shuts it. There's a big silence, and then she closes her eyes and takes a breath.

She finally opens her eyes and starts climbing on her bike. "This was a terrible idea," she says, her voice so soft I almost don't catch what she says. "I'm sorry. Just forget I was here. I'm really sorry."

And with that she jumps back on her bike and starts off down the driveway.

CAROLINE—161 DAYS AFTERWARD

I'M TWO HOUSES DOWN FROM ETHAN'S WHEN I HEAR A VOICE YELLING after me, calling my name.

I slow down but I don't turn around. I think I might be crying, so I take a deep breath and glance up at the sky, blinking a few times real quick to make sure no tears fall.

"Hey, Caroline!"

I glance over my shoulder and, of course, it's Ethan standing in the middle of the street. He's still holding his drumsticks, too.

"Can you please come back?" he shouts. "I can't leave the house."

It's weird to me that he considers two houses down the street "leaving the house," and anyway, I don't think I should go back at all, but the way he says "please" makes me turn around. My heart is hammering the entire time I walk my bike back toward the Jorgensons' house, and by the time I make it to the end of the driveway, I can tell Ethan has a tiny frown on his face like he's trying to figure out some complicated math problem or something.

"Look," he says, "you can't just, like, keep coming to my house without telling me why." He doesn't really look me in the eye when he says it. He kind of glances at me when he starts talking and then finishes by looking at his feet.

"I'm sorry, I didn't mean . . . ," I start. But all of a sudden I hear a buzz, and Ethan pulls his phone out of his pocket.

"God," he murmurs under his breath, and he taps something real quick and slides his phone back into his jeans. "My mom."

"Does she text you a lot?" I ask.

Ethan nods. "Yeah. I mean, when she's not with me." He scratches at the back of his neck and looks up the driveway toward his drum kit. "Actually, this is the first time I've been here by myself since. . ." He doesn't finish the sentence. It just slides into the air, the obvious left unsaid.

"Oh," I say. I guess if I were Mrs. Jorgenson, I wouldn't want to let Ethan out of my sight either. I mean, I still check on Dylan in the middle of the night, and he's not even my kid. The thought of my baby brother makes me clutch my handlebars. Standing there at the foot of Ethan's driveway, I try to silently rehearse one last time what I came here to say. Honestly, if I don't do it now, I won't get another chance.

"Listen, I'm really sorry I showed up here again," I say, my mind searching for the words I rehearsed last night in my bedroom mirror. "And I'm really sorry it was unannounced. Again. But I'm here because I want to see if you can help me. With something about my brother. Dylan?" I don't know why I say his name like a question. Like there's a chance he doesn't know who my brother is. Ethan isn't saying anything. He's just listening, but his eyebrows are sliding together in a little V, like he's trying to read my face. Like he's trying to anticipate what I'm going to say before I say it.

"I'm just, like, this is so weird for me to talk to you about, I know, but I don't know what else to do," I continue. Now that I've started, my words are tumbling out of my mouth, like they couldn't wait to make themselves heard. Like my practice the night before has ingrained them in my memory. "He's been acting so upset lately, and, you know, he's got special needs and everything, so he can't really talk, only he repeats things, you know? Like ever since he was found he keeps repeating the words *piece of cake* and *damn* and I'm just trying to find out, like, what that might mean? What exactly happened to him? I want to know, you know, what that bastard said to him. We don't even know how he was taken, exactly. He's scared to even leave the house now, and he's really scared when we make sudden movements. And my parents don't want to acknowledge any of it, so I feel like it's on me to try and help him. So, I know this is weird, and I'm really sorry to bother you, but . . ." I hear my voice crack. I stop so I don't start crying. Because if I start, I won't stop, and I don't want to be sobbing in front of Ethan Jorgenson.

But at least I've said what I wanted to say.

Ethan doesn't respond at first. Out of the corner of my eye I see the hand not holding the drumsticks is in a tight ball, and his thumb is racing up and down his knuckles, over and over again. He's silent for a good while.

"Well, uh, my memory is kind of, I guess, messed up," he says at last. His voice is quiet.

I nod, listening. I realize I'm holding my breath.

"It was like he was just there one day," Ethan says. "In the apartment. He was scared because he wet his pants. I tried to help him wash them out in the sink. That's kind of all I remember." Then he pauses and closes his eyes. "He had a gun," he says with his eyes still closed. "Marty did, I mean. Marty was . . . in control."

I wince at the mention of that bastard's name. And I crumble inside thinking of Dylan messing himself.

"I hate hearing his name out loud," I say. "Like he's some sort of regular person."

Ethan gives me a half nod, glances over his shoulder and then back up the driveway again. "I'm sorry your brother's not doing so good," he finally manages.

"Me, too," I answer. My voice shakes just a bit again, but

I keep it together. "Thanks for helping him when he dirtied his pants." I swallow down the lump in my throat.

Ethan nods again, but he still isn't making eye contact with me.

"Has he seen, like, a therapist?" he asks.

I shake my head no. "Like I said, my mom and dad want us to just forget it ever happened. Plus, therapists cost money. And probably even a lot more money to find one who'll work with kids who don't even talk."

"Yeah," Ethan says. "I think they do cost a lot of money."

"You see a therapist?"

"Yeah."

Of course his family has the money for it. "Does it help?" I ask.

"I don't know," Ethan answers. "It's okay, I guess. Mine has a dog that's pretty nice."

"Like a dog that sits in on your meetings?"

"They're called sessions. But yeah."

"That's odd," I tell him.

"Yeah, it is. A little bit." He gives me a quick smile. A more smudged-out version of the one from the MISSING poster that I used to stare at for all those years. But still, it's a smile. And for the tiniest sliver of a second, there's a softness between Ethan and me. This tiny moment of normal. As normal as this situation can be. Which is not very. Ethan's hands have relaxed a bit though. His drumsticks dangle slightly out of his right hand.

Just then his phone buzzes again. He shakes his head a bit—is he embarrassed?—and texts back quickly.

"Wow, your mom really likes to check in," I say.

"Pretty much," Ethan says, and he rolls his eyes a little. Then he stops himself and he winces slightly. "But . . . I can't blame her."

"Yeah," I say, and suddenly any bit of normal disappears, and it's weird again. Maybe I should leave. This isn't exactly a comfortable conversation, but I'm not sure how to get out of it. So I nod my chin toward his drums. "What are you working on? I mean, drum-wise?"

His eyes pop open just a bit, and he takes a second to answer. "Uh, just my fills. Getting back to the basics." He stares at the ground again.

"That's cool," I say, glancing back at his drums. I'm realizing how difficult it is for two people to talk to each other when both of them don't know how to make eye contact.

"You really play guitar?" Ethan asks, and I can't tell if he actually wants to know or if he's saying something just because weird conversation is better than awkward silence.

I nod. "Yeah, I play. I mean, I'm not very good or anything." This could be a lie. I might be really great, but I have no way of knowing because no one else I know plays an instrument, and I taught myself with YouTube videos and chord progressions I printed off the Internet. I thought about joining the school band once or twice, but the people I hang out with—people like Jason and Emma—they just aren't the type to join the band. Or join anything. And anyway, I have my job at the farm to keep me busy.

"You're probably better on guitar than I am on drums," Ethan says.

I shrug, and before I realize what I'm saying, I answer, "Well, there would be only one way for us to find out, I guess." As soon as the words come out, I understand what it means. But the idea is ridiculous. "I'm sorry," I say. "I know we couldn't play together . . . I mean, like, you can't have people over, right?"

Ethan frowns. "What do you mean I can't have people over?"

My cheeks warm up. Are there any other people on planet Earth right now having a stranger conversation? "I just . . . ," I stammer. "I didn't think your mom would like it. Maybe your dad wouldn't either, I don't know. He wasn't here last time, but your mom . . . when I was here talking about The White Stripes, I mean . . . I don't know."

"I can have people over," Ethan says, and the way he says it reminds me of a little kid. His voice is soft, but the tone is the same one we all used on the playground when we were younger: *You're not the boss of me.*

"Sorry, I didn't know." Jesus. Does he not remember

telling me ten minutes ago that he wasn't allowed to leave his yard? How the hell am I supposed to know if he can have people over?

"It's okay," Ethan answers, his tone shifting. "I mean, it's fine. It's . . . it's fine."

"So what you're saying is you don't have anyone else to play music with?" I ask, desperate to drag us over this weird patch so we can end this conversation and I can leave.

Ethan shakes his head no. "Do you play with anyone?" he asks.

"No," I say. Which, to be honest, kind of sucks. The whole point of playing electric guitar is to be playing in a band or something. It's definitely not to play along with YouTube videos.

Ethan kicks at some invisible gravel on the blacktop. His Sperrys are new and spotless. The shoes of a guy who never leaves his house. And then I hear his voice. Directed at his shoes but at me, too.

"Maybe we could play sometime," he says. "I mean, if you wanted to or whatever."

I nod, only he can't see it since he's looking at the ground. So I say, "Is there a place for me to plug in my practice amp?"

"Yeah," Ethan says. "The garage has an outlet."

"That's cool," I say.

"Cool," Ethan says. Pause. "You could just come by some afternoon after you get done with school or whatever. Even if I didn't know you were coming . . . I wouldn't be, like, surprised or anything."

I can't tell if he's making a joke about my two unexpected visits, so I just say, "Okay. Sounds good."

There's another long silence, and finally I say, "I guess I should be going."

"Okay," he says.

"Well, take care," I say, climbing on my bike.

"Maybe see you later," he tells me, and as I turn around on my bike and start gliding down the street, my lungs finally taking in a deep breath, I replay Ethan's last sentence to me over and over in my head. *Maybe see you later.* The way he said it—the way it sounded hopeful but mostly sad—it was enough for me to forgive him entirely for not being able to tell me anything new about Dylan.

ETHAN—163 DAYS AFTERWARD

THERE'S NO REASON FOR ME TO TELL DR. GREENBERG ABOUT Caroline. She was gone by the time my mom came home from Dr. Sugar's.

But here I am, sitting next to Groovy and telling Dr. Greenberg about Caroline Anderson biking up to my house two days ago and turning around and leaving and then me calling her back. Explaining to him that we might play music together. Maybe. If she comes back at all.

I didn't think I would tell him about her, but I can't stop thinking about Caroline. About how she showed up out of nowhere and about all the things she said. About how her visit was scary in some ways, but in other ways it was something new. Something different. Something that wasn't therapy or nightmares or tutoring sessions or awkward situations with my parents.

And because I couldn't stop thinking about it, I guess I couldn't fight the urge to talk about it. And Dr. Greenberg is my only option.

"You think you'd like to play music with her?" Dr. Greenberg asks. He tilts his head a little, like that might help him hear my answer a little better or something.

I shrug. "Maybe," I finally manage. "I mean, playing the drums alone or along to music I listen to on my headphones is okay, but it's not like playing it with someone else." And I'm lonely and tired of living my life surrounded by people over the age of forty. But I don't say that to Dr. Greenberg.

"So what did it feel like to ask her to come back?" Dr. Greenberg asks. "After she turned around and biked off?"

I shrug again. Groovy nuzzles up under my hand, and I give him a few pets.

"I don't know," I say.

Dr. Greenberg nods and waits. I stare out the window at the pecan tree. There's a smudge on the window. I wonder if Dr. Greenberg made it with his nose, staring out at the same tree. Dr. Greenberg coughs, but he doesn't say anything. I think he's waiting me out. It makes me want to talk to cut the awkward silence. Which is weird because the awkward silences never used to bug me before.

"I guess I just didn't like how she kept showing up like that, and I wanted to tell her to stop doing it because it kind of pissed me off," I answer. There. I said it.

Dr. Greenberg cracks a smile—you can barely see it through his gray, Santa Claus beard—and he says, "I think that's great. We've been talking about healthy boundaries in here, and it seems like you made an attempt at drawing some."

Drawing healthy boundaries. Whenever Dr. Greenberg mentions that phrase it makes me think of taking a bunch of fruits and vegetables and surrounding myself with them—like a big circle of apples and eggplants and skinny green beans all laid out around me. Healthy boundaries.

"Anyway, she probably won't ever come back," I say. "She could just have been trying to be polite."

"Possibly," Dr. Greenberg says. He waits a beat. Two beats. "Do you want to talk about why she showed up this time? Before she turned around and biked away and then you spoke about playing music together?"

I blink. My brain feels foggy like it always does when Caroline's brother comes to mind, but there's something dark and scary there, too. Something that makes me try to keep him outside of my head as much as I can. If I let myself think of him for a second or two, all I can see are his blue eyes. All I can smell is the stench of his dirty pants when I washed them out in the sink. All I can hear is him crying, sitting next to me on the couch, while I tried to show him the video games I was playing.

"Ethan? You hanging in there with me?"

I place my hand on Groovy's belly. It feels soft and warm.
I take a breath.

"Yeah," I say. "I'm hanging in there." I pause and look
down at Groovy's sleepy dog face. The way his dog mouth is
turned up it looks like he's smiling. Maybe he is. I hear my
voice saying, "She showed up because she wanted to know
about her little brother, but I told her I couldn't remember
anything." I immediately want to take the words back. It's too
much to say. I switch the subject fast. "But we barely talked
about that. We mostly talked about music."

Dr. Greenberg leans over and makes a few notes on his
legal pad. I imagine what he's written about me.

This kid is the weirdest kid I've ever worked with.

Pretty sure there's no hope for this one to ever be normal.

Maybe I should tell his parents they're just wasting their money.

"Okay," he says, setting his pad down again. "So maybe
she'll come back. You two like the same bands?"

He skips over Dylan so easily I wonder if he's going to
come back to him later. I hope he doesn't.

"I don't know if we like the same bands," I say. "I mean,
she likes this one band called The White Stripes. I listened
to them, and they were okay."

"So it could be fun," he says.

I don't respond. I guess it could be fun. It could also be
really awkward. And anyway, she may not even come back,
so why am I even worrying about it?

I think about playing that Ludwig all by myself. I think about listening to Green Day songs in my headphones, closing my eyes and going through them and then opening my eyes and realizing I'm all by myself except for my mom checking on me by staring out the kitchen window every five seconds.

"Maybe," I finally anwer. "Maybe it could be fun." I stare out the window again. I've already said more than I thought I would, and I really don't want to keep talking.

I guess Dr. Greenberg senses as much because he says we can wrap it up. As he walks me out all I feel is exhausted, like I've just run for miles instead of sat on a couch.

. . . .

Because my life couldn't be any stranger, when my mom and I arrive home after my session with Dr. Greenberg, Caroline is waiting for me in the driveway, sitting cross-legged next to her practice amp, her red Fender resting in her arms. Her ten speed is laying on its side in the grass. How did she make it over here on her bike with all that gear?

"Oh my," my mother says as we pull in, and she presses her dark pink lips together like she does when she's nervous or angry or mad. She taps her manicured nails on the steering wheel. "Oh, my," she says again. Then she takes a deep, careful breath.

"Mom," I start, my pulse racing, "I didn't mention it, but Caroline came by the other day when you were gone, and we talked about playing music together, and I want to play with her, and we'll only play here not at her house. If that's okay?" I sound like I'm five years old, begging for a Christmas present that's way too expensive.

My mom's eyes open up a little bit at my speech, and her eyebrows pop up and down a few times like twin jack-in-the-boxes. I'm waiting for her to tell me that she needs to talk to my dad and Dr. Greenberg and Dr. Sugar and maybe the president of the United States before she lets me play with Caroline. But she just takes a breath and peers out at Caroline. Then she finally says, "You're sure you're okay to play with her?"

I nod. "I just want to see what it would be like. To play with another person."

Her eyes well up a little with tears when I tell her that.

I look at Caroline. She's eyeing the Volvo, scrambling to get up, still holding her guitar by the neck.

"Okay, you can play music, but just for a little bit," she says, blinking back tears. "Your dad will be home soon, and we're having dinner together."

When I was little and Jesse would come over, my mom would always invite him to stay for dinner. She won't with Caroline, of course. Not that I think I would want her to.

We get out of the Volvo, and my mom smooths out her khaki skirt and tucks a loose strand of hair behind her ear.

"Hello, Caroline," she says, her voice neutral. "It's nice to have you over to play music with Ethan." Like she knew all along this was the plan for today. Like it was already on one of her To Do lists. *Find Ethan someone to play music with.*

"Thanks for having me," Caroline says. She glances at me and gives me a little half smile. "Hey," is all she says.

"Hey," I say back.

My mom mentions something about being out in a little while with a snack and something to drink, of course, and we both say thanks. She heads for the house, and I realize my heart is still hammering. Maybe this was a stupid idea.

"So," Caroline says, "where do I plug in?"

I like that she wants to get right to playing because that means maybe there won't be too much talking. I point to the outlet and watch as she gets set up. Her hair's pulled back in a ponytail and she's wearing a Violent Femmes T-shirt that hangs off her like a curtain. Her dark jeans are worn out and tight. I'm not sure if she's cute or not. I think she is, but when I try to decide what's cute about her, my body goes numb. I don't know what the hell that means other than I'm definitely, totally not normal in the way every other teenage guy is, and that scares the shit out of me.

I grab my drumsticks.

"You want to count off?" she asks as I sit down at the Ludwig and center myself on my stool.

"Yeah," I answer, nodding as she straps on her guitar. She

pulls a bright yellow pick out of her back jeans pocket. "I can just, like, try a couple of chord progressions or whatever? See what sounds good?"

"Okay," I say. "You ready?"

"Yeah," she says, and she glances at me and for a second we catch each other's eyes, and then I count off one-two-three and I start to drum and Caroline starts to play.

She's good. Like, really good. Like good enough that I'm trying to keep up and watch her play at the same time just to see how she does it. It sounds so much better to hear electric guitar live five feet away from you than in your headphones.

We fool around for a little while and then we come to a natural end, like we're each reading the other, knowing when to stop. After my last wallop on the drums and her last chord, we're still and quiet. She stands there, her Fender hanging low around her waist.

"You're good," I say at last. "Where'd you take lessons?"

Caroline shakes her head. "I didn't. Lessons are expensive. I saved up for the guitar, and I taught myself from watching videos online and everything."

"Seriously?" I ask.

"Seriously," she says. She shrugs her shoulders like it's no big deal. "You're good, too," she says. I'm pretty sure she's just being nice, but I tell her thanks. She peers across the back lawn. "How long before your mom is out here with some snacks so she can spy on us?"

"I'm surprised she's not out here already," I say.

"Well let's see if we can squeeze in a little more playing before she shows up with apple slices and, like, Sunny D or whatever," she says.

"We don't have Sunny D," I tell her. "Only these organic juice boxes."

Caroline grins, and I realize I'm smiling back. Just a little bit.

"Okay, until the juice boxes then," she says. "Go ahead and count off."

And I do.

CAROLINE—183 DAYS AFTERWARD

DYLAN HAS FALLEN ASLEEP ON MY PARENTS' BED, HIS HEAD NESTLED on my shoulder. His episode of *Jeopardy!* is still on, but I'm scared to turn it off in case moving wakes him up.

I listen past Alex Trebek's know-it-all voice. Coming from down the hallway in the kitchen are the hard movements of my mother cleaning up after Thanksgiving dinner. The clatter of plates as they hit the sink. The gush of water coming out of the faucet at full force. The rattle of knives and forks as they're jammed into the dishwasher.

My dad isn't here. He's gone to his favorite place—Out. As in I'm going Out. I've got to get Out. I need to head Out.

Dad is the only person in this house who gets to do whatever the hell he wants whenever he wants to do it.

My phone resting on my stomach buzzes. Trying not to move, I tilt it up so I can read. It's Emma.

Hey

I debate whether I should answer. It's like I'm too exhausted to bother. But I manage a **hey** back. A few seconds later Emma texts me again.

So how was turkey day?

I wish I hadn't answered in the first place, but now I feel like I have to.

Kinda sucked

Why?

My parents got into this big fight cuz my brother wouldn't come out to sit at the table and my dad's mom and stepdad were assholes about it too like it was my mom's fault for not controlling him better

Dylan shifts a little in his sleep and slips off my shoulder. He's still wearing his favorite Superman T-shirt, but not even the promise of his favorite T-shirt and dinner with his usual plate and cup and bowl would get him to sit down with us. My grandmother insisted that Dylan would join us if only my mother didn't "baby him" so much.

I scowl at the thought and lean in to give Dylan a kiss on the cheek. When he's asleep is the only time I can kiss him, and it reminds me of when he was a baby and we didn't know there was anything wrong with him yet, and I could sit on the couch with him cuddled in my arms and I could sing to him while he slept. This was back when people thought we would be the kind of brother and sister who fought over the television or staged elaborate pranks on our parents. Normal stuff.

He's got crust lining his eyes from where mom couldn't wash his face enough and clusters of little freckles on either side of his nose and the lightest eyebrows. He has my mom's coloring, and I have my dad's, so I'm not sure we even look related. But he's my baby brother, and when I think about those days he was gone, those days he had to have been so scared and not knowing what the hell was going on, it makes me want to cover him with a blanket and protect him from everything always.

When I think he's in a deep enough sleep, I manage to turn off *Jeopardy!* Just then, Emma texts back.

Sorry your turkey day sucked . . . mine was okay but my mom bought ham instead of turkey and I was like wtf?

I sigh. When we were little, my problems and Emma's problems matched better. We knew what to say to make each other feel okay about bad grades on spelling quizzes and dumb unrequited crushes on members of boy bands. But it's like as my problems have gotten bigger, Emma hasn't been able to keep up. Like she sometimes has no clue what's the right thing to say.

The banging around in the kitchen has stopped, finally, and I cover Dylan with my parents' bedspread. My mom will probably let him sleep here in the bed with her tonight, and my dad will end up on the couch. The thought of my dad sleeping there doesn't bug me even though the couch, which we bought on clearance, doesn't have a comfortable spot that lasts more than ten minutes.

There's the sound of the television coming on in the family room and the fizz pop of my mom opening a can. My mom doesn't drink that much, but who could blame her for having a beer tonight?

I slide off my parents' bed and hover in hallway, trying to decide what to do with myself. I could go into the family room and talk to my mom, but I know how it would go.

ME: Hey.
MOM: Hey.
ME: Dad still gone?
MOM: Yeah, looks like it.
[LONG PAUSE WHILE DUMB SITCOM WITH FAT HUSBAND AND CUTE WIFE PLAYS ON TELEVISION IN THE BACKGROUND]
ME: The dinner you made was good.
MOM: Thanks, sweetie.
[LONG PAUSE WHILE MOM CHANGES CHANNEL TO DUMB SHOW WHERE WOMEN GET ROSES FROM A DUMB GUY IN A TUX WEARING TOO MUCH HAIR GEL TO BE LEGAL]
ME: Dylan's asleep on your bed.

MOM: Okay, honey, thank you.

ME: I'm sorry things were . . . weird tonight.

MOM: It's okay . . . it's just how they are sometimes.

ME: Yeah.

MOM: . . .

So instead of going to talk to my mom, I creep into my bedroom and put on my pajamas, the red ones with the little white guitars on them. My aunt and cousin sent them to me from Chicago last Christmas and even though I'm not that into cutesy stuff, when I opened them on Christmas morning I let myself smile and love them right there in front of my parents and everything. They've been washed so many times they're softer than soft. And I don't even mind that they reek of the cheap detergent my mom uses. The one that tries and fails to smell of flowers and sunshine.

I crawl into my bed with my phone and fiddle around with it. I could text Emma again, but the idea kind of leaves me empty.

So I start a text to Ethan.

How was . . .

I delete it.

What are . . .

I delete it.

Finally I tap in **Hope you had a good thanksgiving** and hit send before I can think about it too much. It's not open-ended. If he doesn't respond, I can just tell myself I wasn't asking a question anyway.

I flip over on my back and stare at the ceiling. Ethan and I have played music together four times since I managed to bike over there with my guitar and practice amp a few weeks ago. It's weird. We don't even talk that much. I just plug in and we play a little, each one of us figuring out what the other can do. He's actually really good at the drums. Way better than I am at the guitar, which makes me feel kind of self-conscious.

Each time I've gone over there I've stayed one hour, and his mom has come out to the garage about three times. Seriously. One time she came out and watched us play with this hyper excited smile pasted on her face, shifting her glance back and forth from me to Ethan and from Ethan back to me. I got so nervous my fingers slipped like twenty times and I could barely play an A chord.

"I kind of suck," I said, after his mom went back inside.

"No, you're really good," Ethan told me. It was the first full sentence he'd said to me that afternoon. I'm pretty sure he was just being nice, but I just said thanks and tried to keep up.

My phone buzzes from my nightstand, and I grab it. It's Ethan. My stomach flips a bit. I read his text back.

Thanks. Hope you had a good thanksgiving too

I turn over onto my stomach and stare at his words. This

is the first time we've texted about something other than getting together to play music. He was the one that suggested we exchange numbers so we could figure out good times to play. I wonder if his mom knows I know how to reach him.

All of a sudden another text from Ethan pops up.

My grandparents are here from boston. Saw them when I first came home but it was good to see them again

I guess he wants the conversation to keep going. I like texting in general because it's the best mixture of being vulnerable and being safe. I can't even figure out how people communicated before they could text. The idea of having to call on the phone and talk with someone you just met seems so bizarre. But even though Ethan and I are texting, I'm still not sure exactly how to behave.

Cool you got to see your grandparents. I had some family drama. Now I'm sitting here in my room bored

As soon as I send it, I suck in my breath and hold it. I've probably told him too much and now he thinks I'm strange for revealing family stuff out of the blue. But he texts back again a few minutes later.

Sorry. What happened?

Exhaling, I tap the next few words out in a rush before I realize what I'm doing.

My brother. He wouldn't eat dinner with us. My dad left like an asshole. IDK

I bite my lip. It's like Dylan is this taboo topic between us even if that's the whole reason Ethan and I started hanging out. Ethan made it pretty clear he didn't remember much about what happened to my little brother back in May. And anyway, I don't know if the two of us can keep playing music together if the strange thread that ties us together comes up too often.

But when Ethan asked what happened, I thought he genuinely wanted to know. And I thought that it might feel good to tell someone who is actually listening.

Now I'm sure I've scared him off, so I text again, trying to undo the damage.

Hey forget that last text. Let's change the subject

Long pause. Even longer pause.

I sigh and toss my phone toward the bottom of my bed. I shouldn't have mentioned Dylan.

Then I hear my phone buzz again. I jump for it with so much enthusiasm I'm embarrassed for myself. Ethan's texted me back. And he's changed the subject.

Hey I listened to the violent femmes today

Half of my mouth curls up into a smile.

You like them?

Better than the white stripes

Blasphemy

After that last text slips out into the universe, I worry

Ethan is going to think I'm flirting with him or that I like him like that. But I don't. I've never really had guy friends who were just guy friends. Jason McGinty and before him Ryan Huffman and before him Sam Pratt and before him Nick Ortiz weren't friends. We didn't talk much. Mostly we just messed around.

Ethan buzzes back.

Okay the white stripes are pretty good

I'm trying to figure out how to respond when he texts again.

Wanna practice tomorrow?

I do. Then I remember I have to work.

I have a part-time job at jackson family farm and I have a shift tomorrow . . . but I could come over after?

I watch for the word bubble to pop up, anticipating his next message.

That's cool. . . . what do you do at the farm?

Well at xmas time I sell wreaths and cranberry jelly and shit like that . . . the jelly is like 10 dollars a jar

No shit

Seriously it is and people pay for it too . . . whatever

Weird . . . well come over after if you want to

K I will like 3?

Cool

That seems like the last text, so I plug my phone into my

charger, turn off my bedside lamp, and crawl under the covers. Lying there in the darkness, I listen for Dylan's cries or the sound of my father walking in the front door or my mother raising her voice at him. When there's nothing but silence, I allow myself one small smile. Just because there's no one here to see me.

ETHAN—187 DAYS AFTERWARD

I JUST THREW UP IN MY MOM'S CAR. I'VE COME CLOSE TO IT BEFORE, but this is the first time it's actually happened. Grilled cheese sandwich. Dr Pepper. Sour cream and onion potato chips. I can see chunks of it all over the floorboard of my mother's Volvo.

"Sorry, buddy. You were in the wrong place at the wrong time."

"Ethan! Ethan, oh no!"

"Get on the floor. This is a gun on your neck."

"Sweetheart, let me pull over!"

"Don't cry. I don't like crying."

"Oh, honey! Ethan, what's wrong?"

I wipe my chin with my fingers. I'm too humiliated to even look at my mom, who's frantically trying to maneuver her car over to the shoulder.

"Keep going, mom," I manage. "Just get to Dr. Greenberg's. I need to get off the freeway. I don't want to sit here."

She's crying now, trying to weave back into traffic. The rotten smell of vomit rises up into my nostrils, and I feel myself wanting to gag again. I send the car window down, the rush of traffic zooming over and through me as I hang my head out, anxious for any breath of halfway fresh air.

My mother is crying hard now, fumbling through her purse for her phone.

"It was a mistake to let you spend time with her . . . it's . . . too soon . . . I just . . . ," she's muttering, wiping at her cheeks, her eyes darting between me, the road, and her phone.

I don't know how to tell her that every ride to Dr. Greenberg's makes me feel like this. Every ride makes me want to collapse and curl up and barf.

"I'm sorry I puked," I say, miserable.

"I'm the one who should be sorry. I don't think you should be hanging out with Caroline," my mother says, her thumb punching a phone number. "It's too soon for you to have that kind of friendship. And with her, no less." I can't tell if Mom is talking to me or to herself, but I squeeze my eyes shut to try and ignore her.

"Caroline's not the problem," I mutter, but I don't know if she can hear me. I want to scream that the problem is I'm completely fucked up. The problem is this sick guy got a hold of me when I was eleven years old and held me in his closet until I didn't know when it was morning or night and then he did all kinds of sick shit to me that I can barely remember to the point where I can't sleep with the lights off even though I'm sixteen years old. *That* is the problem.

Not Caroline.

Another wave of nausea crawls over me, and I white knuckle it until we're off the freeway and finally find ourselves in front of Dr. Greenberg's. He's sitting on the steps of his front porch wearing that soft, relaxed Dr. Greenberg smile, Groovy sitting next to him. I can see his fingers gently scratch Groovy behind the ears. They both stand up as we pull in.

My mom parks the car and rushes out, meeting Dr. Greenberg halfway up the driveway. I can't hear what they're talking about, but I watch as my mother gestures with her hands and wipes tears away from her face. Dr. Greenberg nods, his face still wearing that same chilled out half smile he always wears, his eyes reassuring. I don't know how he can hear so much messed up shit from people and still smile so much. Still look like everything's going to be okay.

Eventually, he makes his way to my open car window.

"I heard you got sick, Ethan," he says, all matter of fact.

"Yeah," I say. I want to vaporize I feel so awful.

"Why don't we go get cleaned up, okay?" he says. "I've

told your mother she should go get her car taken care of while we talk. Is that okay?"

My mother is squeezing her hands together and looking at me, her face all panicky. I know she's not going to leave until I tell her it's okay. And maybe not even then.

"It's okay, Mom. You should go get the car cleaned up."

"Ethan, are you sure?"

"Yeah."

After my mom drives away, Dr. Greenberg and I go into his house and he gets me a glass of water, and I step inside a small bathroom to rinse out my mouth and take a few sips. Fortunately, I didn't get any vomit on my shirt or shorts. Then we head to Dr. Greenberg's office, and I sink into the couch. Groovy makes his way over and curls up next to me. I don't have much energy to do anything besides rest my hand on his soft fur, but it helps me feel a little bit better.

"Wanna talk about what happened?" Dr. Greenberg asks.

"Isn't that kind of the deal here?" I ask, my voice sharp, a sour taste still on my tongue. I'm still feeling frustrated at what my mom said about Caroline. Hell, I'm just frustrated in general. About everything.

Dr. Greenberg's soft smile grows. "Yeah, that is the deal here," he says.

"I threw up in the car. It was gross." I stare out the window at the pecan tree. I wish I was a bird in a nest in that pecan tree. I wish I was the pecan tree. I wish I was anything but me right now.

"Your mom seems to think it's something to do with Caroline," Dr. Greenberg continues. "I know you've been playing music with her a lot lately. Your mom says she came over this weekend and you played for an hour and a half?"

"I didn't realize she timed it," I snap, instantly feeling like an asshole for saying it.

"I think she just noticed it was a significant amount of time," Dr. Greenberg says. His voice stays soft. Calm. I think I could probably stand up and scream, "FUCK EVERY-THING!" and he would stay calm.

"What's it like playing music with her?" Dr. Greenberg asks.

"It's good," I tell him, offering the quickest, easier answer.

But it's also the truth. It is good playing with Caroline. In fact, when I think about playing music with her, I feel like I do when I reach out to pet Groovy. My mind slips to when I saw her last, a few days ago when she came over after her shift at her job and we tried a White Stripes song because she insisted. The truth is Caroline is a way better guitar player than I am a drummer, but so far she hasn't said anything about it. I can tell she wants to sing, too, because she mouths the words, but so far she hasn't sung out loud yet.

After we struggled through the White Stripes, we took a break. "What made you start playing the drums?" Caroline had asked. She was laying flat on her back on the cement, her skinny legs sticking out in front of her, her pink sneakers still caked with mud. She was wearing her Violent Femmes T-shirt. I think it must be one of three shirts she owns because she wears it so much.

"When I was eight years old my dad showed me this footage of this drummer named Keith Moon from this band called The Who," I answered.

"I know who Keith Moon is," Caroline told me, rolling her eyes and sounding kind of sassy.

"Sorry," I said, rolling my eyes back. "He looked so cool that when my parents said I had to start an instrument, I picked drums. Plus, I thought it would be fun to hit stuff with sticks." Caroline grinned at that.

"So why'd you start guitar?" I asked. I eyed the house. I was giving my mom ten minutes maximum before she came out to spy on us, carrying lemonade or something.

"Honestly, I think girls who play the guitar look badass," Caroline said, crossing her arms in front of her eyes to block out the sun. "And I wanted to look like a badass."

"And you really never took lessons?" I still thought she was too good for that to be true.

"No," Caroline said, most of her face hidden under her arms. "But one year Mr. Case, the band teacher, taught me a few things."

"He was cool," I answered. "He gave me private lessons on drums."

"Did you know he died last year? Car accident."

"Seriously?"

"Yeah."

"Shit," I said.

It was quiet for a moment and then Caroline uncrossed her arms and squinted at me from down on the ground, like she was trying to make out my face through the sun's rays. "I'm sorry. I shouldn't have said that so casually."

"No, it's okay. I mean, I would have found out eventually."

She sat up and frowned, then looked away toward the street. "I don't want to say the wrong thing and upset you."

"It's okay," I said. I liked how she just came out and said it. "Just don't ever bullshit me."

Caroline turned back and looked at me, her dark eyes serious. I wondered for maybe the twentieth time if I was supposed to think she was cute. "I don't do bullshit," she said.

"Good," I answered, and I heard the back screen door bang open and spotted my mom making her way across the lawn with two cans of Coke. I wanted to tell her to turn around and please go back inside because in that moment I felt 50 percent normal and only 50 percent fucked up, which is a better ratio than I feel most of the time.

Caroline isn't the problem.

Caroline isn't why I threw up in my mom's Volvo.

I look up at Dr. Greenberg, trying to get my head straight that I'm here in a session with my therapist. He's sitting there, one leg crossed over the other like he's got all day, which maybe he does.

"Wow, sorry. I was just . . . thinking." I realize I don't even know for how long.

"It's okay," says Dr. Greenberg. "So Caroline . . . she's becoming a friend?"

"Yeah, I think," I say. "She has nothing to do with why I puked. We don't even talk about . . ." I search for the words, "all of that stuff. We mostly talk about music." Dr. Greenberg nods and doesn't say anything. He just soft smiles at me. A minute goes by. Then another one.

"You're being quiet so I'll talk, right?" I ask him.

"I really can't get anything by you, can I?" Dr. Greenberg asks me, and then he laughs. I kind of like that after all these months I've started to figure out his little tricks.

"I threw up because . . . ," I search my head for the words. Maybe I just need to say what I'm thinking. Maybe it's time to try. "I always feel weird when I drive here. I mean, it's not your fault or anything. It's just that we have to drive here on the freeway. That's how Mart . . ." I stop myself. "I don't feel like saying his name anymore."

Dr. Greenberg nods. "You can call him anything you want to in here. By his name. By any word you'd like."

I can feel my heart start to speed up. I give Groovy a rub on the head.

"I feel awful when I come here even though most of the time I can get through it. But it's because that's the way we went. That's the road we took. Even though I was down on the floor . . ." I stare into my lap. My dark jeans. My dorky, navy blue Polo shirt that my mom got me. Sometimes I still can't believe the odds. What happened to me happens to maybe a handful of kids every year. Maybe not even a handful.

I'm the reverse of a lottery winner. I'm the one in a million you don't want to be.

"Ethan, I want to try something, a strategy of sorts," says Dr. Greenberg. "If you want." I glance up. His voice has dropped down now to almost a whisper. He leans forward, his elbows on his knees. His gnarly, old guy hands are clasped tight. "Remember how we talked about intrusive memories? Do you remember what I said they were?"

"Yeah," I answer. "The stuff I feel when I have my nightmares and, like, flashbacks. They're not like normal memories because it's like I'm . . . like my brain thinks it's happening again."

"Yes, very good," says Dr. Greenberg. His voice is even softer now. His body is perfectly still as he talks. Groovy sighs next to me, like he's trying to remind me that he's still there.

"So something we can work on in here is trying to

desensitize you to those memories. To integrate them into your actual memories so they don't bother you like they bother you now."

I nod, and I wonder if he wants to try some new medication. I'm already on four different things. I think being on a fifth has to mean I'm definitely the most screwed up patient he's ever had.

"I want to try something I call my counting method," he says. "It's surprisingly simple, but I've found it to be very effective."

I squirm a little in my seat. "You mean I just count?" How the hell is that supposed to do anything?

Dr. Greenberg nods. "Well, what I do is I ask you to close your eyes or look away from me and listen to me as *I* count. Here in my office. I'll count to one hundred. And what you do is recall the memory from the beginning, from the moment you were taken and put into the truck. Let yourself feel it. Let the memory come to you. And as you hear my voice get to fifty or sixty, let the worst part of the memory build. Eighty or so is the point when the truck arrived at its destination, when you realized you'd survived the drive. Try to let the memory begin to end. When I reach the nineties, you'll hear me say, 'Back here,' and then you should start to leave the past and return to the present."

My heart is racing now. "What if I say no?" I ask.

"Then we won't do it."

I swallow. The sour taste is still there. I clutch some of Groovy's fur in my hand and release.

I want to be okay. I want it so fucking bad.

"I'll try," I say. "But if I want to stop, what do I do?"

"Just open your eyes or look at me and say stop."

"Seriously?"

"I promise," Dr. Greenberg says.

"Okay," I tell him. "Okay."

Dr. Greenberg asks me if I'm ready, and when I say yes, he begins to count.

"1, 2, 3, 4 . . ."

The sun is beating down on my back, and I'm thinking about how maybe Jesse and me can talk our moms into letting me spend the night over there. And maybe we can use his binoculars and spy on his babysitter. Maybe she'll take her shirt off and everything.

Suddenly, there's the sound of a vehicle coming up behind me. I coast to the side of the road to let it pass. I'm still thinking about that babysitter. Monica is her name.

The sound of the roaring engine is coming closer. I glance over my left shoulder. It's a black pickup, moving in toward me. Not too slow. Not too fast. Like early morning fog. Like a shark. Gravel kicks up as it gets closer and hits the back of my shin, and it stings something awful.

"14, 15, 16 . . ."

Now the truck is forcing me off the road. I'm falling down. I haven't fallen off my bike since I learned to ride a two-wheeler in second grade. The wind is knocked out of me, and the heels of my hands are scraped up. I flip them over to check for blood, and that's when I feel a hand on me. It's so strong. It's like Hercules just picked me up. I don't fight. I can't fight.

"28, 29, 30 . . ."

For somebody so strong his voice doesn't sound all that gruff. It's thin and pinched up. Like it doesn't get used much. And it tells me to get down.

"Get on the floor. This is a gun on your neck."

And it is. The metal feels heavy on me. Heavier even than the guy's hands.

There's garbage on the floorboard. Cigarette butts. A wrapper for a Snickers bar. How weird that is, I think to myself. My favorite candy but a gun on my neck.

And we're moving. The truck is moving. Fast.

And then the voice.

"Sorry, buddy. You were in the wrong place at the wrong time."

"51, 52, 53 . . ."

Where is he taking me? How can this be happening? How can this be real? This has to be a joke. This can't be real. This isn't real. This is real!

"72, 73, 74 . . ."

I can see through a rusted out pinhole on the floor of the truck that we are going very, very fast. We are speeding. We are on the freeway. We are moving and this is happening and this is real.

"Don't cry. I don't like crying," *says the pinched up voice.*

I bite my thumb knuckle until I taste blood. And that's how I make myself stop.

"81, 82, 83 . . ."

I can feel the truck stop. Finally. He didn't kill me. I'm not dead. I can hear the key sliding out of the ignition.

"91, 92, back here, Ethan, 93, 94 . . . 95, 96, 97, back here, 98, 99, 100."

I open my eyes. Tears are sliding down my cheeks, but I'm not sobbing or anything. Just crying. It's the first time I've cried in front of Dr. Greenberg.

But I'm not puking.

Dr. Greenberg is in the same position he was when I closed my eyes. His face is just still, neutral. His hands are clasped together.

My body hurts. Like I've just run ten miles or climbed some steep hill or finished a five hour drum solo. I realize I've been touching Groovy's head the whole time, but in the memory I didn't even feel him.

I sit there for I don't know how long. Maybe five minutes. Maybe ten. Dr. Greenberg never says anything.

"So I made it to a hundred," I say. Because I'm pretty sure he isn't going to talk until I say something first.

Dr. Greenberg's eyes crinkle up a little and he smiles.

"You made it there and back again, Ethan." He finally moves, reaching for a pad of paper and a pencil on the stool in front of him. "And if you want to, now we can talk about it."

CAROLINE—199 DAYS AFTERWARD

THE MAIN BEST THING ABOUT LIVING IN TEXAS, MAYBE THE ONLY best thing, is that in December there's a pretty awesome chance that you are still wearing shorts. Which means the weather is nice enough that you can still play guitar in the garage of this guy who is your new friend and who you are linked to because of a bizarre tragedy that made national news.

So there's that.

"You stick your tongue out when you play that chord," Ethan says, wiping his forehead with his shirt sleeve. "Also, you look constipated when you do it."

"It's the F chord, asshole. That's a really hard chord."

Ethan grins. He likes messing with me.

I like being messed with by him, to be honest.

"That sounded good," he says. "Especially the bridge."

"Yeah," I say, and he's right. It kind of sounded totally

amazing, like my guitar and Ethan's drums were chasing each other, daring each other to catch up. "It did."

Ethan asks me if I want to take a break, so I place my guitar down carefully and sit down on the driveway. I eye the back door nestled between two carefully manicured holly bushes. "How soon before your mom is out here with drinks?"

Ethan doesn't answer right away. I glance up at him and he's staring at his lap. In a voice that's a little softer than usual, he says, "My therapist told her not to worry about you."

"Really?"

"Yeah."

I can't decide if I should be glad this shrink guy deemed me worthy of spending time with Ethan or be offended that I'm apparently such an issue that I had to be discussed at all.

Although I get why I'm an issue. I mean, how could I not be?

"Well," I ask, peering down at my shoes, "I mean, that's good, right? That he said we can hang out?" My words buzz like an anxious mosquito. Ethan could say no. He could use this moment to tell me no, it's not good that we hang out.

And I really like hanging out with Ethan Jorgenson. I know it's weird, but I do.

All Ethan says is, "Yeah, it's good," and my heart swells a little, and we sit there in silence for a minute or two. That's one of the things I like about Ethan. We're both okay with being quiet sometimes.

"I'm glad," I say. We're still not looking at each other. It's easier that way.

More minutes pass. I knock my shoes together and a few crumbles of dried mud tumble toward the ground. My shoes are always covered in mud from my shifts at Jackson Family Farm, and I've given up trying to keep them clean. We're heavy into Christmas season now. So many jams and jellies have been sold by the dozen that by the time the holidays are over Enrique should be able to take a cruise around the world and never work again. Plus, in a genius move, he got his cousin Carlos to play Santa, so he's really raking it in on the photographs alone. Me and Jason McGinty having to dress up like Santa's helpers was enough to get us to make up after our fight. And of course, Jason's face and some doctored up Dr Pepper were all it took to get us to make out again, too. Emma told me I should play harder to get, but Emma doesn't seem to understand that I don't think Jason is worth that much effort.

"I've been writing some lyrics," Ethan says, breaking into my thoughts, his voice still quiet. "But I don't know if they suck or not. They probably do."

I finally make eye contact. I don't know how, but he's finally gotten rid of those corny Polos he was wearing and has a normal T-shirt on for once.

"Lyrics about what?" I ask.

Ethan shrugs. "Just shit about my life. You know."

"Yeah," I say, sort of feeling like an idiot. "I can guess."

"Anyway, they probably suck."

"They probably don't," I say. "I'll read them if you want me to. And I'll tell you if they suck. You know I will."

"Yeah," Ethan says. "I know. Maybe that's why I don't want to show them to you."

"Shut up and go get them. I mean, if you want."

"They're in my head," he tells me. "I have to write them down."

I nod. "Well, do it later. Then give them to me. I want to read them."

Ethan considers my request as he scratches the back of his neck. The sweat that built up while he was drumming has lessened, but the dark hair over his forehead is still slick. His cheeks are all pinked up. I look at him without trying to stare, and I think for the millionth time about how he was gone for four years. When he left I wasn't even in high school. I hadn't gotten my period yet, and I still cared about my grades. It seems so freaking long ago.

I hurt for him and I hurt for Dylan, and when I think about the bastard responsible it doesn't seem fair that he got to choose how to end it, with a gun in an alley behind a restaurant.

"I'll write the lyrics down later, I promise," Ethan says,

taking a drumstick and spinning it through his fingers like he does sometimes. I think he does it when he's not sure what to say next. Or when he's trying to figure out what to say next.

"Just show them to me if you want to," I say. "No pressure."

Ethan works the drumstick up and down his right hand three times and then he says, all of a sudden, "Do you think this is fucked up? I mean, that we hang out?" He's talking to the drumstick when he asks.

I draw my knees up to my chin. "Yeah," I say, because it's the only answer. "I mean, it has to be, right?"

"Because of how we know each other?" Ethan asks. The drumstick is still climbing up and down the ladder of his fingers like it's hungry for a workout.

"Yeah," I say. "Because of that."

"But you like hanging out, right?"

"Yeah," I say. "I don't have anyone else to play music with. And you're cool." And funny and nice, I want to add, but I don't want him to think I'm going overboard—even if it is the truth.

Ethan shrugs, but I can tell from the way his cheeks are still pink that maybe I've embarrassed him a little bit.

"So how come your therapist said it was okay if we hang out?" I ask. I really do wonder what this guy thinks of me.

Ethan finally stops spinning his drumstick. "I told him I liked hanging out with you. That it didn't feel weird even if it is weird. He said as long as I liked hanging out, it was good we did."

"How much does this therapist charge, for great advice like that?" I ask. I'm being a smart ass, I know. But there is a part of me that wonders how much therapy costs and how maybe someday my parents could find a therapist like that for Dylan. Not that they ever would, of course, with the way they want to live their lives pretending nothing happened to him.

Ethan smirks, but he says, "I think he costs a lot, but I don't know. He went to Harvard and everything."

"It's weird that there are people out there who actually went to Harvard," I say. "It sounds like going to Mars."

"I know," Ethan says.

I take my guitar and rest it in my lap and start plucking at the strings. I'm not sure if Ethan wants to play anything else. We don't usually talk this much when we take a break, but the truth is, each time we've played lately, we seem to be talking a little bit more each time.

"So," he says, starting the drumstick finger twirling routine again, "how's Dylan doing?"

My throat tightens up. I wasn't expecting that. We haven't spoken about Dylan since that day Ethan chased me down the street.

"Not so great," I tell him. "Still not sleeping so good. Still crying a lot. My mom is hoping that Christmas break will be better because he won't have to go to school."

"Yeah," Ethan says. "Hopefully." Then he frowns and looks down into his lap. "I remembered something the other day."

"Yeah?" I ask. My heart is hammering hard all of a sudden.

"Yeah," Ethan says, still looking at his lap. "I remember the first night he was in the apartment, we got pepperoni pizza to eat, and he ate some of it."

It's weird but this makes me feel better. Because I know how much Dylan likes pizza, especially pepperoni.

"I wish I could remember more," Ethan says, and we make eye contact for a moment. "My memory is just . . . it's fucked up."

"It's okay," I tell him, and I want him to believe me that it is okay. That maybe it doesn't even matter now how much he can tell me about Dylan. That all that matters is that he's trying to get better. But if Ethan can get better, I don't understand why Dylan can't, too. I wish I had a million dollars and could spend it all on getting Dylan better. Or at least try to get him the help he needs, which is more than anyone else seems to want to do.

We stop talking, and there's just the sound of the occasional car passing in front of Ethan's house or the random yip-yip of the Chihuahua who lives next door. Finally Ethan asks me, "You want to play that White Stripes song again?"

"Yeah," I say, getting to my feet and hauling my Fender over my shoulder.

"I'm gonna be watching you," he tells me. "Making sure you don't make any weird faces this time."

I roll my eyes but I'm laughing. "Shut up," I tell him. "And count off."

Hanging out with Ethan is like listening to one of your favorite songs. And you like it so much that fifteen seconds into it you start it over again before you even get to the end. Just so you can hear the beginning again. Because you like it that much.

ETHAN—201 DAYS AFTERWARD

I'M SUPPOSED TO BE WORKING ON THIS ASSIGNMENT FOR Mrs. Leander. Reading a short story and answering questions about it in my composition book. Only I keep getting distracted.

I'm working on these lyrics that maybe (*maybe*) I'm going to show Caroline.

> *I've got a clock in my heart*
> *That I want to turn back*
> *To the start of it all*
> *When it all went to black*

They're probably too cheesy to share. Or too stupid. I rip the page out of the composition book and think about where

I can hide it. I'm pretty sure Gloria isn't going through my drawers, but I can't be sure about my mom.

"Hey, Ethan."

I look up from my bed and there's my dad, standing in the doorway, dressed in khakis and a collared shirt and tie. I blink. Sometimes when I see my parents it's like I can't believe they're real and in front of me. I catch them staring at me sometimes, too, like they're thinking the same thing about me.

"Hey," I say. "You're home early."

"My last appointment canceled."

"Oh."

My dad hovers in the doorway of my room, like he's waiting for me to tell him it's okay to come in. My mom never hovers. She just walks in and starts touching stuff or touching me, like she needs the constant reminder that I'm really here.

"I was wondering if you wanted to go with me to the hardware store. I've got to get a few things for some projects around the house."

My dad loves projects around the house. Even though we could probably afford to hire someone to do most of the work, ever since I was a kid he loved making lists and plans of To Do projects, complete with little diagrams he drew in ballpoint pen on graph paper.

"Yeah, I'll go," I say. A big part of me would rather stay at home and work on lyrics. But I know my dad wants me to say yes, so I do. I push a smile onto my face as we head out the door.

The hardware store is almost in Clayton, so it's not a short drive. But at least it's not on the freeway. The counting thing with Dr. Greenberg was supposed to help me even though when he suggested using the method again, I was too anxious to try. I have no idea if it helped to do it that one day. I mean, I haven't vomited on myself on the way to any of my appointments, but I sure as hell still feel like I could every time we pull onto I-10.

"So," my dad says as we make our way down the two-lane county road heading toward Clayton, "you're still enjoying the drums? Playing with Caroline?"

"Yeah," I say, staring out the window, watching the fields of grass zip by. "It's good."

"That's good. Jesse been over recently?"

"Yeah, the other day he came over after school." Jesse and I never talked again about anything heavy duty since the day he came over for my birthday. But it's all right to just play video games together, I guess.

It's quiet in the car. It's not like when me and Caroline are quiet. Or even when Dr. Greenberg and I are quiet. It's like me and my dad are supposed to be talking. Like he's trying to have a Moment with me.

The truth is, my dad and I didn't hang out all that much

before. He's really into sports and fixing stuff around the house, and even though I like basketball okay, I was always more into music and video games. I still remember the look on his face when I was ten years old and told him I didn't want to play Little League anymore. It was like he wasn't sure we were actually related.

"You know, I never played an instrument," my dad says.

"How come?" I ask.

"Your grandparents didn't think it was a good idea," he says, and he sort of smiles at the memory. Not at me, but just to himself.

"Why wouldn't it be a good idea?" When I told my parents I wanted to play drums when I was little, they never said I couldn't. Just that I would have to play out in the garage.

"They thought it would be better to play a sport. That it would look better when I was applying to college. So that's why I took up baseball."

My dad's dad was a huge baseball fan. He died right before I was taken. During every World Series my grandfather would call our house from his house in Dallas like every day, and he and my dad would talk baseball statistics for hours until my head would go numb and I would be begging for a turn to watch something else on the television.

"If you could have played any instrument," I ask, suddenly curious, "what would it have been?"

My dad laughs a little at the question.

"Drums, honestly. I loved Peter Criss in Kiss. You probably don't even know what I'm talking about."

"Dad, I know who Kiss was. But Peter Criss? The guy whose face was a cat?"

"What's wrong with the cat?"

"It's pretty lame, Dad." But I'm half laughing because my dad is, too, and it feels sort of nice, just the two of us laughing for a second.

We pull into the hardware store parking lot and walk inside, the little doorbell tied to the handle jingle jangling as we do, and my dad consults his list, which is written on a scrap of paper the size of his palm. I'm bored immediately, and I find myself falling behind my dad, running my hands along the cardboard boxes wedged onto shelves. Boxes full of bolts and screws and nuts and nails. I'm staring at the boxes. All of a sudden I look down and realize I've buried my right hand in a box of bolts for no reason that I can figure.

Then, out of the blue, my brain flashes on something.

"Sir, is that your truck double-parked in the front there?"

The police officer is looking right at us, first at him and then at me. He looks young, like he doesn't even have to shave every day.

"Yes, officer, I was just running in to get cigarettes."

He answers the officer like it's nothing. He even smiles a little when he says it. That fake fucking smile he uses when we're outside.

I'm staring at the officer's name badge. R. BAILEY. All capital letters stamped into the shiny gold bar clipped to his chest. He's so close I could reach out and touch that gold name badge. I could whisper and he would hear my voice.

But I can't move. I can't talk.

My whole face is pulsating along with my heart. My whole body is vibrating right there in the middle of the Walgreens.

"Well, you have to move it pronto, my friend. You're lucky it's Friday and I'm in a good mood, or you'd be getting a ticket."

My heart is racing so fast that I can't tell if it's even taking a break between beats. It's one long buzz.

He has to notice me. He has to see me. Can't he see my heart beating?

"Yes, sir, absolutely. Come on, Ethan, let's go, son. Gotta listen to the officer."

No! Can't he see my heart beating? R. BAILEY, can't you see my heart beating? Can't you see it, R. BAILEY? Can't you see it?

"Ethan, you here?"

I turn and there's my dad, his face pale and panicky. He didn't know where I was for a second, I guess.

I swallow and blink and try to take a breath, but I can't. I put my hands on my knees and slump forward a little. Oh, please, please, please don't let me throw up in the hardware store.

"Ethan!" my dad walks over to me, his voice almost a shout. If it were my mom she would be hugging me, rubbing my back, hustling me out to the car. But my dad just stands there, inches away.

"Take a breath, son. Take a deep breath." He's using his best Dr. Jorgenson voice.

I try. My breath comes out shaky.

"One more," he commands. I do. Finally, I'm able to stand up.

My dad is clutching a tub of grout. The words *Pre-Mixed!* and *Improved Formula!* jump out at me in bright red letters across the front. My brain notices the weirdest shit at the weirdest times.

"I'm sorry," I say.

"Should we just leave? I can come back for this." He holds up the grout.

I shake my head no. "Just get what you need." I try one more breath and it comes out a little smoother this time.

"Okay," my dad says, "but why don't you stick close by while I finish up, okay?"

"Okay," I say, and I follow him around for the rest of the trip, trying to blank out my brain.

But when we head to check out, the cashier recognizes me. It's just this thing that happens to me. At the post office and the gas station and the pharmacy. Even though it's been seven months, it still happens all the time.

"Aren't you that Ethan Jorgenson boy who went missing?" the cashier says. She's wearing a sweatshirt that reads *Blessed to be a Grandma.* Her gray hair is pulled back into a ponytail, and she's peering at me over her wire glasses, smiling like no one's ever noticed me in my life and she just has to be the first.

"Yes, ma'am," I say, nodding. My dad glances at me out of the sides of his eyes.

"Well sweetheart, we're just so glad you're back and safe and home with us," she says, like I live at her house or something.

"Yes, ma'am, me, too," I answer, and I'm grateful that my dad is paying with exact change, so we don't have to stand there too much longer.

We head back into the parking lot and get into my dad's SUV.

"I'm sure in a few more months that won't happen so much," my dad says, starting up the car.

"It's okay," I tell him, which is what I always find myself saying when I'm not sure what else to say.

CAROLINE—212 DAYS AFTERWARD

IT'S TWO DAYS BEFORE CHRISTMAS AT JACKSON FAMILY FARM, AND the city folk are out in full force, with a line snaking all the way to the front gate as families line up to get their picture taken with Carlos the Santa.

"Ho, ho, ho, and Merry Christmas, my little one," Carlos says, hauling another toddler onto his lap and managing to grin widely even as the kid bursts into screams and starts crying and clutching at his fake beard. I have to say, he's a pretty believable Santa Claus even though he's only in his mid-thirties.

"Smile now!" coos Emma. "Say 'Merry Christmas!'" She kneels down with the fancy digital camera Enrique bought and snaps three or four pictures in a row before reaching back with one hand to tug at the red velvet elf pants that are slipping down her behind.

"Aren't you so very glad I got you this job, Elf Emma?" I whisper as I hand off one mewling toddler and reach for another one.

"Oh, totally, Elf Caroline," Emma answers, arching one eyebrow.

I spot Elf Jason further down the line, selling photo packages to desperate-faced parents eager to make this the Best Christmas Ever. I wonder how high he is right now. When our eyes meet and he offers a half grin and a lazy wave, I know the answer is very. It doesn't matter. There's still something about him that makes my body thrum.

Only one more hour until we close and then no more work at Jackson Family Farm for a full week.

My phone buzzes, and I break elf protocol to slip it out of the top of my elf boot where I've been hiding it.

Working on lyrics and bored out of my mind

My eyes dart up to make sure Enrique isn't watching me destroy the Christmas image he's worked so hard to create.

I am dressed as an elf right now dude

Not two seconds later Ethan texts back.

Pictures or it didn't happen

I laugh and slip the phone back into my boot.

"Who's that?" Emma asks, watching.

"No one."

"Liar."

"Fine, it's Ethan."

Emma gives me an I-knew-it-was smirk but doesn't say anything. I know she thinks the fact that I hang out with Ethan is strange. I think it's strange, too. But whatever. It's my thing to feel strange about. Not hers. And anyway, I've known Emma long enough to know what she's capable of understanding and what she isn't.

When the last crying Beatrice or Jonas or Alexandra or Caribou or whatever has had his picture snapped, Emma and I are finally allowed to leave. There's a party tonight at this girl Fabiola's house. She's a senior, and there's going to be a keg. As we walk to the bathroom to change, Jason catches up with us.

"I'm going to go try and score some whiskey for this party," he tells us. "Beer will not cut it." He winks at me. Or really, he winks at us.

"Just save some for me, okay?" Emma says. "I hate beer." She pouts a little.

"No, you don't," I argue.

"Well, I like whiskey better," Emma answers.

"I'll make sure you're taken care of," Jason says, grinning.

"Let's go change," I say, annoyed by this exchange. Emma follows me into the bathroom and starts peeling off her elf outfit and sliding into her favorite skintight jeans and a fitted red T-shirt.

"So," she says, "you going to ask Ethan to this party?"

I stare at myself in the mirror. "No," I answer. "I've told you it's not like that."

"I know," Emma says, brushing out her long, thick black hair. "You just get together and play music or whatever. I guess I just find it crazy that you never talk about what happened, that's all."

"We just don't," I say to my reflection.

"So your whole thing was to try and talk to him to find out more about what happened to Dylan, and that didn't happen, right?"

I don't want to tell Emma that Ethan remembers eating pepperoni pizza and not much else. So I just shake my head no.

"I don't get why he can't help you," she presses.

"He doesn't remember a lot," I say, wishing she was done so we could get out of here.

"Okay, maybe he doesn't remember everything, but can't he remember anything about your brother?" Emma says, scrunching up her forehead in confusion as she eyes her reflection.

"Emma, he went through some serious shit. Like, trauma. For four years." The same trauma my brother went through, even if it wasn't for as long. It kills me that she doesn't have sympathy for that.

"I still think it's weird he never ran away after he had the chance. I think that is fucked up." She tosses her hairbrush into her duffel bag and digs around until she finds her lipstick.

"Well, you're not him, so, whatever," I tell her. I don't know why I didn't think ahead and pack something cute to wear. All I have are my sad jeans with the threadbare knees and an old Jackson Family Farm T-shirt that reads EAT WHAT'S SWEET and has a picture of smiling strawberries on the back.

"I'm ready now," Emma announces, ignoring my irritation, and I follow her out to her car, half of me wishing I could just go home, even if that would mean hiding out in my room listening for Dylan to cry out or hearing my mom on the phone complaining to her sister or feeling the silence of my dad not being around.

The party is typical Dove Lake High School bullshit which means red Solo cups and a few people smoking weed outside and dudes playing video games and Fabiola running around telling people not to go into her parents' bedroom. It's boring, actually. Maybe there was a time my freshman year when I thought these parties were fun. But that feels like a long time ago.

Emma gets sucked into some conversation with some other girls in our class the second we get there, and soon I find myself maneuvering through the crowded house alone, nodding my head and offering a quick smile as I pass people, not feeling much like talking to anyone.

After a while, I try to find Jason, who should have gotten

the whiskey by now. I'm not sure why. It's like I think I'm supposed to, I guess. I can see myself finding him on the back deck. I can picture myself slipping off to the side of the yard to smoke and make out. I can imagine ending up in some dark corner somewhere, our faces and bodies pressed together like mechanical parts on autopilot.

I finally spot him through the sliding glass patio door, standing on the deck right where I thought he'd be, tucked into a circle of kids from our class. Emma's there, too, laughing loudly out of her perfectly made up lips.

I don't go outside. Instead, I get myself a full cup of beer from the keg and shut myself in a small back room that looks like some sort of home office for Fabiola's mom or dad. There's a futon in the corner next to a bookshelf full of self-help books with titles like *The Magic of Thinking BIG* and *The Motivation Manifesto*. I turn off the light and settle in on the futon, sipping my beer.

I wish there was some way to know what's going on at home. I wonder how many land mines I would have to avoid if I showed up there right now. The thought makes my stomach hurt.

I slide my phone out of my back pocket and rub my thumb up and down the glass.

I'm so fucking lonely. I admit it inside my head. Then, just to be sure, I say the words out loud.

"I'm so fucking lonely."

I listen to the words and I stare them in the face and I know they're true. They really are.

Holding my phone, I tap out a message.

What are you doing?

A few moments later, Ethan texts back.

Wrapping my presents for my parents

Presents. I have to go by the drugstore tomorrow and get my dad some new razors. While on a break today I got my mom some jars of jams with my employee discount. The only gift I got in advance was for Dylan. Last week I bought him some more wooden blocks for his block collection.

I read Ethan's text one more time and write back **That's nice what did you get them?**

As I wait for him to text back, I wonder if I should have bought something for Ethan, too. Or maybe that would be too strange. A few seconds later his response pops up.

I got my mom a framed picture of me and her from not too long ago and my dad this book about the band Kiss

I grimace. Kiss? I type back another message.

Omg I hate kiss . . . and that drummer looking like a cat

That's my dad's favorite guy

What the actual fuck

I know right?

I smile a little at that last text. Then I hear shrieking

outside, coming from the kitchen. I think someone is doing a keg stand. Ethan texts me again.

So you're off elf duty?

I'm at a stupid party

Why is it stupid?

Just dumb . . . drunk people. Boring. Idk

And I'm lonely. And sometimes I think I have no real friends except for you.

Whose house?

Fabiola Hernandez . . . two years ahead of you . . . you remember her?

There's a longer pause.

Maybe. Sometimes I think it would be cool to go to a party instead of being in my house with my parents every day

Music thuds outside the door. You're not missing much I text back.

There's a pause, and I worry Ethan will be pissed at me for that. After all, shouldn't he get to be the one to decide what he's missing? But a second later a text pops up.

Maybe someday I'll go to a party and see for myself . . . but for now my mom wants help decorating the tree . . .

The only tree my family has managed to put up this year is this little half-sized fake one on top of the coffee table. It's like my mom didn't have the energy for anything else.

Have fun

Have a merry xmas caroline

You too ethan

I finish the rest of my beer and head outside into the dark hallway. A door to the bedroom next to the office is halfway open. The front porch light streams through a window, and on the bed I can make out the image of two people kissing.

Gross, I think to myself. *Shut the door at least.*

As I lean in for the doorknob to do everyone a favor, my eyes figure out exactly who it is rolling around on the bed drunk and groping each other like two eighth graders under the bleachers at a Dove Lake High School football game.

It's Emma.

And Jason McGinty.

I don't even slam the door. I just shut it and turn around and walk down the hallway toward the kitchen, hoping that whichever dumbasses were doing a keg stand are finished now because my cup is empty, and I need something else to drink.

ETHAN—224 DAYS AFTERWARD

IT'S SO MILD, EVEN FOR JANUARY, THAT DR. GREENBERG ASKS ME IF I want to take Groovy for a walk during our session.

"Yeah, okay," I say. My mom has gone to run a few errands, which she's finally started doing when I meet with Dr. Greenberg. I guess for my mom to leave me alone with someone, the only thing they have to be is a Harvard graduate who is also a famous specialist in healing trauma.

"So, did you have a nice Christmas?" Dr. Greenberg asks. We hadn't met last week because of the holidays.

"Yeah, it was okay," I say, my hand holding tight to Groovy's leash. He trots out in front of me at a happy dog pace, the pace of a dog who could probably walk without a leash because he knows exactly how to get back home.

"Did you get any neat presents?"

"Some books and a new laptop. A couple of gift cards."

"Sounds nice."

"And Caroline got me something, too. I mean, she dropped it off two days after Christmas, but it was a set of new drumsticks."

"Those will come in handy."

"I feel bad I didn't get her anything," I admit.

"You can always get her something later. I bet she wouldn't mind."

"Probably," I say, wondering what I would buy her. Maybe another Violent Femmes T-shirt. The one she wears so much is so worn out there are holes in the armpits.

"You're still enjoying hanging out with Caroline?" Dr. Greenberg asks.

"Yeah," I say.

"That's good."

We keep walking. I feel like it's my turn to talk next, so I ask Dr. Greenberg what he did for Christmas.

"Well, I'm Jewish," he says, "so I don't celebrate it, really, but I went to visit my son in Atlanta."

It's weird to learn these things about Dr. Greenberg like his religion or that he has a kid. It's like that moment when you're little and you realize your teacher doesn't live at your school.

"Is your son a therapist, too?"

Dr. Greenberg smiles. "No, he's a Unitarian Universalist minister."

"But I thought you were Jewish?"

Dr. Greenberg shrugs. "I am. But my son isn't."

"Oh. What's . . . Unitar . . . um . . . what did you say?"

"Unitarian Universalist," Dr. Greenberg repeats. "Oh, it's a fascinating faith tradition. It supports the idea of everyone being on their own faith journey. So there really isn't any dogma. Any set of beliefs. It's very interesting."

It sounds like a strange kind of religion to me, but I don't say that out loud. My parents and I go to church sometimes, to First Methodist of Dove Lake. We went pretty regularly after I got back, but lately not so much. I guess I don't mind not going. I mean, it was fine, but it was just another place for people to look at me and talk to me like that cashier did at the hardware store. Just one more place to remind me how not normal I am.

We walk for a half block more or so, and suddenly I hear my voice say, "I wonder how some people decide they don't believe in God." Groovy stops to pee on a tree. Maybe that's his way of telling me he doesn't approve of what I've just said.

"It's a question a lot of people have," Dr. Greenberg says. He slips his hands into the pockets of his khaki slacks. "My wife was an avowed atheist. She didn't debate God's existence in her mind at all. But I think most people do."

"I didn't know you were married," I say.

"Well, I'm widowed. My wife passed away five years ago from pancreatic cancer. I miss her quite a bit."

It's the first time he's ever really said anything to me about his own emotions. I like that he thinks he can say that to me. That he doesn't mind me knowing.

"I'm sorry," I say. "About your wife."

"Me, too." He points to the big school building at the end of the block. "She taught tenth grade biology there for years. She loved it."

Groovy tugs at the leash, and we're off again. I kind of want to ask Dr. Greenberg if he believes in God just to see what he would say, but I think maybe that's too personal, no matter what he's just shared with me. So instead I ask him, "If your wife was an atheist, does that mean when she died she didn't think she would see you again? I mean, in Heaven?"

"Yes, I'm pretty sure. I mean, I never asked her, but I can only assume it to be the case."

"Does that make you sad?"

Dr. Greenberg nods. "Yes, it does. But in Judaism when someone dies, we say, 'May her memory be a blessing.' I love that saying. Her memory is a blessing every single day. So I try to focus on that."

We're almost back to Dr. Greenberg's house again. A little breeze kicks up as we pass a mom pushing her baby in a stroller. She smiles at us, and I smile back. Dr. Greenberg offers a soft, "Hello." I wonder if the lady knows Dr. Greenberg is a therapist and if she realizes I'm one of his messed up clients. Maybe she thinks I'm his grandson or nephew or something. I guess I kind of hope she does.

When we climb the steps to Dr. Greenberg's porch, he suggests that if I'm up for it, we sit in the big, blue Adirondack chairs he has and talk outside.

"Sure," I say. It's like taking the walk. It feels less formal. Less like therapy.

"So when you ask about people not believing in God, is that because it's something you wanted to talk about?" Dr. Greenberg asks.

I stare at my shoes, considering the question. "I don't know," I say. Maybe I do. But not right now.

"We can always put it on the back burner and come back to it."

I look up and give Dr. Greenberg a curious look. "You make it sound like questioning God's existence is like trying to decide what I'll eat for lunch a week from now."

Dr. Greenberg smiles a little. "All I'm saying is it's a very typical question, and you have time to wrestle with it."

"So it's normal," I ask, "to question God?"

"I like to stay away from the word *normal*," says Dr. Greenberg. "Like I said, it's typical."

I don't know if that's supposed to help, but I do know I'm not normal even if I wish I were. I guess I'm not typical either. I'm one in a million. So I don't know why it matters what we call it.

My eyes glance at the house across the street and then fixate on the dark wood of the front door. The Christmas wreath of red and green ribbons is still hanging there, waiting to be remembered and put away until next year. I think about what Dr. Greenberg said about having time to figure out God.

I don't know if I can figure out God, but I remember God. Or I remember my idea of God from before. He was this nice guy in the sky who would help me out with math tests.

When I was in the closet, though, I prayed to God so much, begging for help. For someone to find me. And it didn't happen.

So eventually I gave up. And I think I started to hate God. Maybe I still do.

I sense my hands are gripping the edges of the Adirondack chair. I close my eyes. I wish I hadn't thought about the closet. The closet makes me think about his rough hands. His fake smile.

My brain is buzzing. I can feel the weight of words at the back of my tongue, anxious to be spoken. Begging to be spoken. I think they've been there for a very long time. And I've been ignoring them as much as I possibly can. My heart, which had been beating along at a pretty normal pace, is suddenly racing at hyper speed.

"Dr. Greenberg," I begin. The words sound weird outside my ears, like I'm hearing them underwater. "For the first few months after I came back," I say, not believing I'm actually admitting this out loud or finally even to myself, "there was a part of me that thought that he could read my mind. Even though he was dead. I mean, I *knew* he was dead. I knew it, like, logically. But it was like he was still there. In my head. Watching me. And I'm worried that it means I'm crazy."

I swallow and wait, and Dr. Greenberg doesn't say anything right away. I must be right. I must be totally nuts. He's probably got a form in his desk that he's going to fill out to admit me to the psych ward. When my mom pulls back into the driveway, he's going to have to speak with her privately and call ahead to the hospital to let them know I'm coming.

The thought makes me panic. Even more than being away from my parents again, I'm afraid that I'm beyond getting better. If they take me away, doesn't that mean normal or typical really can't happen for me? Ever?

Dr. Greenberg readjusts in his seat, crosses one leg over the other. I watch him from the corner of my eye. I can't face him.

"You're not the first client of mine to have these thoughts," he says.

My whole body goes loose all at once, so fast my legs feel rubbery and I'm not sure I could stand if I tried.

"Yeah?" I ask.

"Yes," Dr. Greenberg says, and I finally manage to look at him. He looks at me, too, his grizzled face serious. "That's a common reaction when someone makes it through something like what you've gone through. I once worked with a young woman who was part of a suicide cult, and almost a year after she survived and the leader died, she still felt that the leader could read her mind, even though she had the rational thinking skills to know that such thoughts weren't logical."

"Shit," I murmur under my breath. It dawns on me that I might not actually be the most screwed up patient that Dr. Greenberg's ever had.

"You remember how we've talked about how, when someone goes through extreme trauma, the brain is capable of coming up with all sorts of unusual thoughts to try and make sense of things and just survive? I know it seems odd to you now that you thought that about the kidnapper, but ultimately, Ethan, the important thing is that you survived. You managed to survive and come back from something horrible."

"Yeah," I answer. I do know this. Logically. But that I once thought he could read my mind feels absurd to me. Really, when I try to see my situation through other people's eyes, the whole story seems absurd. "People think I just could have left," I continue, and I feel my hands ball up into fists. "Sometimes I think maybe even my mom and dad think that, even though when we have our family therapy sessions, they tell me, 'Oh, Ethan, we get it.' But, like, how can they get it, really?"

"No one can, unless they've been through what you've been through," Dr. Greenberg answers, "but I think some people will try to understand."

"I mean, I was able to walk around alone outside, and I never asked for help even when I could have," I argue back. My throat is tightening. My body is trying to decide if I should cry. "Just the other day I remembered this time we ran into a cop, and I didn't say anything. People think that's bullshit. Sometimes I think that's bullshit."

Tears start streaming down my face.

"Ethan, do you believe me when I tell you that I've studied the human mind and trauma and captivity and all of these things for years and years?" Dr. Greenberg says, his brow furrowing. He leans forward in his chair. His voice is steady and sure of itself.

"Yes," I say.

"And do you believe me when I tell you that the way you behaved is the way that countless victims of similar crimes have behaved? That all the research shows that what you did was what you had to do to survive?"

I shrug and wipe away some tears with the edge of my sleeve, not really convinced.

"Ethan, let me ask you, you do know that sometimes in wartime people in the military get taken captive, right?"

Sniffling a little, I turn and frown at Dr. Greenberg.

"What?"

"You've heard of prisoners of war? It happens to tough guys, right? Army soldiers? Marines?"

"Yeah."

"So how old do you think those soldiers, those Marines are, when they're taken captive?"

"I don't know," I answer.

"Are they eleven?" Dr. Greenberg presses.

"Of course not," I snap back. "They're adults."

"Right. So what if I told you there are many documented cases of prisoners of war behaving just as you did after they've been imprisoned? Who reacted just as you did? What would you say to that?"

I squeeze my eyes shut for a minute and try to stop crying. I know Dr. Greenberg is trying to make me realize it's not logical for a kid to be stronger than a Marine. But I still wish I had been able to walk away. Maybe it wasn't possible. I guess.

"You survived war, Ethan," Dr. Greenberg tells me, his voice quiet. "You survived the unimaginable. Which makes you a pretty incredible person in my eyes."

We sit there for a while longer, and I keep my eyes closed. I feel better about the fact that Dr. Greenberg doesn't think I've lost my mind, but some days the heaviness of all of it is so much I can't stand it.

Finally I open my eyes and look at Dr. Greenberg.

"I feel like I'm never going to be normal again."

"Remember what I said about the word *normal*. I like the word *typical*. You might not be typical in your life experiences, but that doesn't mean that you can't experience life in ways that will bring you fulfillment. Happiness and joy."

"Yeah," I answer. "I guess."

We sit there for a while, both of us staring forward at the house across the street. Letting time pass. I can feel the temperature shift, and it gets a little chillier, but I don't want to go inside yet. Something about sitting on Dr. Greenberg's porch makes it easier to unload some of this stuff. Lay it out right there in all its weird, deformed fuckedupedness.

"Ethan," Dr. Greenberg finally says, "I'm not going to try and reduce the weight of your burden, but I'm going to help you grow strong enough to carry it."

I repeat the words in my head over and over. I picture myself scaling Mount Everest with a pack that's double my body weight. The breeze picks up again, and the places on my face where the tears snaked down my cheeks feel extra cold. I imagine going home tonight and getting into bed and having to sleep with the lights on. I'm not sure how I can climb a mountain or carry some huge burden if I can't sleep with the lights turned off like a normal person. Or like a typical person. Or whatever.

But I don't say that to Dr. Greenberg. I just nod, and the

two of us sit there not saying anything else, waiting for my mom's Volvo to appear at the end of the street. When it finally does, my tears are all dried up, and I'm glad about that because I don't think I could handle having to deal with my mom if she sees that I had been crying.

CAROLINE—224 DAYS AFTERWARD

THERE'S SOMETHING ABOUT THE FIRST DAY BACK AT SCHOOL AFTER winter break that truly makes a person want to move to a remote island where no schools exist, so school attendance is not only not required but also impossible.

This morning when I woke up, the idea of going to Dove Lake High and dealing with Emma and Jason and the way my US History classroom smells like the crushed dreams of thousands of hopeful Proactiv users was just too much. I still don't know how I managed to do it. When I got home, I went right to bed, and I've been here ever since.

My phone buzzes. I stick my hand out from under my bedspread and grab it off the nightstand, hoping maybe it's Ethan wanting to talk about some of the songs we're going to work on. He still hasn't shown me those lyrics like he promised. But it's just Emma with her twenty millionth let's-be-friends-again text. The day after Fabiola's party she texted me like everything was normal, and it wasn't until after I told her I saw her messing around with Jason that she even acted sorry about it.

I ignored her all break and all day today at school. But the truth is, I'm not even ignoring her to prove a point. Honestly, the past few weeks without Emma in my life haven't been that lonely. Which makes me think maybe all the years we were friends were sort of bullshit. Which actually *is* depressing to think about.

Jason McGinty hasn't texted me, and at work he's read my silent treatment as the real deal this time.

Emma being out of my life burns a little. Jason being gone just feels like nothing.

I read Emma's text.

Girl come on don't be ridiculous over this. I'm gonna say it again but I was drunk and Jason was too. You were never totally BF/GF—let's not throw our friendship away over this.

I almost want to laugh at how easily Emma can justify anything.

Stop texting me I write back, and then I toss my phone aside. I can make out the muffled sounds of my parents fighting down the hall in the kitchen. Their voices are building in volume until I can hear everything they're yelling at each other. When this used to happen before Dylan was taken,

I would go find my baby brother and distract him with *Jeopardy!* on the television or one of my whistling songs. Right now I'm too frozen with my own sadness to move, but as my parents' fighting escalates, the sadness transforms into anger. I twist my face until it hurts and beat my fists against my bed, wishing voluntary temporary deafness were a real thing.

> DAD: Mindy, it's nothing. You're freaking out over nothing. Stop reading meaning into shit when there's nothing there.
>
> MOM: Andrew, don't talk down to me. And don't curse with the kids in the house.
>
> DAD: It's not like Caroline doesn't use the exact same words, and he doesn't even know what the hell we're saying.
>
> MOM: He does know! He does understand! God, you're the reason he started cursing at all. And he has a name, you know. He's your son!
>
> DAD: You don't think I've had to live with that for years?
>
> MOM: Go to hell.

And commence door slamming in three, two, one . . .
SLAM!

Yup.

The house is still for a while, and I imagine the players acting out the rest of this drama. Is MOM grabbing her phone and stepping outside to the back deck to call her sister in Chicago and cry and smoke one of the cigarettes she thinks I don't know she keeps hidden inside the doghouse from back when we used to have a dog? Is DAD driving aimlessly through the streets of Dove Lake thinking up ways of how he could be a bigger dickhead? And BROTHER, where are you? Who is watching out for you?

That last thought forces me up out of my bed, suddenly filled with guilt. It's not like Mom asked me to watch him, but whenever it hits me that I'm not 100 percent sure where Dylan is, I'm reminded of that miserable day in May when my mother popped her head into my bedroom, a small frown on her face.

"Caroline, have you seen Dylan? I thought you were keeping an eye on him."

I make it down the hallway and find him on the back porch with my mom in the last sunlight of the day, playing with his favorite wooden alphabet blocks, including the new ones I gave him for Christmas. The way Dylan plays isn't by making castles or towers like other kids. He likes to take the blocks and line them up in one long line, like a train going down railroad tracks, and if you interrupt him, he gets super frustrated. It's weird, I guess, but I think he finds it soothing, and I'm glad that he's doing something that relaxes him at least.

My mom is standing by the fence, talking on her phone.

When she hears the back door slam, she comes toward me. Her eyes are pink from crying.

"Hey, I'm going to go inside and talk to Aunt Josie for a sec, okay? Will you watch Dylan?" She hesitates a little as she says this. Like for some microsecond she's debating if leaving me responsible for him is a good idea.

The hesitation is like a knife in my gut.

"I'll watch him, Mom. I won't even go to the bathroom. I promise."

I plop myself down on the white plastic lawn chair dotted with bird poop and draw my knees up to my chin. Dylan doesn't even look up to see I'm here. The back of his hair is curling down over his collar. He needs a haircut bad. My mom likes to take him to this kids' stylist in the city who's trained to work with kids who have autism because anyone else who tries to cut Dylan's hair usually can't handle him.

When we were younger, I had to get my hair cut by that stylist, too, and I hated how she always cut my bangs too short. But I couldn't say anything because it didn't make sense for my mom to have to drive all the way into the city for Dylan to get his hair cut and then spend some other Saturday afternoon driving some place local for me. Eventually, I stopped getting my hair cut at all, letting it grow out super long and trimming the bangs myself.

Dylan tries to line up a block and something goes wrong,

and suddenly he's yelping in frustration. He throws the block across the yard and starts thumping the ground in anger.

"Hey!" I say, sliding off the chair. "Hey, Dill Pickle, I'll get it."

I race across the backyard for the small blue block. It has the letter D on it.

"Look, it's a D!" I say, heading back, showing Dylan the block. The doctors told my mom to read and talk to Dylan because it would help if he was ever going to develop real language, and even though he's old enough now that I doubt that's ever going to happen, I still like to help remind Dylan of letters just in case. "You threw the *D* block. Duh, duh, duh. *D*! Dylan! *D* is for Dylan! Duh, duh, *D*."

Dylan snatches the block out of my hand and knocks it a few times on the wooden deck of our porch. Then he adds it to his line, nice and straight like he likes it, and keeps going, his tense limbs relaxing again. I sit back down in my chair.

I like watching Dylan work on his block lines and his marble lines and his Lego lines. His little fingers with the dirt-filled fingernails move the blocks around carefully. Precisely. Like a surgeon but for blocks. I keep staring at the curls of hair at the back of his neck, and something about them makes me feel like crying. He looks so helpless with his hair all long like that. My throat tightens up, and I fight my brain, which wants to think about what happened to Dylan when he was gone. To find out whatever it is that still upsets him so much.

And then I want to explode in fury at the way my parents seem more caught up in their own stupid drama instead of Dylan.

Finally, Dylan finishes, and he looks up at me, and his eyes fix on mine. My mom likes to call it a magic moment. When he seems to be acting like he really understands you. Like whatever fog separates him from us has lifted for a minute or two.

His light eyes blink once. Twice. And then Dylan moves over to me and presses his soft cheek against my calf.

Hesitant, I reach out to ruffle his too-long hair. I'm worried he might flinch or pull away. But Dylan stays put.

"Dylan, you made a nice line of blocks," I say, petting him and trying to take in the moment. "I love this nice line of blocks."

As quickly as it starts, it's over, and Dylan scoots away, taking the blocks and moving them in a different direction, starting a new line from scratch. I watch him and his curls and his little boy hands, and I wonder how anyone could ever hurt someone like him.

ETHAN—226 DAYS AFTERWARD

I'M NOT TOTALLY SURE, BUT I THINK DR. SUGAR HAS BEEN WORKING on convincing my parents to take time for themselves or something, because lately on Friday nights they've been going out for an early dinner and leaving me alone in the house. And when we have our family sessions we talk about how to create a functional family or establish trust or whatever. Dr. Sugar is okay, but he's not Dr. Greenberg. Everything he says sounds like he's repeating it from a textbook or a website about mental health. With Dr. Greenberg, it just feels like we're talking.

So anyway, my parents have gone out to an early dinner at Tony's, the one sort of fancy restaurant in Dove Lake. I told them to drive into the city if they wanted to, but I don't think they feel ready for that yet.

I'm whacking away on my drums, as usual, singing my latest lyrics in my head. I still haven't gotten the guts to show them to Caroline, but maybe tomorrow when she comes over I will.

Like a face without a name
And you think that I'm to blame
But I will not feel the shame
You want to put on me
I'll walk the street so free forever
As those bonds I start to sever
What happened to me ain't a measure
Of the man that I can be

"Hey."

I look up. Caroline is standing just under the garage door, wearing that stained Violent Femmes T-shirt again, and her face looks busted up somehow, like she's been crying. She isn't carrying her guitar, but a red backpack is slung low on her shoulders. She chews on her bottom lip.

"Hey," I say, smiling. "Did you bike here?"

"No," she says. "Walked."

I want to be glad she's here. I am glad. But Caroline doesn't seem like herself.

"Wanna go down by the creek?" she asks. I know she

means Dove Lake Creek down behind my house. She looks me right in the eyes, and I think she's daring me to say yes. She's like a force tonight.

I peer out beyond the open garage door at the empty street. The sun is just starting to set. I know my parents are going to be home soon. Going out without permission will mean huge trouble with them.

"What's wrong?" I ask.

"I need to get out of here. I need to just walk by the creek, and I don't want to be alone."

"Okay," I say. "I'll go." My hand goes to my phone to text my mom, but I can't do that. She'll freak and tell me not to go anywhere. And I feel like going somewhere for once. Like a normal teenager would. So I tell Caroline to hang on and I go inside, grab a jacket, and leave a note on the kitchen counter.

Went out with Caroline. I won't be gone long. Don't worry.

I think about my mom reading it and I add *Love, Ethan* at the end.

Caroline doesn't look at me as we walk down the sidewalk to the place where the muddy path begins that ends by the creek bank. She just holds her backpack tight to her shoulders. It's weird because I've never really been anywhere with Caroline except my garage. Seeing her outside like this, outside of where we normally hang out, feels strange. Sur-real, even.

"So what's up?" I ask.

"Shit at home." The words come out quick, like she's spit-ting them out instead of speaking them.

"Okay," I say. I have to double step to keep up even though I'm taller.

She leads the way, and we make it down to the creek bank and she slips her backpack off her shoulders and tosses it onto the ground. She sits down, and I follow her lead because what else am I going to do? The bank is wet from the rain we've just had, and the dampness seeps through the bottom of my pants. The smell of fresh mud is strong.

Unzipping her backpack, Caroline pulls out a 20-ounce plastic bottle of Diet Coke and unscrews it. She takes a neat sip, and I know it's not just Diet Coke in there.

"Want some?" she asks.

"Yeah," I say. I take a swallow from the bottle. The taste is metallic, but I know it will relax me.

Sometimes he used to get me to drink.

No, don't think about that now.

We sit there staring at the creek for a while. Plastic bags and a couple of empty cans of Busch are trapped in the tree roots that disappear under the water. Caroline matches me three sips for every one.

"Why'd you have to get out of your house?" I ask.

Whatever Caroline gave me to drink has made my bones and muscles feel all loopy and numb.

"My parents got into a fight this afternoon and my dad left, and then he came back and they got into their most epic fight of all time, and then my dad left again. I think, like, for good."

"Oh man," I say. "I'm sorry, Caroline."

"I don't want to talk about it. I actually don't want to talk about anything. I just want to sit here. And drink."

"Okay," I say, and I'm almost relieved because I don't know what else to say to her.

Maybe half an hour passes but it's hard to say. We don't talk. Just drink. Darkness falls around us. Finally, Caroline starts to screw the cap back on the mostly empty bottle, but as I watch her, I can tell she's struggling.

"Let me do it," I say, reaching for it. But Caroline flings the bottle into the creek in one sure motion.

"Hey," I say, "what the hell?"

But she just digs into her backpack and finds her sunglasses and tosses those into the water, too. She smiles a little half smile.

The weird thing is that something about it makes sense somehow, and the next thing I know I'm sliding my Sperrys off my feet and throwing them into the creek, too. One and then the other. I hurl them so hard one makes it all the way to the other side of the creek where it smacks a tree and lands with a splash into the water. Something about that is satisfying.

Caroline takes off her shoes, too, and tosses them one and then two. Next she jumps up and peels her T-shirt off and whips it around her head a few times and throws it toward the creek bank where it falls like a deflating balloon.

Caroline has on a bra. A plain, old white one. I've never seen a real girl in a bra before. I'm not breathing really well. She slides back down onto the mud and doesn't look at me. Her little half smile has changed into a full-on frown.

"Shit," she says. "I liked that shirt."

"I can go get it. If you want."

"No, it doesn't matter."

"Okay," I say, not sure where to look. So I look at the shirt sinking into the water. I can barely make it out now because the sun has gone away almost completely. It's starting to get cold, too, but it's hard to tell just how cold since we've been drinking.

"Hey, can you come here?" Caroline says to me, and her voice is soft and slow.

I look at her face and glance down real quick at her breasts. They don't seem too big or too small, but I'm not sure because I don't have a lot of experience to go on.

"Come here like how?" I ask. My heart is up in my throat. I try to swallow it back down to where it belongs.

"Like over here," she insists, and she reaches out for me kind of clumsy and not sure of herself.

Let me be able to do this. I want to be able to do this. I should be able to do this.

Caroline is touching my shoulder all tentative, but then she reaches over and puts her face near mine, so close I can smell the liquor on her breath. Her lips are stained cherry-red and they're open, but just barely.

"Kiss me," she says, and she sort of leans into me and we're kissing. We're kissing. Her tongue is in my mouth, and she's putting her hands on my shoulders and my back. Her body feels so small next to me, and warm, too.

We fall back into the mud and roll toward one another, and we're kissing like it's our job. Pushing into each other all insistent.

This should feel good. I want this to feel good. Please make it feel good.

I can feel myself getting hard. Caroline is making little noises in the back of her throat.

This is different. This is a girl.

Suddenly Caroline's hands are down by my waist. She doesn't do anything, but I feel them there, almost hovering her touch is so light. Her hands are so small. A girl's hands. I push into her, kissing her harder than before.

"Wait," she says, and she falls back a little. I pull away. I have to catch my breath.

"I'm kind of drunk," she whispers. But she reaches for me again, and we kiss some more. It's the first time I've kissed a girl. Or anythinged with a girl. And it's Caroline and we're drunk and I don't know what I'm feeling except I want it to be the right thing. It has to be.

Hands on me. Rough hands. Big hands. Not stopping. Not when I pleaded for them to stop and then gave up because the pleading only made it worse. No, not now. Don't think about this now.

I kiss Caroline so hard I don't think it counts as kissing anymore, but it's like if I kiss her hard enough I can push the other thoughts out of my head.

"Ethan," she says, drawing back and sitting up, "that hurts."

Any good feeling I had in my body flickers off immediately.

"I'm sorry," I say. "I'm sorry." Suddenly, I feel kind of queasy. Please don't let me throw up.

"It's okay," she says. "But this is fucked up." She blinks a few times, and I look down at my bare feet caked in mud. She's right. This is fucked up so many times over I can't even figure out where to start counting.

"I didn't mean to hurt you," I say. My head is starting to throb, and I close my eyes. But all I can think is that I hurt her. I can't turn into someone who hurts people.

"I kissed you," Caroline says. "I started it."

She stands up and wobbles a little. I stand up, too, and

reach out to try and steady her. Only I'm not sure if I should touch her.

"I need to go," she says.

"What about your shirt? Our shoes?" It's full on dark now. I'm not sure we could even find them by the creek.

"Don't worry. It doesn't matter."

"Let me walk you home."

"No, just go. Your parents will be worried."

Her words make me reach for my phone. There are so many texts from my mom I'm surprised my phone hasn't melted. Shit.

Caroline grabs her backpack and slips up the creek bank pretty fast for someone not wearing any shoes. When we make it to the top, she looks at me but I have a hard time looking at her.

"I'll talk to you later," she says. I don't know if I should kiss her or hug her or just stand there. But Caroline turns around and darts off into the night, still dressed in her jeans and white bra.

I race home, and about fifty yards from my house I see the spinning blue and red lights of a police car. Shit shit shit.

"Megan, he's here! He's right here!" My dad is standing in our front yard, holding his phone, yelling in the general direction of our house. He looks at me and takes a deep breath.

I'm going to be in so much trouble.

The screen door bangs open and my mom comes running out, crying and pretty much hysterical. She screams my name and starts clutching at me, her fingers digging into my back, hugging me like she did when I was found. I hug her back.

"Mom, I'm fine," I say. "I'm okay. Didn't you get my note?"

She doesn't answer, just pulls back a little like she's making sure it's me, and then she hugs me again. Over her shoulder I can see my dad talking to the police officer who gets into his car and drives off. Then my dad walks over to my mom and me.

"You okay, son?" he asks. He pats mom on the back. He's wearing his "It's all going to be great let's just focus on how great it's going to be," smile which isn't really a smile but this expression that makes him look like he threw out his back and doesn't want us to know.

"I only went on a walk. With Caroline." I'm waiting for one of them to notice I'm not wearing any shoes. But they're too busy staring into my face. Mom's touching it, still sniffling and blinking back tears.

"Honey," she says, "when we text you, you have to text us back. Immediately. You understand that, right?"

I exhale. I want to take off. Run. Run back to that creek and jump in and sink to the bottom and hide there with the frogs and the dead leaves and the rusty, empty cans of beer. I'll transform into a swamp creature that never has to figure out what to do with girls and never hurts his parents. And when I die I'll be swallowed up by the muck and the mud and it'll be an easy way to go.

Forget what Dr. Greenberg said about me being okay and enjoying life like a normal or typical person. I am too fucked up for that.

"I'm sorry I didn't text back," I say. "I'm sorry."

We go back inside the house, and I realize I'm still feeling a little weird from whatever was in Caroline's Diet Coke bottle. "Caroline and I were walking by the creek. I got some mud on me, so I'm going to go take a shower, okay?" I say. My mom nods. I have a feeling she's going to wait for me right outside the bathroom door.

I make the shower as hot as I can stand it and get in, turning my face upwards, letting the water pound down on me. I think about Caroline and her breasts and kissing her. I wait for my body to react again but nothing happens. I don't know why. I'm scared to wonder what it might mean. I stay in the shower, letting the hot water run until there's no hot water left and my mom is knocking on the door, asking me if everything is okay.

CAROLINE—232 DAYS AFTERWARD

IT'S ACTUALLY REALLY EASY TO SKIP SCHOOL. I TELL MY MOM I'M going, and then I just don't go.

Every morning I get dressed like I'm heading to Dove Lake High, and then I walk to the bus stop and I just keep walking. I walk all the way into downtown, and on the way there I call the school attendance office and fake my mom's voice and say I'm sick. The attendance clerk must be deaf or stupid or both, but it doesn't matter which because she never acts like she doesn't think I'm a depressed woman in her late thirties with two screwed up kids and one asshole husband.

I wonder if when I'm older, I will sound like my mom. For real. I won't even have to fake it. My voice will just sort of morph into hers and my life will morph into hers, too, and I'll end up living in Dove Lake, and I'll marry a really big asshole, too.

Maybe I deserve it.

For the past three days that I've been cutting class, I've been heading to this easement between the public library and a strip mall. There's a scattering of trees I can hide out in, and if I get hungry, I can always head over to the Stop N Go and get a bag of chips or a Mountain Dew or something.

Today I curl up on a spot of damp earth in the deepest part of this little forest, and I pull out my phone.

No texts from anyone.

Definitely not from Ethan.

I can't believe I've fucked this up so bad.

Friday night when I got home, I thought about texting him, but I was so out of it I just got into the shower and tried to get my head straight. After I got out and into my pajamas, I peeked inside my mom and dad's bedroom and saw my mom and Dylan asleep together in her bed. My dad wasn't anywhere. Their second epic fight of the day really had made him leave for good.

I hid in my bedroom and tried to text Ethan, but everything came out sounding stupid. Finally I just texted him the only words I could come up with.

I'm so sorry. I feel like the biggest jerk

Nothing. No message saying it was okay he just needed some time. No message saying I was a total bitch and don't ever bother him again. No message from Ethan's mom saying I should never contact him again.

Nothing at all.

Finally I dozed off and I woke up with my head pounding and I spent all weekend miserable and not hearing from Ethan and when I woke up on Monday I knew I wouldn't be going to school.

And now it's Thursday and I'm still not at school and Ethan still hasn't texted me back.

I spend all day in the easement messing around on my phone and reading old magazines and walking over to the Stop N Go to get something to eat when I'm hungry. It's actually a lot more enjoyable than school, and if I'm going to be honest, I think I'm probably learning a lot more just doing this instead of sitting in English class trying to figure out the theme of a stupid poem. Like poets write to have you figure out a theme. I'm pretty sure they write just to write.

I keep replaying Friday night by the creek in my mind. The way I pushed myself onto Ethan. The way I could tell he didn't like it. Wasn't even sure what to do. What was I even thinking? I squeeze my eyes shut, and my throat seizes up like maybe I'm about to cry, but I don't. It's like I'm too numb for it.

I pull my phone out again.

Ethan, I'm really sorry. If you want me to stop texting, just tell me. And I will. I'm not sure if I'm being a bigger creep by texting you but I'm so sorry. I just want to say I know what I did was awful. You're the only friend I've

had lately and I've totally fucked it all up. Part of me wants you to hate me forever because it's what I deserve. But part of me hopes you don't because it would suck if we couldn't hang out again. And I really like hanging out with you.

I rub my thumbs on the smooth surface of the phone, willing Ethan to write me back. Finally my phone buzzes.

Hey I need time so please just leave me alone for right now

I read the message over and over before tossing my phone into my backpack. I stare out at the stretch of easement in front of me, full of empty aluminum cans and plastic bags from the Stop N Go, and I think about the fact that I have no friends. No fake friends like Emma or real ones like I thought I had in Ethan. I mean, sure, if I went to school tomorrow I would have people to sit with at lunch. People would loan me a pencil in class if I needed one. It's not like I would be mocked openly as I walked down the hallway or anything.

But I wouldn't have anyone who I just liked hanging out with. Who I could be myself with. Who I could relax around because I felt like somehow we just got each other. Like it is— like it *was*—with Ethan.

At around the time school is about to end, I walk home, scraping my feet along the sidewalk just because it feels good to do it. When I head inside the house, I find my dad sitting at the kitchen table, going through the mail.

"Hey," I say, sliding my backpack off and setting it down on the floor. I haven't seen him in days.

"Hey," he says, barely looking up at me. He just leans forward and puts his head down and scratches at the top of his balding scalp with his big, thick hands. His football player hands. Back when he went to Dove Lake High he was quarterback and king of the school. He and my mom got together during their senior year, and in their senior yearbook there's a picture of them being crowned Prom King and Queen. They were each grinning like they'd won a contest and the prize was each other. They were thinner. Prettier. Handsomer. Like two different people.

And then my dad never got a college scholarship and I was born a girl and my brother was born not normal. And everything I guess fell apart.

"So you're back?" I ask, opening the refrigerator to see if there's anything I want.

"Caroline, let's just be cool, okay?" His voice is tired. Irritated.

"Okay, Dad. I'll be cool."

I wish it were true that things weren't always like this. I wish that in the family albums there are pictures of my dad carrying me on his shoulders or pushing me on my first two wheeler. But there aren't. I wish that when I was younger my dad tucked me in at night and sang me lullabies. But he didn't.

We've just lived in the same house together for sixteen

years, and I'm pretty sure he's been miserable for most of them.

I take a beer from the refrigerator just to see if he'll notice, which he doesn't, and I head back to my room. When I get there I drink half of it until I start to feel like a cautionary tale from one of the terrible and hilarious movies we had to watch in health class sophomore year where everything was set in the nineties and nobody had a cell phone. So I pour out the rest of the beer in the bathroom sink and hide the empty can at the back of my closet. Then I crawl under the covers and try to imagine myself melting away into nothing.

ETHAN—233 DAYS AFTERWARD

IT'S RAINING, SO EVEN THOUGH I WANT TO SIT ON THE PORCH WITH Dr. Greenberg, we're in his office. Groovy is there with us, this time curling up on top of my feet.

"He's your own personal foot warmer," Dr. Greenberg says, grinning.

I nod and try to laugh. But I feel the weight of Caroline and everything else on my shoulders and it's so heavy. I know talking with Dr. Greenberg can help, but sometimes it's just so tiring to try.

"How's your week been going?" he asks.

I shrug. Silence. I don't know what there is to say. Dr. Greenberg doesn't say anything.

On Wednesday I'd squeezed my hands together to work up the courage to tell Dr. Greenberg what had happened with Caroline. I told him about drinking with Caroline and about her taking off her shirt. About Caroline kissing me and about me kissing her back. About my brain being invaded with the worst kinds of memories. Of pain and fear and hands groping for me. Hurting me.

I expected Dr. Greenberg to be totally weirded out or shocked. But he'd just nodded, like he was listening really hard.

Suddenly, I didn't want to talk about it anymore, and when I asked Dr. Greenberg if we could stop, he said of course.

After that session on Wednesday, I came home and did my homework. Caroline had texted me once, right after, saying she was sorry and a jerk, but I had just ignored it. Because I didn't know what to say. And I was mad at her.

But also, I missed her.

I didn't play the drums on Wednesday night. I just sat with my parents and watched television with them. I wasn't even paying attention to what we were watching. When my mom and dad laughed a little, I laughed, too.

On Thursday morning she texted me again. A long text where she said she was sorry again and she understood if I never wanted to see her again but if I didn't she would be sad.

Reading that text made my stomach hurt. So I told her that I needed her to leave me alone for a little while.

On Thursday, I didn't play the drums either.

And here it is, Friday, and I'm back with Dr. Greenberg. Pretty much everything sucks.

I'm just staring out the window when Dr. Greenberg asks, "Have you spoken to Caroline since our last session?"

He's so direct I answer before I realize I'm doing it. "No," I say, "but she texted me that she feels bad about everything, so I texted her back that I need some time and to please leave me alone."

Dr. Greenberg's big bushy beard cracks a small smile. "I think that's good," he says. "You're making those healthy boundaries."

I think about sitting in a circle of fruits and vegetables again. I could really stand to never hear that phrase "healthy boundaries" again, to be honest.

"You don't agree?" Dr. Greenberg asks. I guess I must be frowning.

I don't want to be a jerk to Dr. Greenberg. But I don't know what I'm supposed to say. And there's this weight in my stomach. I mean, I think there's always a weight in my stomach, but this weight that's been sitting inside of me feels new. And it doesn't even have anything to do with Caroline and me and our friendship. Or maybe it does, I don't know. But it's a weight that hurts. That's been making itself known more and more since last Friday.

I keep hoping for it to disappear, and it doesn't.

I reach out for Groovy's soft fur. Dr. Greenbeg waits. I

hear the sound of the house's old furnace churn on, and a gust of warm breath slips out from the grate above my head. Dr. Greenberg waits.

I've been meeting with Dr. Greenberg for almost nine months, and I've never talked about anything having to do with sex or anything like that. He's never pushed it, but it's like it's always there with us in the room, only he isn't going to bring it up unless I do.

I can't talk about the details. It's like the worst details are erased from my mind. Sometimes I remember just a rush of sounds and smells and phrases. Snippets of darkness. Pieces of awful.

But since that night at the creek . . .

I cough a little and close my eyes for a moment, working up the nerve.

"Caroline is the first girl I ever kissed," I say.

"Okay," says Dr. Greenberg, nodding.

I feel my face flushing. I look down at Groovy but my cheeks are still on fire.

"It's awkward talking about this, isn't it?" Dr. Greenberg asks.

"Yeah," I say, grateful he's named the problem out loud.

"What could make it easier to talk about it?" he says. "Would you rather write it down, maybe?"

I think about it. "Could you maybe, like, stand over there

by the window? Stare out the window so we can talk and you can hear me but maybe I'm not having to look at you when we talk about it? I mean, no offense."

"None taken," Dr. Greenberg says, and he walks over to the window and stares out at the pecan tree and blue slice of sky above it. He slips his hands into his back pockets. I can only see the back of his gray head and the two skinny shoulder blades that pop out from under his worn out blue button-down shirt with the sleeves rolled up. I notice he missed a belt loop, and for some reason this makes me feel more relaxed. Makes talking easier.

"When Caroline and I kissed, my body, like . . . it felt . . . it . . . uh . . ."

I pause. I can't say *erection* in front of Dr. Greenberg. I really can't.

"Your body responded?" he says to the window.

"Yeah," I say, thankful.

"Okay," he says.

"But then when it got weird it didn't," I say. "And when I thought later about kissing her, it didn't either."

"The way our bodies respond to sexual situations is complicated," says Dr. Greenberg.

Well that doesn't help me very much. But Dr. Greenberg doesn't say anything else, so I keep talking.

"The thing is . . ." I pause. I take a deep breath. If I say it, then it's out there and I can't take it back. "When I was with him, sometimes my body responded then, too. Even though I hated what was happening."

I push myself back into Dr. Greenberg's couch, and I want to evaporate I'm so embarrassed. I'm so thankful Dr. Greenberg isn't sitting across from me.

"This comes up a lot with people who've been the victims of sexual abuse," Dr. Greenberg says, his voice soft and a little bit sad, even. "Their bodies respond to the abuse, and they get very worried about what it means."

"So I'm not the only one?"

"No, not at all," Dr. Greenberg says. My shoulders sink with relief, and suddenly I actually want to talk about this. But I'm not sure about the right words to use.

"But because my body . . . responded, I . . . I just . . . ," I struggle, then give up.

"Let me give you this comparison," Dr. Greenberg says. "Imagine I burned myself on the stove. I don't want it to hurt, but it does, doesn't it?"

"Yeah," I say.

"Just because I don't want to feel the pain of the burn doesn't mean that my body is going to listen and respond the way I want it to. Even if your body responded to the abuse, even if what happened to you physically felt good sometimes, that doesn't mean it was okay or that you wanted it or that you were somehow complicit in it. You weren't, Ethan. Not at all."

I exhale. A big, shaky exhale. I work Dr. Greenberg's words over in my mind.

"But I still wonder . . . I mean . . . like . . . if you've worked with other guys who were, you know . . . molested by guys? And their bodies . . . responded . . . or whatever? Do they wonder if that means they're gay?"

The back of Dr. Greenberg's head nods. "Yes," he answers. "That's a question I get a lot. And the answer is that being molested by someone of the same sex doesn't make you gay."

"I'm not saying there's anything wrong with being gay or whatever," I say, blushing again. I know this is the right thing to say. I feel sort of bad about being worried about being gay.

"I know you don't mean anything hurtful," says Dr. Greenberg. "But just so you know, many men who were molested by other men when they were boys go on to have fulfilling sexual relationships with women."

The words *fulfilling sexual relationships* make me think about people making out in a room full of candles with terrible jazz music playing. Suddenly, I don't want to talk about any of this anymore.

"This conversation is really exhausting," I say. "Can we stop for a while?"

"Sure," says Dr. Greenberg.

"Okay," I say.

"Should I turn around from the window?" he asks, and it suddenly strikes me as sort of ridiculous that I've been talking to his back this entire time.

"Yeah," I say.

He turns around and sits back down. "I just realized I really need to wash my windows. They're filthy."

I grin a little.

"Is that funny?" Dr. Greenberg says, but he's smiling, too.

"Do you ever think how totally weird some of these sessions are?" I ask. "Everything we're talking about and then we're talking about washing windows."

"Sometimes we need a little humor at just the right time," Dr. Greenberg says. "Just a pause in the intensity. One time during a very difficult session with a client just when we needed a break, Groovy passed gas. It was so loud and very foul."

"Jesus!" I say, and Groovy looks up at us like he knows we're talking about him, which makes me actually laugh some.

But then when I stop laughing, I realize that even though I feel better about one thing, I still feel horrible about a million other things.

"I'm still not sure what to do about Caroline," I say.

Dr. Greenberg nods. "From her actions, it sounds like Caroline is hurting."

"Yeah," I say. My mind thinks about Caroline's family and how screwed up it sounds, but I don't let my head go there too much, because it makes me think about Dylan. And thinking too much about Dylan scares me because I don't know what kind of memories it might bring up.

"I can see why Caroline would want to reach out to you," says Dr. Greenberg. "But sometimes when we're going through something difficult, we become reckless without meaning to be. And we can hurt others."

"Yeah," I say. Caroline told me in her text I was the only friend she had. Sometimes I wonder if that's the truth for me, too. I mean, Jesse still comes over once in a while and we just play video games and barely talk. But it's not like how it is— was—with Caroline.

Soon our time is up, and Dr. Greenberg walks me out. On the way home, I close my eyes and try to clear my mind. But I can't stop thinking about Caroline, so I open them again and count the brightly colored billboards for churches and truck stops and lawyers who specialize in personal injury.

When we get home, I get out of the car and pause in the driveway. I glance at the garage, the door shut tight, my drums trapped behind it. I imagine Caroline zipping up on her bike, her ponytail flying behind her head like Superman's cape, ready to play. I can almost feel my drumsticks in my hands. I can almost hear the sloppy whine of her Fender getting in tune.

"I'm going to play some video games," I tell my mom, and I head inside the house. Soon I'm numbed out with a plastic controller stuck in my hands, the blips and beeps riding in and out of my ears like bugs on some mindless journey.

CAROLINE—238 DAYS AFTERWARD

EITHER THE ATTENDANCE CLERK MUST HAVE GROWN A BRAIN OR someone at Dove Lake High got wise to me, but after a week off I'm back at school. Back at the dull, beige grind of graffiti-covered desks and teacher handouts and lockers slamming shut over and over again.

My vacation was nice while it lasted.

I had to start back at school, but I quit Jackson Family Farm. I was probably going to be fired anyway after missing three shifts in a row, but when I called Enrique to tell him I wasn't coming back, it kind of sounded like he felt sorry for me. Maybe I was just imagining it.

So today, after my third day of in-school suspension (my punishment for skipping), I bike over to the frozen yogurt place in the same strip mall as the Tom Thumb because they have a HELP WANTED sign in their window. When I walk in, I see this guy named Jesse who's a year younger than me working the counter.

"Hey," he says. There's no one else in here but us. I stare at the sign above Jesse's head.

NEW FLAVOR EXPLOSION! SUPER CHOCOLICIOUS MINT FREEEZ!

"Do you really explode when you eat that kind?" I say, motioning at the sign.

"I don't actually consume this stuff," Jesse says, rolling his eyes. But he kind of grins when he says it.

"I'm here for an application," I say. "I saw the sign in the window."

Jesse nods and heads in the back and then comes out with a piece of paper.

"Most places let you apply online, but when I called, the owner said I had to come in," I say, taking the paper and sitting down at one of the sticky tables so I can fill it out.

"Yeah, the boss is sort of old school, but she's cool," Jesse says. "Hey, you're Caroline, right? You're a junior?"

"Yeah," I say, and I'm not sure if he knows me because of what happened with Dylan or because it's Dove Lake, and knowing people you've never actually talked to before isn't all that weird.

"I'm Jesse," he says.

"Yeah, I thought so," I say. "You're a sophomore?"

He nods.

"So working here's not so bad?"

"Honestly, no. It's pretty easy and you can have two cups of free frozen yogurt on each shift. But I've heard the sugar-free stuff gives you diarrhea."

"Gross," I say, wrinkling up my nose. "Thanks for the warning."

"No problem." He laughs and so do I. I leave my application with him and say goodbye, then bike home and head inside my empty house. As I shut the front door, my phone buzzes, and even though I know it's stupid, I can't help but think maybe it's Ethan. But it's only Jesse from the frozen yogurt place.

"Hey, I just gave your application to Jana, and she says can you start tomorrow? She wants you Tuesdays and Thursdays after school until close and Saturdays 10 to 6."

"That was fast," I say.

"Well, you're the only one who's applied, so . . ."

"Oh," I say. "Yeah. I can start tomorrow."

"Okay, cool. I'll tell her."

Jesse's voice is cute. He's pretty cute in the face, too, I admit, but his voice is even cuter. Like all buttery and breathy and dreamy and soft.

"Do you work tomorrow, too?"

"Yeah," Jesse says. "I'll show you the ropes."

"Okay. Just make sure to point out the sugar-free stuff."

"No doubt."

I hang up and throw my backpack on the floor before flopping down on my bed.

Even if he is a sophomore, Jesse is cute.

As soon as I have the thought, I roll my eyes at myself. Jesse seems a lot more together than Jason, but the truth is when it comes to guys I'm pretty sure I don't know what I'm doing. Maybe I need to stop thinking about whether boys are cute or not. Maybe I just need to get a job at this yogurt place and start doing my homework and be normal for a while. If only I could figure out what exactly normal is.

I hear the front door open and the heavy-footed sounds of my dad coming in. Since he moved back last week it's been the usual: moments of relative peace interrupted by fights late at night and frowny scowls and uncomfortable silences, their meanings as thick as milkshakes.

I stare at the ceiling of my bedroom trying to think about what I need to do to get my shit together. Calm down about Jesse. Maybe put forth some effort on a homework assignment for once. Keep practicing guitar in case Ethan wants to be my friend again. A moment later the front door opens again, followed by the yelps and shrieks of Dylan crying. My stomach sinks, and I wonder if Dylan's freak out will be enough to make my dad turn around and move out again. Whether he stays or goes doesn't matter to me, but I wish he would just pick one and stick to it.

"Caroline, will you help, please!" My mom's voice is strained. On edge.

I don't want to go out there. I'm the worst sister on Earth. The worst person, actually. Because at this moment I would rather hide in here all night and go to bed starving than go out there.

But I think about my little brother and I force myself to get up and go down the hall into the kitchen where Dylan is flapping his arms over and over, which is something he does when he's trying to calm himself down. He's making little squeaky noises and his face is twisted up in pain and worry.

"Damn, damn, piece of cake," he's saying. "Piece of cake, damn, damn." This again.

My dad is sitting at the kitchen table, still in his work shirt and jeans, watching it all like we're a movie and he's just part of the audience.

"Dilly, Dilly, Dill Pickle," I say, crossing the kitchen floor to stand near him. If Dylan's really upset, like he is right now, like he is so much lately, he doesn't want anyone to touch him. He moves away from me, flapping his arms and scrunching up his face so hard I know it has to hurt.

"I stopped to get some pizza for dinner, and he just started melting down by the cash register," my mom says, sliding a greasy cardboard box onto the kitchen counter along with her purse and car keys. "I almost left without our food."

I can see my dad's body slump with frustration. "Pizza, Mindy?" he says. "There's seventy-five dollars in the checking account until next week."

My mom acts like my dad hasn't said anything. As if he's still gone the way he was most of last week. She just pushes past me and starts getting stuff out of the refrigerator to make a salad. Frustration burns inside. It would be nice if she at least appreciated me for helping.

"Dill Pickle," I say, touching him gently on the shoulder, "let's go watch *Jeopardy!*, okay?"

He scowls and flaps some more.

"*Jeopardy!*, Dill Pickle. *Jeopardy!*"

This is enough to get him to stop flapping. And after a little more pleading on my part, he heads down the hallway toward my parents' bedroom.

"Thanks so much for your help," I remark to my dad as I walk past him, my voice sugary sweet. He shoots a don't-mess-with-me look, but we both know there's not enough energy behind it to matter.

Dylan crawls onto my mom and dad's bed, and I find the *Jeopardy!* episode he loves so much. When the opening song flickers on, he scoots to the edge of the bed, his sweet, light eyes fixated on the action, his little boy face finally relaxing into something of a smile.

Down the hall, I hear the hum of one of my parents' fights

starting to build, and I shut the door so Dylan and I don't have to hear it.

I can't take much more of this back and forth between my parents. My dad is worse but even my mom acts selfishly sometimes. It's like she cares more about getting the last word in with my father than making this house a halfway tolerable place to live. I wish she'd just kick my dad out.

There is so much of me that wants to jump up and dart out of here, get on my bike, and pedal as fast as I can away from all of this. But I don't. I can't. I just keep my eyes on my baby brother as he nods along with the electronic game show theme song. I swallow him up with my eyes and my heart, and I promise myself that I won't ever let him get hurt again.

ETHAN—260 DAYS AFTERWARD

EVEN THOUGH DR. GREENBERG'S SESSIONS HAVE GOTTEN A LOT better, the family sessions with Dr. Sugar are still totally uncomfortable and weird. He's always giving us assignments. He actually calls them action items, and my mom taps them into her phone so she can review them later.

The last time we met, we talked about all of us needing to practice being independent, especially me. Like how I should be able to be alone for stretches of time. And how my mom and dad can text me while I'm alone but only a reasonable amount. And how if they text me, I have to text right back.

"It's about building trust and establishing those functional and healthy relationships with each other as a family again," says Dr. Sugar. Unlike Dr. Greenberg, Dr. Sugar wears some fancy new suit during each session, and he has a secretary who wears perfume and keeps track of all his appointments in a MacBook Air. Dr. Greenberg schedules stuff himself in a spiral notebook.

One of Dr. Sugar's action items is why I'm here now, climbing out of my mom's Volvo and onto the sidewalk in front of the frozen yogurt place where Jesse works.

"I'm going to go to the Tom Thumb and get what we need for dinner and a few other things, just what's on this list, and then I'll text you when I'm ready to leave, okay?" my mom tells me, only for the five millionth time. She waves a pink piece of paper in the air with *eggs, milk-skim, milk-2%, whole wheat bread, soy sauce* and a bunch of other stuff written on it.

"Got it," I say, nodding. We stand there outside of the yogurt place, neither one of us sure who should move first. My mom not wanting to move at all. Her cheeks are pink, and she swallows and looks at the space between me and the yogurt shop. It's maybe twenty feet. And I think she's going to stand here on the sidewalk and watch me until I make it inside.

"Mom, go get the groceries," I say, and I force a smile to try and encourage her. "I'm going right in. It's okay."

"You have your money and your phone?"

I nod. She's asked me that five million times, too.

"All right, well, have fun catching up with Jesse!" she says, her voice trying way too hard to make it normal. Like most sixteen-year-old guys get dropped off at a frozen yogurt place by their moms so they can hang out there for thirty minutes.

Like that's what all the really cool, normal teenage guys are doing.

I'm not cool. Or normal.

"Okay," I say, and I turn toward the yogurt place and she turns to go, but as I make it to the door and pull open the handle, I catch a glimpse of her, and she's walking toward the grocery store looking over her shoulder, keeping an eye on me. As soon as she catches me catching her, she waves. Like, *oh, see you, honey, just have a great time at the yogurt place, la la la, it's no big deal.*

I love my mom so much.

And she drives me crazy.

And this makes me feel terrible.

I walk in. It smells like plastic and something super sweet, and really terrible music from at least ten years ago is playing on the radio. Jesse is behind the counter and when he sees me walk in, he gives me a little wave. He knew I was coming. When Dr. Sugar suggested I go somewhere alone, my parents thought going to visit Jesse at work would be a good idea. So I texted him to let him know I'd be stopping by today. We don't really text. Not like Caroline and me texted. But he wrote me back right away and said okay.

"Hey, man," Jesse says, giving me a good-natured grin. Over his clothes he's wearing a bright pink apron with pictures of smiling, dancing spoons on the front.

"Hey," I say, feeling awkward. Hanging out and playing video games at my house with Jesse is okay, but seeing him here out in the world means we have to talk, which we don't do when we're playing video games.

"Man, how's it going, man?" he says. I think Jesse is nervous, too, which is probably why he keeps saying man.

"Okay, I guess." I'm trying to act cool, but I'm not sure how. My mind flashes on Bennie and Narciso at the apartment complex. They were cool. I felt cool sometimes hanging out with them. Even though I always wondered when they were going to guess the truth about me, even though they never did. But when the three of us would hang out and chill behind the abandoned strip mall near the apartment complex, I was the happiest I could be in the worst time of my life.

I'm not sure if Bennie and Narciso were my friends. Can you be friends with someone when you're so messed up you don't even know who you are, really? And if I'm still messed up, can I be real friends with Jesse again?

Or Caroline?

"You want some fro yo?" Jesse says, busting into my thoughts. I'm just standing there like a weirdo. He's probably wishing I wasn't here.

"Yeah, I guess, chocolate," I say, just to be saying something. The idea of actually eating any of this stuff makes my stomach knot up.

"Sprinkles?"

"Sure."

Suddenly the door opens behind me and I turn and if it isn't Caroline herself running in. Like she knew I was thinking about her. I stare. It's been weeks since that night at the creek.

"Sorry I'm late, Jesse," she says, not even realizing I'm standing there. "I had to talk to Mrs. Garcia about making up some math homework."

"Hey," I say. And she looks up at me and actually jumps.

"Oh!" she says, her eyes wide. "Hey."

I think about the last time we saw each other and what we were doing. My cheeks warm up just thinking about it. I think Caroline's do, too.

"Hey, you know Caroline?" Jesse says, sliding a cup of sprinkle-covered yogurt across the counter. Then it's like he does the math in his head. "Oh, yeah, of course you do." But Jesse only knows about what happened with me and Dylan. He doesn't know about those months when Caroline and I played music. Became friends.

"How much for the yogurt?" I ask.

"On the house," says Jesse.

"Thanks," I say. I take the plastic spoon he hands me and shovel some into my mouth. It tastes like ice-cold chemicals.

Caroline is heading behind the counter and tying on one of those pink aprons. She takes her long hair and puts it up in a ponytail. Just then a mom and her little girl walk in, and

Caroline gets to helping them. I stand to the side and force myself to finish the frozen yogurt, feeling out of place. Almost wishing my mom would text me just to give me something to do. I'm kind of surprised she hasn't yet.

"So how's everything going?" Jesse asks.

"Okay," I say. Caroline is ringing up the mom. I'm sure she can hear us.

"Still working with that tutor?" Jesse asks.

"Yeah, I am. It's going okay."

"You think you'll be coming back to school next year?"

"Maybe," I say. "It's only February. So there's time to decide. And I have to make sure I'm caught up enough to be in regular classes."

"You were always in accelerated when we were kids," Jesse says. "I bet you can do it no problem."

After the mom and her kid have walked out, Caroline busies herself wiping down the already clean counter. When I glance over at her I feel my throat tighten up. Like if I were all by myself I would let myself start crying.

"Don't you think Ethan is ready to come back to school?" Jesse asks her. "Don't you think he could handle it?"

Caroline scrubs the counter even harder and doesn't look at me. "I'm sure he could handle it," she says. She glances up for a half second and catches my eye. Then she looks back down at the counter again.

I think about what Dr. Greenberg said. How when you're

going through something difficult, you can become reckless without meaning to be. I remember what Caroline told me about her parents fighting. I remember how it sometimes seemed like she never wanted to go home.

My phone buzzes. Grateful for the distraction, I look down. It's my mom checking in.

Almost done with the shopping. I'll be outside the yogurt shop right by the Volvo in a few minutes. I'll text you when I get to the Volvo.

She mentions the Volvo twice, like she thinks I might forget and go to the wrong car or something. I text her back a quick okay and that I'm fine.

I finish the yogurt, and Jesse and I talk about video games and how he's almost saved up enough for this used car his cousin wants to sell him and a little bit about college basketball. The whole time Caroline acts all busy, taking boxes into the back, cleaning stuff she's already cleaned once, helping customers as they walk in. Each time Jesse tries to help, she says she's got it.

"It's okay. Take a break and talk to your friend." The way she says the word *friend*, it sort of hangs there, lonely and sad.

While I try to make small talk with Jesse, my mind drifts to thinking about playing music with Caroline in the garage. Talking to Jesse is okay. It's fun to play video games with him, and he's always really nice and everything. But hanging out with him won't ever be like the way it was when Caroline and I were hanging out.

When my mom texts me that she's waiting, I tell Jesse I have to get going.

"Let's hang out soon," he says. "Or stop by whenever."

"Okay," I say. Caroline is cracking open rolls of coins to put in the register.

"Bye, Caroline," I say, and when she hears her name she looks up and nods, uncertainly.

"Bye, Ethan," she says, giving me a tentative half wave.

I actually witness my mom's whole body relax when she sees me walk out of the frozen yogurt place in one piece. Alive. Safe.

"Was it nice seeing Jesse?" she says as I help her load the bags into the back of the car. Her voice goes all sing-song, and I can already hear her telling Dr. Sugar how well everything went during this action item.

"Yeah," I say, trying to sound upbeat.

"So great, honey," she says as we get in. "I'm so proud of you. So proud of us!" She's almost giddy driving home.

Later on that night in my bedroom after dinner, I put on some White Stripes and lie on my bed, staring at the ceiling. I pull out my phone and text Caroline.

Hey

A minute later I get a hey in response.

How's it working with Jesse? What happened with the farm?

Quit the farm. Working with Jesse is pretty good . . .
but that frozen yogurt tastes so fucking terrible

I know . . . I ate mine just to be nice

Long pause. Then another text pops up.

I'm still sorry about what happened

It's ok

Seriously?

Yeah

Long pause again. I can tell from the word bubble popping up and going away that she's trying to figure out what
to say next. Finally, her next text appears.

I miss hanging out

I stare at the words she's sent me. I read them over and
over again.

Playing with Caroline was never hard. Even the very first
time we played. I mean, I was nervous about proving I was
a good enough drummer to keep up with her. Then there
was always the strange, dark cloud of how we knew each
other hovering over us, never totally gone. But once we
started playing, it was the easiest thing in my life. Easier
than catching up in my schoolwork, easier than being with
my parents, easier than anything. And I know the shit at
the creek was messed up. I know I don't want it to get weird
like that again.

But if we can stick to playing in the garage. If we can stick
to closing our eyes and filling the air around us with power

chords and progressions and music. If we can stick to talking about the future and never the past.

If we could do that. I take a deep breath and text Caroline again.

You want to come over Saturday night and play?
Yeah?
Yeah
I would totally love to
Cool
Like after dinner or whatever?

I grin to myself and write her back.

Yeah after dinner is good
K sounds good . . . I have to go. To help my mom with Dylan

That last text—that mention of Dylan—makes me freeze up a bit. The words slice through my little moment of happiness. I text her back, but I don't say anything about her brother. I just respond **See you Saturday.**

After I take my medication and say goodnight to my parents, I climb into bed with the lights on and the door halfway open just like I need it. I check my phone one more time but the only message I see from Caroline is her last one. I squeeze my eyes shut. I wish I hadn't reread it.

As I wait to fall asleep, I try to fill my head with the songs I want to play with Caroline. Tonight I want to try and have good dreams.

CAROLINE—262 DAYS AFTERWARD

I HEAD OVER TO ETHAN'S RIGHT AFTER WORK ON SATURDAY, AND MY heart is pounding the whole bike ride over. I'd left my practice amp at his house the last time we'd played all those weeks ago, but my guitar is balanced on my handlebars in its soft case, and I'm trying so hard not to tip over. Maybe I should have walked.

Maybe I shouldn't even be doing this.

Instead of dumping my bike on the front lawn like I normally do, I wheel it up toward the garage. I'm trying to be a good guest, I guess.

Ethan's sitting at his drums, twirling his drumsticks like he sometimes does when he's nervous or quiet or doesn't want to talk much or just because. He hears me approaching and glances up.

"Hey," he says.

"Hey," I say back.

We don't talk. I just plug in and start fiddling with my guitar, and Ethan nods his head a little, listens to me as I pluck a few strings and get comfortable. It's a White Stripes song we've played before, and when he realizes where I'm going he shoots me this look and rolls his eyes a little. I roll mine back.

We play the whole song, but after that first glance we don't look at each other while we play. I stare down at my fingers moving across the frets. I'm a good enough player that I don't have to watch my fingers, usually. But tonight I do. It's easier than looking anyplace else. It's definitely easier than looking at Ethan.

We finish playing, and he crosses his drumsticks in his lap.

"Really? That's what you want to play?" He's trying to make it jokey.

"Ethan," I say, and the guitar feels like a shield. Like I can say anything I want as long as I'm holding it. "I messed everything up."

He tries to force a grin. To make me see it's okay. But he can tell I'm not going to let it go. I'm not going to just pretend nothing happened.

"Okay, so yeah, it got weird. It did."

"It won't happen again," I tell him.

"What won't? You getting drunk or you forcing me to go on some random walk to the creek or us kissing?"

I flush. It all sounds even stupider when he puts it like that. "All of the above."

Ethan twirls his sticks.

"Kissing me must have been really awful," he says, and I can barely hear him his voice is so small. And it's meant to be a joke. But, like, not a joke at the same time. I swallow and stare at my guitar.

"No, Ethan, it wasn't," I say, and I see his eyes dart up in surprise and then dart down again, embarrassed. "But . . . ," I keep going, "I think us playing music . . . it's better than kissing. It's more than that, even. And maybe we shouldn't mess with that. And kissing sometimes messes things up."

Ethan stares at his knees and nods, and it gets quiet for a good long while. So quiet that even though Ethan and me are usually pretty good at being quiet together, I can't stand it anymore. "So," I say, "I'm trying this new thing. Where I try not to be stupid and kiss boys without really thinking about why I'm doing it. Without really knowing exactly what it means."

Ethan nods. "That sounds like a good plan."

"Yeah?"

"Yeah," he says back, and I can tell he wants to change the subject. He nods to a cooler off to the side. "You want a Coke?"

"When did you get a cooler out here?" I ask, eager to talk about something so basic.

"A few days ago," he says. "I convinced my mom it was easier than her walking out here every ten minutes to offer me something to drink. Not that that's why she's coming out here, really."

I don't know what to say to that, but Ethan hands me a can, its sides still slippery from sitting in ice water, and I unstrap my guitar and sit down on the cement to drink.

"I feel bad sitting up here, and you're on the ground," he says.

"No, I like it," I say, taking a slurp of my drink. I stretch out on my back, the coolness of the pavement making its way through my dark blue hoodie. I really do like being on the ground. I like watching the tops of the crepe myrtle trees hanging over the roof of Ethan's garage. I like how their naked, skinny wintertime branches stretch out like witches' fingers.

"I could always get you a chair," says Ethan, and I can hear him take a swallow from his drink.

"Your neighbors don't mind us playing so late?" I ask. Dusk is starting to settle.

"No," he says. "They're ancient and deaf. They have a Chihuahua that barks all the time, and I swear they never hear her."

"We used to have a dog," I say to Ethan and to the tree branches hanging overhead.

"What kind?"

"A mutt," I answer. "Only she got cancer, and we had to put her down."

"Can't they treat cancer in dogs?" Ethan asks.

"If you have, like, thousands of dollars," I say, and I immediately feel bad for saying it. Ethan's family does have thousands of dollars. At least I'm pretty sure they do.

Talking about our old dog makes me think about Dylan. He and the dog—Trixie was her name—loved to watch *Jeopardy!* together, and Dylan used to be calmer when Trixie was around. At least he didn't have more meltdowns and scream out, *"Damn, damn, piece of cake, damn,"* all the time. No matter what my mom thinks, in my gut I know those words have something to do with the kidnapping, and I wish Ethan could explain them to me. I wish I could understand what they mean. I'll probably never find out. I'll probably never know what happened to my little brother.

I sit up, antsy all of a sudden. I can feel my fingers itching to play. But I'm not sure what.

"If we formed a band someday," I find myself saying, "we could play for money. Like, there's a school dance tonight. We could find a bass player and play something like that." It's nonsense talk, I know. Ethan will probably never come back to school, and I would rather have nothing to do with anything involving the school gym, even if it is decorated in paper streamers and the lights are dimmed. But talking about it is fun, somehow. Picturing myself in front of a big crowd, my hair done up some really cool way I could never actually manage to do. My makeup all gorgeous so I look like someone else.

"What's the dance for?" Ethan asks, and I think for a moment of all the things he hasn't done in years. Slam lockers. Take notes. Text in class. Skip gym. And my heart breaks for him for the ten thousandth time.

"It's for Valentine's Day."

"Oh," he says, and as soon as he says it I realize how totally awkward it could be to mention Valentine's Day after everything that's happened between us.

"They probably have a terrible deejay," I say, anxious to fill up the space. "He's playing, like, terrible music with some thumping bass and the teachers are wandering around making sure no one is doing anything inappropriate."

"My parents met at a dance," Ethan says. The sky is getting all purple and gray, and it's getting chilly, too. I'm glad I have my jacket.

"Like a dance in high school?" I ask.

"No, college," Ethan says. "It was a party at my dad's fraternity, and my mom says they danced to this song by Air Supply."

"Air Supply?"

"Oh, shit, you have to hear it," Ethan says. "I mean, it's terrible. I'm warning you right now. Your ears could possibly bleed."

He finds the song on his phone and soon the two of us are sitting there, listening to a tinny male voice singing about being all out of love and so lost without you.

"They fell in love to this?" I ask, horrified. The song is so awful that I sit up, stunned.

"Yeah," Ethan says, shrugging. "My mom still loves to sing it."

We sit there and listen to the entire song, and when it's done, I find myself humming it, then trying to mimic the words. It's terrible and overproduced and cheesy, but the truth is it's catchy as hell. "I'm all out of love, I'm so lost without yooooouuuuu," I start. I stretch the "you" out as far as it will go.

"No, don't do it," Ethan starts, holding up his hands in mock surrender, but I can tell what he really means is sing my guts out, and he starts up a slow and steady beat on the bass drum.

"How does the chorus go again?" I say, standing up and strapping my guitar on again.

"Something about it can't be too late to say that I was wrong," Ethan says, nodding his head to the beat he's creating.

"Something something something . . . and blah blah blah!" I sing, managing to mimic the tune.

"Just make it up!" Ethan insists.

"This song is so bad . . . I have to keep singing!" I belt out. "I cannot ignore . . . the pain it is bringing!"

Ethan cracks up and keeps drumming.

"The words to this song . . . are so totally lame!" I try. "After hearing it now . . . I won't be the same!"

I'm laughing so hard that Ethan takes over until he's out of ideas and I make up another stupid verse for this very stupid love song, playing the chorus over and over again with new and ridiculous words until Ethan's mom comes out to see what the hell we are doing. It's almost dark now, and she stands in the circle of floodlight shining down from the back of the house. It's late, but she still has her hair in a neat ponytail and her lipstick is still perfect.

"What is going on?" she says, her hands on her hips. But I think she might be smiling a little, too.

"We're recreating your first date with dad in honor of Valentine's Day," Ethan says. "You mean you couldn't tell?"

"Air Supply sounded very different that night," Ethan's mom says, shaking her head, but I can see her eyes light up a little when she says it. It's almost like maybe she is liking me for the first time. "Not too much longer," she says, "or even the Fletchers will hear."

But after she turns to head back inside, Ethan insists on another made up verse and then another one after that. And the both of us keep playing. By the time we finally finish our epic Air Supply cover, we are drenched in sweat and we are making stupid faces at each other and we are laughing so hard we can't breathe.

ETHAN—264 DAYS AFTERWARD

AFTER MY MONDAY MORNING LESSONS WITH MRS. LEANDER, MY MOM and I sit down to eat lunch at our kitchen table. She makes us roast beef sandwiches with tomatoes and lettuce and mayonnaise on thick baguettes. My mom cuts her sandwich in half and wraps the first half in aluminum foil, saving it for later. I plow into mine, knowing I'll finish all of it.

"Famished, huh?" she asks.

I nod, wiping a drop of mayonnaise off the side of my mouth with my thumb. Four hours with Mrs. Leander and I'm starving. She's tough in a good way, and I know from the quizzes and tests I'm acing that I'm catching up fast, but when you're the only student in the room, you don't get the chance to slack off.

"You're planning on playing with Caroline later?" she says, taking a tiny bite and chewing carefully.

"Yeah," I say. "Don't worry. No Air Supply this time."

"It was funny," she says, smiling. "I can tell you like playing with her."

"Yeah, I do," I say, and I know from the way that she pauses to speak and then takes a sip from her can of Diet Coke instead that she wants to say something. Maybe about Caroline. But she's second guessing herself. I wonder if it will always be like this between my mom and me. And my dad and me. Always hesitations. Always things under the surface. Things said but not said.

We keep eating and we don't talk. My mother takes these small little bites. She's put together as usual. Her hair is always perfect, her nails are always done, she always has her lipstick on. When I was little, she would get dressed nice just to take me to the park even though the other moms were in T-shirts and sweatpants. Before I was born she did something in banking. Investing or something, and after I was born, it was like she still dressed as if she were going to some fancy office even though she was just staying at home with me. Maybe it's because she'd dressed for work for so long she didn't know how to stop. My mom didn't have me until she was thirty-eight, and my middle name is Joseph after the doctor she and my dad went to back in Austin when they couldn't get pregnant right away. It's a weird fact about myself, I realize. Sometimes I wonder if Dr. Joseph saw all the headlines about me. And if he did, I wonder if he remembered my parents were his patients and if he realized who I was.

I stand up to take the lunch dishes to the sink. One of my chores before I was gone was to clear the table after meals, and I fell right back into it when I came home. At first my mom didn't want me to do it. Didn't want me to do anything, really. But I like making things clean and putting things away. I like how after the table is cleared off and the dishes are in the dishwasher, I take a dishtowel and the all-purpose cleanser and wipe down the counters and the white kitchen table where we eat. And everything looks just like it should.

I'm admiring my work when I turn and find my mom is sitting there staring at me. She does this a lot—the staring—but now I think her eyes are a little glassy with the start of tears.

"Mom?" I manage. "Are you okay?"

She smiles a little. "Your shoulders, Ethan," she tells me. "I was looking at you as you did the dishes and your shoulders . . . your shoulders are like a man's shoulders. You're so grown up."

I'm standing there, blue and white checkered dishtowel in my hand. My mom's cheeks are red and splotchy and her eye makeup is starting to soften. She takes a deep breath.

"I've been thinking . . . that you need to have more freedom," she says. She folds her napkin and then unfolds it and folds it again. "I know I drive you crazy. I know I follow you from room to room in this house and I check on you thirty times a night. I know I can't do these things anymore. But I don't know how to stop."

I put the cleanser and the dishtowel down on the kitchen counter. I walk toward her and sit down with her at the kitchen table. She blinks a few times until her eyes aren't glassy anymore.

"Mom," I say, and then I don't know what to say next.

"I annoy you sometimes, don't I?" she asks.

I look down. I'm giving myself away.

"It's okay, Ethan," she says. She reaches over and she squeezes my hand, and it's nice. I remember when I was a little kid and she would squeeze my hand at the doctor's office whenever it was time for me to get a shot. One tight, sure squeeze.

"Sometimes," I say. "Yeah, sometimes you do, Mom."

She exhales.

I think about Dr. Greenberg. How he always seems to know the right words at the right time. How he has all these little tricks like brushing Groovy or going on walks so that somehow when our session is up I feel better. I wish I could be like Dr. Greenberg right now, but I just sit there, my throat clenching in sadness.

"Mom," I whisper, "I'm sorry that I didn't leave."

My mom blinks hard and stares at me, her eyes widening.

"No, Ethan," she says. "No. No! That's not what this is

about. I know you couldn't leave. I wish you could have, yes, but I know you couldn't. I do understand that. I really do."

"I don't know how you could when I don't always," I say. We're still holding hands. But it's not bugging me.

"Ethan, the doctors have explained it to us," she says. "Your reaction was so common. It happens to victims of trauma—"

"It happened to me," I interrupt. I'm not used to interrupting. But I do it now. "And I know what the doctors say, and sometimes I get it and sometimes I still don't understand. I don't know why this happened to us either. I went on that website for missing kids the other day—do you know something like a hundred kids a year in the United States are taken like I was? By a total stranger? And I was one of them? It's like being struck by lightning."

My mom looks into my eyes and studies my face carefully, like she'll never get sick of looking at it. Because she never will.

"Did you know when your dad and I tried to have you, the doctors told us we had less than a 10 percent chance of getting pregnant?" she asks. "Did you know we did IVF three times?"

I shake my head no.

"So it's something with you and odds. Both good and bad, it seems."

"So you're saying I should play the lottery and never get

on a plane," I try. She smiles and I smile, too. Careful, half smiles. Like we're testing them out just to see how they feel.

"It's a long road, isn't it, sweetheart?" she says, and her half smile is real even though her eyes are sad.

"Yeah, it really is," I say, and I wonder what happens to kids like me that don't get to come home to moms like my mom and dads like my dad. My mind flashes on Dylan and the stories Caroline has told me about her family. I shut my eyes for a minute to try and lose the thought.

After one more squeeze of our hands, she takes the napkin she's already folded twice and starts folding it again, even more neatly this time.

"I'm trying to be better with all the hovering," she says. "I'm really working on it."

"I know," I say.

"For example, have you noticed I don't come out to check on you and Caroline all the time anymore?" she asks. "I only came out last night because of Air Supply."

"Yes, mom, I noticed. You get an A for effort there."

Now her half smile turns into a full smile, and so does mine. Her eyes light up, too. We sit there in the kitchen, just smiling and breathing together, with the refrigerator humming and the ice maker plunk-plunking its ice. There's no rush to get up.

CAROLINE—288 DAYS AFTERWARD

JESSE AND I ARE WORKING THE LAST SHIFT AT THE FROZEN YOGURT place on Thursday afternoon. He closes out the register, and I mop the floor. The mop is so in need of replacing that it's dark gray, not remotely white, and I don't think my mopping does much more than push dirty water around in circles, but finally I finish and dump out the filthy water in the mop sink, and Jesse comes out of the back office and says we can lock up.

Normally I bike home and Jesse drives, but today he's waiting for his mom to pick him up because the car he just bought from his cousin is in the shop getting new tires.

"Sorry I can't give you a lift," I say, nodding at my handlebars. "This sweet ride only fits one."

Jesse grins. "It's cool, Caroline. I can wait for my mom."

I like how he says my name in his buttery voice. How he

sounds like a radio deejay with some secret bad habit. Just the right mix of good boy and not-so-good boy. But I'm still not doing anything with Jesse. Anyway, I'm not sure he wants to do anything with me. Sometimes when we're working together and I say something funny he winks at me, and I think there's a chance. But really, I want to put the brakes on my romance life until I figure out exactly if I'm capable of having one without screwing it up.

It's only early March, but I can already sense a hint of summer heat in the air as I bike home. When I walk inside my house, I find my mom sitting in the family room drinking a beer, staring glumly at the wall in front of her. The television is on the local news with the volume turned way low, and I can barely hear the big-boobed news anchor talking about the upcoming city council meeting. Dylan is in the corner doing his line-up-the-blocks game.

My mom doesn't look at me. She just takes a sip from her beer.

And then, her voice even, she says, "Your father is having sex with someone else."

I wish she'd at least said he was having an affair, just to gross me out less. But I'm not surprised. This is exactly the type of thing my dad would do even though it makes him even more of a stereotype than I ever thought possible.

I let my backpack slide to the floor. I slump down on the couch next to my mother and look at her profile. At the tiny double chin that's come into form these past few years. At the scraggly ponytail she keeps permanently stuck to the back of her head. I remember the picture in the yearbook of my mother being crowned Prom Queen. She was the best kind of skinny, with curves just where they needed to be. Her eyes were alive like she knew she was special. Like her life wasn't going to be like everyone else's.

I guess that part was true.

"Mom, I'm sorry," I say.

"Yeah," she says, taking another sip of beer.

"Who is it?"

"The woman who answers phones at his work," she says. "He finally admitted it this afternoon."

"Is he here?" I ask.

"I kicked him out," she says. "He's staying at his brother's, I think."

I breathe a little easier now because I'd rather put up with sad, drinking mom than screaming mom and shouting dad. But the reality of the situation is already worming its way into my head. My mom hasn't worked in years, not since Dylan was born. Even though we needed the money, probably.

"What are we going to do?" I ask. I don't have to tell her I'm talking about the rent or the grocery money or the gas money.

"I don't know," she says. "But I'll figure it out."

I look over at Dylan moving his blocks into order. I will

him to not make a mistake, to not freak out. That's the last thing we need right now.

"I never thought things would turn out like this," my mom says, and it's weird how she's talking to me like a girlfriend or a sister. Like we're besties or something. I don't like it.

"I'm sorry," I say because I'm not sure what else to say.

"Everything went to shit after Dylan was taken," my mom says, and suddenly it occurs to me that this isn't her first beer. She hardly ever swears in front of us, and her cheeks are red and her eyes are glassy and I've been sitting next to her for a few minutes and she still hasn't made eye contact with me. "I mean, it was bad before," she continues, "but it all really fell apart after that."

I wait for her to say what she isn't saying but has to be thinking. The unsaid words hang over us like bad weather.

Why weren't you watching him?

It was something she'd asked me to do a million times. Something I'd learned to do with my eyes still on my phone or my ears still listening to my music. Where was Dylan going to go, anyway? He didn't know how to open the door. He didn't know how to unlatch the window.

I'd been on my bed, probably texting Jason about something stupid. Trying to make myself sound the right mix of sexy cute. And Dylan had been wandering around my room, messing with my fifth grade rock collection that I kept on top of my dresser. The one that I'd always been meaning to throw out. The one I didn't even give a shit about. He was pounding the rocks on the dresser and humming to himself and in general distracting me from whatever important thing I thought I was doing.

Dill Pickle, give me a second, okay? Can you let me finish something? Go play somewhere else, okay?

And he'd disappeared somewhere down the hall, and I hadn't thought much of it. I'd had the hazy feeling that he was somewhere just beyond my line of sight. Maybe in the family room. Maybe in the kitchen. The sound of my dad mowing the lawn rumbled through the house. In the distance, I heard a neighbor's dog barking.

Caroline, wasn't Dylan in here with you? Weren't you watching him?

And then my mom and me are running through the house and we can't find him and my mom is running out the back door into the backyard yelling at my dad to turn off the mower, and I am in the front room of the house and the door is open so wide I can see all of the street in front of us and the Mackenzie's dying lawn across the road and my heart is thumping and my knees are almost certainly about to give out. A breeze comes and the door swings open even wider, like it's laughing at me.

And then my mom and my dad and I are running, my mom and I in bare feet, circling the house, chasing each other in a hide-and-seek game where no one can win because the one we're looking for isn't there to be found.

And the whole time my mind is on fire.

It's your fault, Caroline. It's your fault. It's your fault. It's your fault.

And here, right now, is the end result. Dylan is messed up and my parents are splitting up. It's still my fault.

My mom finishes her beer and gets up to open another one.

"Has Dylan eaten yet?" I ask.

"He had some frozen pizza," she says.

I cajole Dylan into putting his blocks away, and I wipe down his face and his hands. I skip brushing his teeth because I just don't have it in me. I get him to use the bathroom and I help him with his pajamas and then after he crawls into bed and I turn on all three of his nightlights, I sit with him on his bed. I make sure he has his pink horsie blanket and his three stuffed dogs. I try to sing to him, but the only song I can think of is the stupid Air Supply song Ethan and I played the other night. So I hum that for a little while, and I watch as he finally drifts off.

I thank the God I'm pretty sure I don't believe in that at least Dylan had an easy night.

I'm not hungry, so I go hide in my bedroom. I want to practice guitar, but I know it'll make too much noise. I've been getting better about finishing my homework lately, but there's no way in hell I'll tackle that tonight. I could go out and see how my beer-drinking mother is doing, but I can't see that being anything but crazy depressing.

I pull out my phone and turn it over in my hands. I want

to text Ethan. I want to think things aren't so fragile between us after the last time we hung out. But what if he thinks I'm too much?

I don't care. I text him anyway.

So big news my dad is having an affair and I'm pretty sure my parents are splitting up

He doesn't respond for almost half an hour, but finally my phone dings.

Sorry eating dinner with my parents . . . shit I'm really sorry Caroline

I'm envious that he gets to eat dinner with his mom and dad. Me. Jealous of Ethan. That's pretty screwed up. I text back.

It's my fault. Everything was awful before but after Dylan got taken it just got worse, and I should have been watching Dylan that day. He got taken because of ME

My stomach knots up just typing that. I probably shouldn't bring up Dylan with Ethan but right now I don't care. I see a bubble pop up as Ethan is texting me back, but it goes away and comes back like five times before he finally replies.

I'm really sorry . . . maybe they could work it out?

His response annoys me. Then again, I'm not sure how I would respond to me if I were him.

I'm hoping they don't get back together because it's hell when they fight

Pause.

Yeah I can only imagine

Yeah, he can only imagine. Because he doesn't have parents who scream and fight even though their son was gone for four years. Because he has a nice house and a new drum kit and a fancy, expensive therapist.

I'm being a brat, and I don't care.

I search around in my closet for the bag of weed I got from Jason all those months ago. There's only enough for the tiniest joint in the world, but I think it's enough. I smoke with the window open and by the time Ethan texts me again asking me if I want to come over the next night to play, I ignore him. I don't feel like doing anything but blanking out my brain and closing my eyes and imagining myself floating away somewhere into the stratosphere like a satellite that's slipped out of its orbit. Like a star burning up in the sky.

ETHAN—289 DAYS AFTERWARD

MY MOTHER AND I ARE DRIVING THROUGH THE STREETS OF Dr. Greenberg's neighborhood. It's a bright Friday morning, and I'm feeling pretty good. I even made it on the freeway okay. Maybe it's because Dr. Greenberg and I have tried his counting thing a few more times, I'm not sure. But as we turn the corner onto Dr. Greenberg's street, really, I'm feeling pretty good.

Suddenly, we spot a woman on the sidewalk, yelling. She's tiny, dressed all in black. When she sees our Volvo approaching, she waves her hands in the air like she's saying hello, but her expression is anxious.

"I wonder if she needs some help," my mother says, and she pulls the car over to the side of the road.

The way the car lurches to the side. The way my body presses against the door, following the car's movement. The way there's a person there, outside on the sidewalk, just next to the car.

Suddenly, my heart starts to pound.

The automatic window slides down easily, with barely a whisper. "Are you okay?" my mother says to the lady.

I can hear my mom's voice, but it's muffled and strange. My heart hurts it's thumping so hard.

"I'm just looking for my dog," the lady says.

I blink and try to focus on her face, but my vision is blurry and I can only hear her voice, soft and worried. She keeps talking. "She's a black lab. Her name is Princess if you see her. She's very friendly. My electrician left the gate open, and she got out."

I'm running my thumbs over my knuckles. I'm holding back my own vomit. I'm dying inside.

"We haven't seen her, but we'll keep an eye out," my mother says.

The lady says something back—thanks, I think. I don't know. I'm just trying to stay upright.

"I hope she finds her dog," my mother says, pulling the car back into drive.

"Yeah," I manage. I wonder if she can see the sweat beading around my forehead. I wonder if she can tell how close I am to passing out.

Finally, after all these months, my mom is okay with just dropping me off at Dr. Greenberg's front porch where he always sits, waiting for me. Then she spends our session time running errands to the sorts of stores and places we don't have in Dove Lake. When we pull up, Dr. Greenberg is on his porch with Groovy. I slide out of the Volvo and manage to wave goodbye to my mother. I walk the few steps up to the porch on spaghetti legs. And then I feel a tidal wave of nausea come over me.

"Dr. Greenberg, I'm going to puke." I haven't even said hello.

"Sit down," he says, his voice commanding. "Sit down and put your head between your knees. Take slow, deep breaths."

I do exactly as he says. I'm staring at the peeling gray paint of Dr. Greenberg's front porch. My breathing is quick and shallow.

"Slow breaths, Ethan," he says. "Deep breaths. And don't lift your head up just yet. I'm right here, Ethan. I'm right here with you."

A minute passes. Maybe five. I don't know. I close my eyes. Finally the swimminess in my skull starts to pass. I tell Dr. Greenberg I think I'm okay to sit up.

"Slowly," he says. "Very slowly."

I sit up and blink, then glance at him. "Sorry," I say.

"Nothing to be sorry about," he answers. "What's going on?"

"Dr. Greenberg," I start, my voice cracking, "I just re-membered something so bad. I just had this memory, and

I . . . I just . . . it's so terrible, Dr. Greenberg." I fight back one more wave of nausea.

"Ethan, do you think you can talk about it?" Dr. Greenberg asks, his forehead furrowed deep.

"It's about Caroline. About her brother, really."

I shift in my Adirondack chair and think about Caroline texting me last night about her parents splitting. I think about what she said about Dylan. How him getting taken was her fault. My stomach lurches again.

I work my thumbs over the arms of the chair. I try to focus on my breathing.

"Dr. Greenberg," I start, and I'm fighting back tears. I hate that I cry all the time now. Those years I was gone I'd completely stopped crying. I gave up on it because it didn't help anyway. And now when I cry, it's like my body's exhausted the minute the lump starts to build in my throat.

"Ethan, whatever you need to say, I'm here," he tells me, his voice soft. "We can figure this out together."

I choke on a sob and Dr. Greenberg asks if I want to go inside, but I shake my head no. I feel better outside. Outside with the fresh air and the sun.

"Last night Caroline texted me that her parents are splitting up," I say. "And she said it's because of Dylan getting taken. And she thinks that it's all her fault. Because she was supposed to be watching him that day, and he made it out of the house when she wasn't looking."

Dr. Greenberg nods.

"But Dr. Greenberg," I say, and my body heaves. I'm crying now for real. "I remembered something. It just came back to me in the car. It isn't Caroline's fault Dylan got taken, Dr. Greenberg. It's mine."

Dr. Greenberg frowns a little. "Ethan, how do you mean?"

I close my eyes and let hot tears slide down my face. I don't know if there's enough courage inside of me to tell this story. I run my thumbs over my knuckles. I let more tears fall. And then, somehow, in a quiet voice I start to tell Dr. Greenberg exactly what came rushing back to me when my mother stopped to talk to the lady who'd lost her dog. The moment the car made its way over to the side of the road. The moment the car window went sliding down.

We're in the black truck, him and me. We're driving through Dove Lake.

The streets are familiar. Like I can place them but not really. Like I saw them in a photograph in a history book, back when I used to go to school.

There's a gun in the glove compartment. I know it real well. It's the same gun he's trained on me. The same gun he's held at my head more times than I could ever count. The same gun he told me he would use to kill me. And kill my parents if I ever tried to run away.

The gun that was waiting for me whenever he took me out of the closet.

The gun whose evil eye stared me down so many times that even when I stopped seeing it all the time it was still there. Still watching me.

The man is hunting with the black truck. He is looking for my replacement.

What do you do when your car gets too old?

You get a new car.

Suddenly, he spots him. I can see him, too. Light-haired boy, skinny frame. Walking down the sidewalk all by himself. He looks like he is lost. He is flapping his arms like he is trying to fly.

"Tell him you're looking for your lost puppy," the man in the driver's seat says, and he doesn't have to open the glove compartment. He knows he doesn't even need to bother with that part anymore. He knows I will do exactly as told.

The truck slides over to the side, casual. The automatic window sinks down and the hot May air seeps in.

"Hey," I say, my elbow leaning out the window. "Hey, kid. My dad and I are looking for my lost dog? A big black lab?"

The kid turns to look at me, and I know something is off. Something isn't right. He puts both hands in his mouth and starts sucking his fingers. He steps right up to the truck, but he doesn't say anything.

The voice behind me speaks up. "Open the door. Right now."

I do. Of course I do. I open the door and when the man reaches over me to grab the kid by the shirt, I am reaching down and helping him, too. The kid starts to yelp and kick and when I'm told to get the gun from the glove compartment and aim it at this kid, I do.

Of course I do.

And we are speeding out of these streets that look familiar and strange at the same time, and the kid is on the floorboard, crying and making noises that I know will annoy the man, and the gun is heavy in my hands. My finger is on the trigger. The boy starts calling out, over and over, "Lost dog, lost dog."

"Shut up!" I shout. "There's no dog. So shut up." I tell the boy this because I know what will happen to him if he doesn't shut up. And then I think it is stupid to warn him. Because it's already too late. It doesn't matter what he does or doesn't do. The worst part isn't over. It is just beginning.

I can see the back of the boy's neck and the way his light hair falls down over it, like it needs to be trimmed. I can see his whole body shaking. I can smell the scent of cigarettes on the man and I can hear the truck's engine roaring. Roaring as we move and we move and keep moving.

"Damn," says the man in the driver's seat. "That was a piece of cake."

By the time I am done telling Dr. Greenberg, I'm not crying anymore. The words tumble out, and when I'm done my whole body aches. I've been tensing my entire self as I've been talking, and it feels like I've just run a marathon or hiked through the jungle.

Dr. Greenberg's eyes are pink. He's the one crying now.

"Ethan," Dr. Greenberg says, his voice a whisper. "Ethan, I'm so sorry that happened to you."

I shake my head, confused.

"What do you mean, what happened to me?" I shout. "What about what I did? What about what happened to Dylan? I did that, Dr. Greenberg! I did it!"

Dr. Greenberg takes a deep breath and leans toward me. "Ethan," he says, "I can see how you would feel that way, but think of it like this. Is Caroline to blame for what happened to her brother?" he asks me.

"No, of course not," I say.

"But she feels like she is, doesn't she?" Dr. Greenberg asks.

"Yeah," I admit.

"And you feel like you're to blame even though you were under severe psychological stress the likes of which most human beings will never have to experience in their lifetimes, right?"

I shrug.

"Who are we not blaming, Ethan?"

"What do you mean?" I ask, confused.

"Should we blame Dylan for running out of the house?"

"No," I answer. It comes out almost like a shout.

"So who are we not blaming?"

I stare across the street. I wipe at my runny nose with my sleeve. "You're saying I should blame him. The guy driving the truck. The kidnapper."

"Yes," says Dr. Greenberg. "In fact, I think he's the only one we could blame."

I shrug, working Dr. Greenberg's words over in my mind. I want to believe them, just like I want to believe his words about why I didn't try to run away.

"I want to believe you. But I don't know if I can."

Dr. Greenberg nods. "I understand that. But with time I think you will start to believe it. I really do."

We sit in silence for a while, and Dr. Greenberg finally says, "I'm glad you shared this with me, Ethan. The truth is, the fact that this memory came back to you now is a sign you're getting healthier. Your mind knows you're in a safe enough space to process that sort of memory now, so it's letting you have it."

"I wish it had kept it," I mutter. Dr. Greenberg doesn't say anything. I shift my feet and more silence passes. I wonder how much time has gone by. How much time is left before my mom comes back. I want her to come and take me home where maybe I can escape into playing my drums or my video games or some medication-induced sleep. But at the same time, it's like I know being here and talking about this makes me feel better, too. Even if I do need a break.

Still, I know I can't really take a break because there's been something gnawing at me ever since the memory came back to me in my mom's car. Thinking about it brings on a wave of panic, and I know the only way to slow it down is to tell Dr. Greenbeg about it.

"The thing is, I don't think I can keep hanging out with

Caroline if I don't tell her about this," I say. "I feel like I need to tell her how Dylan was taken." I grip the arm rests of the chair.

At this Dr. Greenberg starts scratching his chin, and he seems a little lost in thought. It's happened. I've finally stumped my Harvard-educated therapist.

Eventually, he looks at me and says, "Ethan, you have to understand that Caroline may react really poorly to this. You have to know that this won't be easy for her to hear."

I nod. That's stating the obvious.

But I can't imagine playing music with Caroline and singing stupid songs and sharing Cokes in my garage again if I don't share this. If I don't stay 100 percent honest with her. Because if I've figured one thing out about Caroline and me these past few months it's that the two of us—we don't do bullshit.

"I know, Dr. Greenberg," I say. "But I want to tell her. I think I have to."

"What if this ends your friendship?" Dr. Greenberg asks gently. "What if that's the outcome? Do you think you could handle that?"

I look at the floor. The idea makes my insides hurt. "I think I could," I say. "At least, I know I could handle that more than I could handle being friends with her with this secret."

Dr. Greenberg nods and then takes a deep breath.

"I think you and Caroline must be in the same karass," he says.

"What?" I ask, confused.

"It's from this book by one of my favorite authors, Kurt Vonnegut," he says. "In his novel *Cat's Cradle*. He invented a religion just for this particular story." At this Dr. Greenberg grins like he is remembering the story for the first time in a long time. "In this religion, people who were linked cosmically, who were put together in teams of sorts to do God's will, were said to be in the same karass."

"Like fate brought Caroline and me together?" I ask. "Like God?"

"That's what Vonnegut would say," Dr. Greenberg answers. "Or what the religion he invented for this book would say, anyway."

I think about Caroline and me and, really, Dylan, too. I think about the three of us connected by some invisible thread, and I wonder why God or fate would have connected us in such an awful way. What it could possibly mean.

"I don't know about a karass," I say. "But I know if we're going to keep being friends, I have to tell her."

Dr. Greenberg doesn't say anything. He just nods, and I try to read his face to see if he thinks this is a good idea. But I can't be sure.

CAROLINE—291 DAYS AFTERWARD

I DON'T GO TO ETHAN'S ON FRIDAY NIGHT OR SATURDAY NIGHT, BUT by Sunday afternoon I'm missing him. I feel bad that I haven't texted him back. From my bed where I've been trying to do some homework, I finally do.

Feel like playing?

I'm ready to get out of the house. My dad is gone, there's nothing in the house to eat except frozen pizza, and my mom has spent all day on the phone with her sister while Dylan zones out in front of the television with his *Jeopardy!* episode playing over and over again. At least I got to spend most of Saturday at work, distracting myself with orders and Jesse's easygoing smiles and jokes. But a few hours at a yogurt shop aren't enough to make home easy to take.

I glance at my phone, wondering what's taking Ethan so long to write back. Finally, it lights up.

Sure. Come over whenever.

It's dusk when I bike over with my guitar, my knees bumping into the soft guitar case that I balance on my handlebars.

"I'll be glad when the time changes, so we can have more daylight to play in," I say as I plug in and get ready.

"Yeah," Ethan says, and something about the way he says it makes me look at him more closely. Like something is chewing away at him. But maybe I'm just imagining it. And anyway, Ethan counts off like nothing's up.

We fiddle around for a while, but it's like we're playing when we first met. Hesitant. Careful. Ethan keeps stopping, steadying his cymbals, and counting off again.

"I'm just off tonight," he says.

"It's okay," I say.

We struggle through a song or two and then all of a sudden Ethan's arms go limp, and his drumsticks drop to the floor by his feet with a clatter.

"Caroline, I have to tell you something."

I'm standing, still holding my guitar. "Should I sit down?" I ask.

"I think so, yeah," says Ethan, and his voice is tight and quiet.

Maybe Ethan's therapist thinks we shouldn't hang out together anymore. Or maybe his parents want to move back to Austin. Maybe his mom found out somehow what happened that night at the creek, and she hates me so much now I'm never going to be allowed over again. My heart starts pounding hard. I slide my guitar off my body and sit down on the cement. Ethan isn't looking at me. I can tell from the way his chest is moving under his black T-shirt that his breathing is coming quickly. Maybe too quickly. I'm worried he might pass out.

"Ethan," I say, "do I need to . . . like . . . go get someone?" I picture myself sprinting across the backyard in the fading sunlight, rapping my knuckles on the back door until his mom or dad comes to see what's the matter.

But Ethan shakes his head no. He just starts talking.

"I have to tell you this, Caroline. Because . . . I like you." He flushes and shakes his head, embarrassed. "I mean . . . you know what I mean. I like playing with you. You're my friend, and it's so easy to be around you. I can't say that for a lot of people right now. You're funny. And you're smart."

I nod, my eyes big.

"When you first came here," he pauses, takes a breath, "you wanted to know what I remembered about Dylan. About how he was taken. And the truth is I couldn't remember much. Not then. But my memory . . . it's weird sometimes. There are holes in it, and sometimes the holes get filled in when I don't even expect it. Dr. Greenberg says that's what happens with traumatic memories."

I nod again because it's all I seem able to do, and I

wonder if Dylan is having the same sort of feelings and memories as Ethan, only he doesn't know how to voice them.

But why is Ethan mentioning Dylan now?

And then, suddenly, I feel it. Like when you know someone is walking up behind you. Or when you sense that it's just about to rain. I know that Ethan is about to tell me something I don't want to hear but have to listen to. My heart starts hammering away inside my chest.

Now Ethan's mouth is moving and words are sliding out, lining up one right after another. I want them to stop coming, but they won't. He's careful how he puts them in order, with pauses in between. He isn't looking at me as he talks, just staring at his drums.

He tells me a terrible story with the scariest monster in it. Scarier than the wolf in *Little Red Riding Hood* or the evil stepmother in *Cinderella*. Scarier than Jason in those old eighties horror movies Emma and I used to watch. Scarier than anything I've ever seen or heard.

And in the story, Ethan is the scary monster's helper.

And my brother is the prey.

I blink. I blink again.

Ethan isn't crying, but it's like he's going to.

"I understand if you never want to see me again," he says at the end of the story. "But I wanted to tell you this. So you wouldn't think it was your fault what happened. And Dr. Greenberg tells me it's not my fault either, but I don't know. Either way, it isn't yours." His voice is barely a whisper.

We sit there in silence, and I find myself reaching for my guitar. How can I be here, with Ethan? How can I sit here with him after what he's just said he did?

How can I want to reach out to him and want to cover him with a raincoat or my arms or something and protect him? How can I want to scream at him, yelling at the the tops of my lungs, my fists clenched? How can I feel both wants tugging at my insides?

And then I hear myself saying, "I have to go," and I'm standing, somehow, my guitar still strapped on. "I'm sorry, but I have to . . . go."

Ethan is nodding like he expected as much, and I am on my bike and I am pedaling and I am crying so hard. I can barely see to make it home, and the darkening sky doesn't help. As I reach my street my entire body is gripped with panic. I have to see Dylan. Now.

I dump my bike and guitar in the front yard and race to the door, trembling. I can barely manage the key in the door. I imagine walking in and finding all the windows wide open, my brother vanished, my mom racing up and down the halls of our house calling his name.

But inside all that's happening is the television is on, and I catch a glimpse of my mom's ponytail and her hand clicking away at the remote.

I dart up to Dylan's bedroom and open the door. He's curled up around his pink horsie blanket, gripping it tight. The glow of his nightlights makes him look golden. Peaceful. Perfect.

I sink to my knees at the side of his bed, and I watch him take breaths as I try to catch my own. My mind is frantic with questions. How could anyone frighten my brother? How could anyone hurt my brother?

And how can I be friends with someone who did?

ETHAN—306 DAYS AFTERWARD

MY DAD SHUTS THE FRONT DOOR AND TURNS TO LOOK AT ME AND MY mom. He's smiling, of course.

"I think that went well, right?" he says.

My mom is smiling, too, but I know she's trying too hard. Maybe not as hard as my dad, but still.

"I think it's good," I say, and I do, actually, but I look down and see my thumbs traveling up and down my knuckles.

"That's great!" my dad answers, and he sits back down on the living room couch and picks up the pieces of paper that Principal Berry and the school's counselor have just dropped off. He leafs through them even though we've spent the past two hours talking about every single word that's written on them. Everything from optimal schedules to classroom seating to locker placement.

"So you're ready to be a junior in high school next fall?" he asks me.

I shrug my shoulders. The idea to go back to school came from Mrs. Leander. She said I was ready—that I'd made tremendous progress over the past several months. When she asked me about going back, even part-time, it was like she was asking me if I wanted to run for president. Technically, it was something I was able to do. But in actuality, I wasn't sure I wanted to.

What if I don't go back? Do I just stay at home every day, visiting Jesse at the frozen yogurt place when Caroline isn't there? If I don't go back to school, do I live here with my parents for the rest of my life? If I don't go back to school, and I don't have Caroline, do I never have another real friend again outside of my semi-awkward, semi-cool video game and frozen yogurt friendship with Jesse, who probably still wonders if everything that happened to me is his fault?

"What do you think about the schedule, Ethan?" my mom asks, taking a yellow piece of paper where Principal Berry has sketched some times and course names.

"I think it's good. It's good to go in for the stuff I feel I'm strongest at for now, and keep meeting with Mrs. Leander in the afternoons for everything else." That means homeroom, Spanish I, English Literature, and US History in the mornings, then lunch in the cafeteria—maybe—and then home to work on math and science with Mrs. Leander.

My mom stares at the paper and then looks up and across the room like my dad and I aren't there.

"I can't believe we're here already," she says, finally. "Talking about going to school."

I nod. I can't believe it either, really.

"I think it's good that Principal Berry will be meeting with the students first and letting them know your schedule and that you're excited to be going back," my dad says, "but that you don't necessarily want to talk about what happened." The words *what happened* are as close as my dad can get to naming my kidnapping. Dr. Greenberg says my dad is probably having a harder time dealing with everything than my mom because he likes to pretend he's all right all the time even when he isn't.

"Maybe," I say. "But maybe I should just go there and not stand out? I mean, it's not like everything wasn't already all out in the news and everything." My parents glance at one another but don't say anything. I imagine Caroline sitting in on a student meeting in the auditorium about how to handle the Kidnap Victim. I'm glad she's a year ahead of me and there's no chance we could be in any of the same classes. But still. I imagine walking past her in the hallway and her ignoring me, like we never knew each other at all.

My throat tightens like it has the past few weeks, whenever I've thought about Caroline. Suddenly I need to stop thinking about school. I need to stop talking to my parents about it at least.

"Can we take a break and come back to this?" I say. This is something we talk about with Dr. Sugar. That any of us are supposed to be able to "take a break" from talking about something when it gets too stressful as long as we "come back to it" later either at home or during a session. Whenever I ask to "take a break and come back" to something, I think I sound like I'm forty years old.

"Sure," my mom says, taking the papers off the table and making a nice stack. She'll probably alphabetize them later and flag questions for Dr. Sugar with Post-its.

"Hey, Ethan," my dad says, "why don't we go by that frozen yogurt place? The one Jesse works at? You've been going over there to hang out and say hi?" This is what my dad does best: sensing a need for a change in our family rhythm and planning an outing.

It's not Tuesday or Thursday or Saturday, so Caroline won't be there. And maybe I could stand to get out of the house, although the idea that my dad thinks I "hang out" at the frozen yogurt place is both funny and sad.

"Okay," I say, and my mom smiles like she always does when the two of us do something together. Like she's fighting the urge to take a picture with her phone.

We take the Volvo, and on the way there, my dad and I make small talk. About my drumming. (It's going good.) About March Madness. (Kentucky will win.) About one of his patients that he saw that morning (a kindergartner who bites). I wonder if I had never been taken if I would have different kinds of conversations with my dad. Or if we would still just be having these forced talks about nothing much. Like I said, we didn't hang out a lot before. So maybe this is just the way it is and was always meant to be.

What sucks is not knowing for sure.

"Hey, I haven't seen Caroline around," my dad says suddenly. To him it's just more of the same. Small talk. He can't know how much her name makes me catch my breath.

"Yeah," I say, staring out the window. "She's been busy."

"I think you guys sounded really good together," my dad continues. "I hope she comes back soon."

"Yeah," I answer again. I haven't heard from Caroline since that night she ran off crying, and I haven't tried to text her or anything.

I stare out the window of the car. Caroline. Playing drums isn't as much fun without her. Writing lyrics isn't as easy. Even if I never got the guts to share them with her, it was like I was writing them for her to read eventually.

Nothing is as funny or interesting without her. We hadn't even really hung out outside of my garage, unless you count that one weird night at the creek. But even though I only really ever saw her at my house, it's like I feel her absence everywhere I go.

And it hurts like hell.

Dr. Greenberg says I have to give her time just like she

gave me time after that night we kissed. That I have to be willing to respect her need for space if we're ever going to be real friends again.

And I want to be real friends with her. Even if our friendship is based on the weirdest, most horrible thing. The idea of not being friends with her is actually more than I can let myself think about.

But it's been weeks, and she hasn't gotten in touch. And I'm scared I know what that means.

We pull into the Tom Thumb parking lot, and my dad starts steering the car toward the frozen yogurt place.

"Dad," I say, "can we not get frozen yogurt?" The idea of walking inside and maybe having to make small talk and force smiles with Jesse is so tiring.

My dad pulls into a parking spot and turns to look at me.

"Sure. I mean, yeah, we don't have to get any." He looks confused. "You mean you don't like it?"

"It's okay."

"But I thought your mom said you liked coming here?"

I shrug. "It's just a good place to come and practice, you know, being independent. While mom gets the grocery shopping done. But the stuff tastes like frozen cough medicine. Covered in sprinkles."

My dad laughs. "That does sound pretty nasty."

"It is."

I want to tell him, too, that being there reminds me of

Caroline. That I'm feeling down without her. But I don't tell him that part.

We sit there for a moment, staring at the mostly empty Tom Thumb parking lot.

"I have an idea," he says, all of a sudden, "for practicing independence."

"What?"

"You want to drive the Volvo?"

I give my dad a look. My eyebrows must be way up because he nods and says, "No, I'm serious."

"Is that even legal? I don't have a license or even a permit."

"What the hell," my dad answers, which is so unlike my dad. To swear, even a little, and to not care about the rules.

So before I can really realize it's happening, we are switching seats and my dad is showing me how to adjust the mirrors and the seat positioning. It feels so weird to be in the driver's seat.

"Okay, you want to ease on the gas very lightly," my dad says, and before I know it the car is moving, and I'm the one who's moving it.

"Hey!" I shout.

"Okay, okay, why don't you turn up there, over by the Dollar Tree."

I give the steering wheel a turn but it's too much, and we start heading toward the Payless instead.

"That's fine, I wanted a new pair of very cheap shoes

anyway," my dad says, and we both crack up a little. I maneuver the Volvo around for a good ten minutes until my dad says that's probably a decent amount of practice time. As I put the car in park, it hits me that my desire to learn how to drive is a lot stronger than my interest in going back to school. If I enroll as a high school junior next fall, I hope I can still keep getting behind the wheel of a car.

"That was so cool," I say, and I look at my dad and he is grinning so wide. A real grin, not one of his fake ones.

"That was cool," he tells me. And we sit there for a minute, me and my dad, and the rims of his eyes get a little red. "I never thought," he says, and his voice cracks, but only for a second, and he catches it. "I'd *hoped* for it, of course, but I never thought . . . I mean, I wasn't sure, that I would ever get to teach you to drive."

"Yeah, I bet," I say, not sure what to say. I reach out and pat my dad on the shoulder. Two quick pats. He looks at me and smiles and nods. We sit there for a while, the Volvo's engine humming. I think my dad has been trying to have Moments with me ever since I got back, but the thing about Moments is that when you try to have them, you can't. They only sneak up on you when you don't expect them.

"Okay, let's switch," my dad says, and when he gets back in the driver's seat and we start heading for home, he says, "Maybe let's not tell your mom about this yet. I mean, I'll tell her. I'm just trying to think of how to phrase it." He gives me a little wink.

"Okay," I say. "I won't tell her." I grin a little.

We drive the rest of the way home in a comfortable silence. When we pull into the driveway of our house, my dad says, "Ethan, I'm so glad you're home." As easy as anything. I mean, he's said it lots of times since I got back. But this time, it sounds different.

"Me, too, Dad," I say.

We get out of the car and I find my hand slipping into my pocket, checking to make sure my phone is there. I take it out and glance at it. No messages. I imagine texting Caroline and telling her all about getting to drive the Volvo and how cool it was. Maybe later I could even tell her that it actually felt good to hang out with my dad, just the two of us. I imagine how she would respond (*okay, mister volvo, does this mean you can come pick me up for practice so I don't have to lug my guitar to your house on my bike?*). Imagining this makes me smile a little.

But of course, there's no Caroline to tell anything to, so I let the smile fade from my face, and I follow my dad inside the house.

CAROLINE—312 DAYS AFTERWARD

AS I GLANCE OUTSIDE THE FRONT WINDOW, I CAN SEE MY DAD IS pushing the last box of his stuff into the back of his work van. I'm not sure what's inside, but it's one of five boxes he's taking from our house. My mom actually helped him pack everything up, and they're being, like, weirdly civil about everything. She just stands there, barefoot in jean shorts, her hands on her hips. Like my dad is just a houseguest who's lived with us for a while, and now it's time for him to move on.

I turn back toward the kitchen to check on Dylan when I hear my mother's voice calling me from the driveway.

"Caroline, do you know where I put the duct tape? We need to make sure this box is really closed."

Dylan is watching television. I grab the tape off the kitchen counter and head outside, anxious to go back in as soon as possible so I can keep an eye on my little brother.

"Here," I say as I come to the front door. I toss the tape, and my mother catches it. My dad doesn't look up.

I go back into the kitchen and start making grilled cheese sandwiches for lunch. It's been a few weeks since my dad moved out, and today is just about him coming back to get all his stuff. It's been a few weeks, too, since I last spoke to or hung out with Ethan. It's weird how only one of those things makes me sad, and it's not the one most people would assume.

My dad leaving isn't the only big change. My mom got a job last week, too, as the attendance clerk at the middle school where Dylan is supposed to go in the fall. She was so excited after she got her district employee badge, she wore it home.

"Check it out!" she said, spinning around in the kitchen, pointing to the laminated tag she had pinned to her collar. It was one of the first times I'd really seen her smile since my dad left.

I take one of Dylan's blue plastic plates and put a grilled cheese sandwich on it and then take it over to the coffee table in front of the television set.

"Here, Dylan, eat your sandwich."

Dylan shakes his head no and pushes the plate and the sandwich off the table to the floor where it falls with a clatter. He immediately begins sucking his fingers.

"Dylan, no, that's not nice," I say, and I pick the plate up off the floor and put it back on the coffee table. I brush the dirty sandwich clean and put it back on the plate. When I turn around I hear a clatter again. I look back and the plate is on the floor again.

I roll my eyes, fighting frustration. Just then my dad walks in with my mom behind him.

"Hey, guys," my dad says. He's wearing one of his shirts from work. It says Bugs-B-Gone and has a picture of a sad cartoon roach on its back kicking its legs in the air. That shirt has always icked me out. I'm glad I won't have to see as much of it anymore.

"Hey," I say. Dylan eyes him from the couch where he is sitting.

"Can we talk for a sec?" he says.

"I thought we already did the divorce talk," I say, just to be a snot, and my mom sighs, which is the only reason I give in and go and sit down next to Dylan.

"Listen, I know you understand I'm not going to be living here anymore," my dad says, and I sort of zone out for a minute as he talks. It's so weird to be sitting here, the four of us, when I've never really felt like we're much of a family to begin with. Maybe when I was little, when Dylan was really tiny, before everything started to totally fall apart. Maybe then. I remember my dad would sometimes barbeque in the backyard and stop to spray me with the garden hose. I was really little, but I remember. So I have that.

"I want you to know we can still see each other, and I'm going to come by each Wednesday to take you out to eat," he says.

No you won't, I think to myself. But it doesn't matter. I only wonder if Dylan understands anything he's saying.

"The important thing is that your mom and I love you both a lot," he says, and I swear, he got this speech from the Internet or something it's so scripted.

After he's done he stands up and reaches out to hug me and I hug him back and he smells like sweat and guy deodorant.

"Bye, Dad," I say, and my throat clenches up for the tiniest moment and I will it to stop and it does. I step back and watch as he rubs Dylan's hair. "Bye, buddy," he says, and Dylan just nods and sits there.

My mom walks him to the front door, and I hear some low voices and the door shutting. When she comes back to the kitchen her eyes are wet, but she's not hysterical or anything.

"I'm going to pack school lunches for tomorrow," she says, and I can tell she is anxious to be busy.

"Well don't pack grilled cheese," I say. "He's not eating it." I nod my head toward Dylan.

"Okay," my mom says. I lean back against the kitchen counter and take a bite of my own sandwich and watch as my mom packs our lunches.

"You doing okay, mom?" I ask.

"Oh," she says, her voice cracking a little. "Yeah, mostly."

I finish my sandwich in silence and think about what it's going to be like to live here just the three of us. It's already been a little bit better these past few weeks. No fights or screaming. No late night slams of the door that wake up Dylan and make him scream. No beer for my mom, who got rid of all the alcohol in the house. That means no beer for me, either, which is probably a good thing.

I put my dish in the sink and tell my mom I'm going to my room.

"Okay, sweetheart," she says, and I admit she looks kind of sort of okay. I never really realized it before, but my mom is kind of tough.

In my room, I take out my guitar and pluck away at it. I left my amp at Ethan's, and I've thought about going to get it. But I don't know what I would say if I saw him there. And let's face it. He's almost always there.

I pick at the strings and let the images from the horror story he told me flicker through my head like I sometimes do—even when I don't want them to. I squeeze my eyes tight and slide my guitar to the side. Then I curl up in bed, my eyes on the wall where I've tacked up pictures of Kathleen Hanna and Poly Styrene that I cut out from magazines my cousin sent me. I think about trying to make peace with Emma just to have someone to talk to, or texting one of the girls who sits at the same table as me at lunch and who does stupid class group projects with me. I even think about texting Jesse, just to feel less lonely.

But the only person I honestly want to talk to is Ethan.

I think about the stuff I would text him if I were texting him right now. About my dad. About my mom's new job. About the level of disgust achieved by this new frozen yogurt flavor at the store called Peanut Butter Shazaam. About songs I want to play with him.

I miss texting Ethan. I miss being around him.

But how could the Ethan I like be the Ethan who did what he did to my brother?

Ever since he told me what happened, I haven't felt less guilty. Just more guilty. More guilty that I wasn't watching Dylan that day. More guilty with the realization that if I had been watching him, he wouldn't have had Ethan put a gun to his head.

I shake my head in frustration. No, that's not right. Not really. If Ethan couldn't even figure out how to run away from that bastard, how could he find a way to help my brother? He couldn't even help himself.

My stomach knots up, and I wish it were hours later and I could just drift off to sleep. But it's three in the afternoon on a Sunday, and my dad just moved out for good. In the kitchen my mom is trying to keep things going, and my little brother won't eat.

My throat freezes up again like it did when I hugged my father goodbye, only this time, all alone in my room, I let the tears snake their way out. I cry until I'm all cried out. Until no tears are left.

ETHAN—315 DAYS AFTERWARD

DR. GREENBERG KEEPS A CALENDAR HANGING ON THE WALL BEHIND his messy desk. It has pictures of birds, and I know from what he's told me that he's a "birder." Sometimes he drives down to High Island on the coast, which is a good spot to see exotic birds. He keeps track of the ones he sees in a notebook.

"Why do you write them down?" I'd asked him once.

"I guess to make it official somehow," he'd said with a smile. "Of course, that's not a very good answer. But that's the best one I can come up with."

That was the weird kind of answer that left me sort of unsettled when I'd first started seeing Dr. Greenberg. Made me wonder if he was even qualified to be a therapist. But now it's the kind of answer that makes me think I can trust him more than anyone. Because he doesn't do bullshit.

Dr. Greenberg's calendar is turned to April. A black-and-yellow bird is perched on a tree branch, and its mouth is open in a forever chirp.

April. Almost a year since I came back.

When I say as much to Dr. Greenberg, he nods.

"I was just thinking that the other day," he says. "I don't know how you feel, but when I think about it, it seems like yesterday. And in the same moment as if it were a very long time ago."

"Yeah," I nod. "Exactly. Sometimes I try to picture it and it feels real and sometimes it feels like a dream."

Dr. Greenberg nods. "I remember the first time I saw you at your house. You looked very different."

I must frown because Dr. Greenberg smiles. "You did. I remember I walked into your living room and you were sitting on the couch next to your mother, and you looked so small and scared, like you were going in sink into the couch cushions."

I try to pull back that time. Those first days home. Staring at my parents. Blinking my eyes over and over again like I was trying to wash off some film that made everything feel slightly unreal. Convinced if I fell asleep I would wake up and be back in a nightmare.

"It's been hard," I say. "Like, exhausting."

"It has been," says Dr. Greenberg. "And you've done it with so much grace, Ethan. So much strength."

I glance down, embarrassed. "Maybe," I say.

We sit there, and Groovy climbs up onto the couch and nuzzles me under my hand. He's just been groomed, so his fur is super soft.

"You're feeling okay about school in the fall?" Dr. Greenberg asks.

"It's still four months away," I say. "But mostly, yeah. I mean, I'm curious."

"About what?"

"About being around a lot of people my age. About what high school is like. I mean, high school is this thing you're supposed to experience, you know?"

Dr. Greenberg grins. "You're right. The prom, senior prank day, things like that."

I smile. "Wait, senior prank day?"

"I'm old, but I'm not from the Dark Ages," Dr. Greenberg says. "My classmates and I filled the entire main hallway with balloons. We spent hours blowing them up. We were so light-headed. Then the next day no one could get to class. It was marvelous."

I try to picture a teenage Dr. Greenberg, and all I can imagine is a skinnier, younger body with an old Dr. Greenberg head.

"Did you get in trouble?" I ask.

"No," he says. "The principal was very forgiving, fortunately. The class the year before had let chickens run through the building, so really, he was grateful."

"Chickens?"

"Yes!" he says. "Live chickens, can you believe it?" Then he chuckles and says with a sigh, "Teenagers."

I scratch Groovy's silky head. "It seems so weird that teenagers back then would do stuff that was so stupid," I say.

"Really?" Dr. Greenberg says. "What makes you say so?"

I shrug. "I don't know. Old movies and stuff. They always make the olden days seem, like, more polite or something."

Dr. Greenberg shakes his head. "Teenagers have always been teenagers. Every generation thinks it invented adolescence," he tells me. "But the truth is, it's been around for a very long time."

We're quiet for a while, and then I bring up Caroline. Or rather, I bring up the fact that nothing much has changed since our last session.

"We still haven't talked," I admit.

"Let me ask the classic therapist question," he says. "How do you feel about that?"

"It kind of sucks," I say. "I mean, it sucks a lot."

"How come?"

"Because . . . ," I struggle to find the right words, "even if Caroline and I had this strange thing that bonded us, even if things got weird between us for a while, the truth is, I just liked being around her. She made me feel . . . calm somehow. And she was pretty funny, too. And really good at guitar.

I don't know. I just liked being with her. I liked being friends with her."

Dr. Greenberg listens and nods.

"Before you told her what happened with her brother, we discussed the possibility that telling her about what happened would mean you wouldn't be friends with her anymore, right?"

I nod.

"Right now, you and Caroline aren't talking. Aren't friends. How are you handling that?"

I think about it, and there's an ache at the back of my throat.

"It's shitty," I tell him. "But I'm getting through it. I'm playing my music. I'm thinking about what might come next for me. School. Learning how to drive."

Dr. Greenberg nods, his expression firm and certain. "You are getting through it," he says.

"Do you think that people are really fated to know each other?" I ask. "To be in the same . . . what did you call it?"

"Karass?" Dr. Greenberg says. "I don't know. The issue of fate versus free will is something that the human race has puzzled over since we had words for these things. I suppose what some people call fate others call God."

"I still don't know what I believe," I say. "Like, if I was fated to get to be friends with Caroline, to be in the same karass with her, that means I was fated to be taken. And if I was fated to be taken, what was the point of it if my friendship with Caroline only lasted a few months anyway?"

Dr. Greenberg crosses his legs one way and sighs and then crosses them the other way and sighs again.

"You ask really hard questions," he tells me.

"Well, you went to Harvard," I shoot back with a smirk, and he laughs with his whole body for a minute. When he calms down he says, "Thank you for making me laugh. It freed me up to remember this quote. Do you know who Voltaire was?"

"No," I say.

"He was a French writer and philosopher during the Enlightenment."

"Oh," I say. "So I guess a bigger deal than Harvard."

"Maybe a little," Dr. Greenberg agrees. "Anyway, there's this quote that's attributed to him that I've always liked. 'Each player must accept the cards life deals him, but once they are in hand, he alone must decide how to play the cards in order to win the game.'"

I ask Dr. Greenberg to repeat himself, and he does, and then he asks me what I think Voltaire meant.

"Well," I say, "I think he's saying that bad stuff is going to happen to us and good stuff is going to happen to us, but how we handle it is what matters in the end."

"Exactly," Dr. Greenberg says.

"But Dr. Greenberg, that's so obvious," I say, throwing

up my hands. "I mean, I don't mean to be a dick about it, but come on. I mean, yeah, in the end all that matters is how you deal with it. But that idea doesn't make anything better when bad things happen."

"No," Dr. Greenberg says, shaking his head. "It doesn't."

I slump down on the couch.

"But that sucks."

"Yes," says Dr. Greenberg, "it does."

"Sorry I picked on Voltaire," I say.

"It's okay."

"The card metaphor was interesting."

Dr. Greenberg's eyes crinkle up and he laughs. "You don't have to humor me, Ethan."

Groovy sighs and rolls on his back, stretching all four paws into the air. I chew on my thumbnail for a minute. "Dr. Greenberg?" I ask. "Do you think I'm getting better?" I think about all the reasons I'm not. I still sleep with the lights on. I still have nightmares that make me wake up sweating. I still don't feel normal or like other kids, and I'm really nervous about what going back to school will be like.

His eyes go soft. "Oh, Ethan, when you first started coming here you were as quiet as a mouse," he says. "You stared out the window more than you looked at me. And now you're wrestling with difficult questions, and you're doing a really good job at it. You're talking about how you feel, you're thinking about the future in a healthy way, you're working on relationships with the people around you, and you're honest as hell. Yes, Ethan, I think you're getting better. As much as any of this can be measured that way."

"Yeah?" I ask.

"Is my approval important to you?"

"Yeah, I think," I say. "I don't know why, but it is."

"I hope you believe that I'm telling you the truth, because yes, I think you're getting better, and I mean it."

I nod. I let myself smile a little, and I tell Dr. Greenberg thank you.

We spend the last few minutes of my session talking about nothing all that interesting, like how hot it's already starting to get and what I'm reading with Mrs. Leander. But what I really want to tell Dr. Greenberg in that moment is that I'm so glad he's my therapist. That I'm so glad he's a part of my life. I don't say it because there is a small part of me that thinks it could be weird to say it even if there's a bigger part of me that knows he wouldn't mind. But maybe I don't say it because I don't have to. Maybe, probably, he already knows.

· · · · · · · ·

When my mom pulls into the driveway of our house, I'm not surprised to see Caroline pulling up on her bike, her dark ponytail flying out behind her. It's the weirdest timing. If she'd come a moment sooner, I wouldn't have been home. Maybe she would have left. But the timing is perfect.

"Caroline's here," I say, like I want to prove it to myself.

"She hasn't been here in a while," my mother says. "Do you want to ask her to stay for dinner?" I glance at my mom all surprised because this is the first time she's ever offered.

"I don't know if she'll want to," I say. "But I can ask." We get out of the car.

"Hey," I say to Caroline.

"Hey," she says back. I read her face, trying to find a smile in her eyes or anywhere, but her expression is neutral.

"I'm going in the house, but let me know if you need anything," my mom says, and I notice as she walks away she doesn't look over her shoulder ten times to see if I'm still standing where she left me.

"So what's up?" says Caroline.

"I just got back from therapy," I say.

"Was it a good meeting? I mean . . . session."

"Yeah," I say.

The April sun is beating down on us. I ask Caroline if she wants to go to the garage where at least there's some shade. She says sure. I notice she doesn't have her guitar with her, and I realize maybe she's just here to pick up her amp. Disappointment tugs at me.

I sit down at my drums, and she flops down on the cement

like always, which makes me think at least she's not just going to grab her amp and take off.

"So my life is basically pretty shitty," she announces all of a sudden. "My dad finally left, which is good, but which is also shitty. My mom got a job, which is good, but it also means I have more responsibility around the house, which is also shitty. My brother has good days which are good and shitty days which are shitty. So . . . there you go."

"That's a lot of shitty," I say.

"No shit," says Caroline, and I know for the first time that things are going to be okay.

"Caroline," I start, "about the last time we hung out . . . and what I told you . . ."

Caroline looks up at me, her face open. Her expression hopeful.

"I wish I hadn't told you sometimes because I feel like you aren't ever going to forgive me. But at the same time, I know I wouldn't have ever been able to keep being friends with you otherwise. It would have felt like I was lying."

Caroline tips her head forward, drops her chin on her bent knees. Her long ponytail slides over one shoulder in an S. It's quiet. Not even the dog next door is barking. All I hear is the air conditioner at the side of the house cycling on, rattling around like it's working up the strength to survive a long Texas summer.

"I forgive you," she says. "But I don't think there's

anything to forgive you for, really. You were in a horrible situation. You were scared for your own life."

I reach down for my drumsticks to have something to do with my hands. I run my thumbs on the wood, and I flip the sticks through my fingers.

"I still wish I hadn't done it," I say, my voice quiet.

"Well, I still wish I hadn't taken my eyes off my brother that afternoon," says Caroline.

"I still wish I hadn't taken that bike ride all those years ago," I respond.

"I still wish my brother didn't have so many problems," she answers.

It's quiet again, and Caroline looks up at me, her eyes glassy.

"I was talking about this stuff with my therapist today," I tell her. "Like what's free will and what's fate and how do we cope with the cards we're given in life."

Caroline sighs. "Sounds heavy duty."

"Yeah, but in a good way," I tell her.

"If you hadn't taken that bike ride and if my brother hadn't had problems and run off like he did, maybe we would never have gotten to really know each other," she says. "Which is weird to think about. Sometimes I wish we'd just met at the pool."

I grin for the first time since we started talking. "Yeah. Maybe in some parallel universe, we do."

I twirl my drumsticks but one of them slips from my hands and lands with a clatter near Caroline's feet. She reaches for it and hands it toward me.

"We could try to make this a good summer, Ethan," says Caroline. "We could try to make it great."

"Yeah," I say, "I'd like that." And I smile at Caroline and she smiles at me.

We sit there for a bit, and then I ask her, "How come you didn't bring your guitar?"

"I was picking up an extra shift at work," she says. "I felt this urge to come by after."

"Why?" I ask.

She shrugs her shoulders. "It was like a little voice told me it was time," she says. "And I had to listen to it."

"I'm glad you did," I tell her.

"Me, too," she says.

I tell her my mom wants her to stay for dinner and she shoots me a mock shocked expression, and I laugh. And then before I know it we are talking about my parents and school and music and it's so easy, just the two of us in my driveway on a late spring afternoon.

CAROLINE—329 DAYS AFTERWARD

WHEN I GET HOME FROM SCHOOL, MY MOM IS THROWING A FEW LAST ingredients into the slow cooker. Dylan is lining up his blocks by the television. He looks up when I come in, and I give him a little wave. He goes back to his blocks.

"Hey," my mom says.

"Hey," I answer.

"Mom," I tell her, motioning to her collar, "you still have your work badge on."

"Oh, jeez, I forgot," she says, unclipping it and placing the laminated card carefully on the counter, like it's something valuable. And maybe it is. I know she likes her job. Likes getting up and going somewhere every morning. Likes earning her own money. I think my dad is sending checks once in a while, but I'm not sure. The other night after I put Dylan to bed, I caught her at the kitchen table, adding and subtracting numbers on a sheet of lined paper. When I asked if everything was okay, she nodded but her smile was forced.

But still, life in our house has been so much quieter since my dad moved out. I'm not constantly counting the minutes until the next big scene. Even Dylan has seemed a little better. But he still melts down more than he used to. He still screams and shrieks at the most unexpected moments.

"Job's going okay?" I ask, taking out plates to set the table.

"Yeah, real good," she says, stirring what's inside the pot with a large spoon. I smell tomato sauce and chicken. I don't miss frozen pizza.

"I think it's really good that you're working," I tell her. I know it's cheesy, but I add, "I'm proud of you."

She glances up at me suddenly, like she's really looking at me for the first time since I walked in. "Hey," she says, and her cheeks dimple. "That's real nice. Thanks, Caroline."

"Sure," I say.

"You have work tomorrow?" she asks.

"Yes," I tell her. "And then maybe hang out at Ethan's."

Before my dad moved out, I didn't even tell my mom I'd been biking over there. It was like she couldn't handle knowing more than the day-to-day basics of our lives, and sometimes not even that. But ever since it's been just the three of us, it's all "Where are you going?" and "When will you get back?" Which is annoying and comforting at the same time.

"You're playing music with him, hmm?" she asks.

"Yeah. He's good at the drums."

My mom thinks it's weird I go there. I know she does. I haven't told her anything he's said about Dylan, and I don't know that I can. At least not yet. I told her I just drove by one day because I was curious, and we started talking. And anyway, his dad is our dentist, and it's Dove Lake. So it's not like any of us are actual strangers.

But still. I'm pretty sure she thinks the whole thing is weird.

"You know, Ethan sees a therapist," I say, folding paper towels into neat rectangles and setting them next to my plate, my mom's plate, and one of Dylan's plastic blue plates. "His whole family does."

"Well, that makes sense after everything they went through," my mom says.

"He says it really helps."

"I'm sure it does." Her voice is tight. She's staring at the slow cooker and moving the ladle in little circles. Her mouth is in a firm line.

"Mom, we went through something, too," I say, my voice even. "We did."

My mom takes the ladle out of the cooker and sets it down on the counter. I swallow, my throat dry. She holds her hands up to her face and presses her fingers against her eyes.

"I just wish . . . ," she starts. She takes a breath. Then another. Then her shoulders start to shake a little.

"Mom?" I ask. My eyes glance at Dylan, but he doesn't seem to notice what's happening. "Mom?" I leave the table where I've been putting down the napkins and move toward her. My mom and I aren't huggers. We've never been, like, BFF mom and daughter. I've always thought that kind of duo is gross, anyway.

But she's my mom. And she's made mistakes, but she's never left us. She never would.

She's doing the best she can.

Like Dylan.

Like Ethan.

Like Ethan's parents.

Like me, too.

I put my hand on my mom's shoulder and give it a little squeeze.

"I just want . . . things to be okay," she says to me in a whisper, her hands still covering her face. For the first time, I notice a white line where her wedding ring used to be.

"I want things to be okay, too," I say. "But maybe things could be okay faster if we got some help. Someone to talk to. I think it could be good."

"I don't know," my mom answers, and finally she lowers her hands and looks across the room at Dylan. Her eyes are wet. She chews at her bottom lip a bit. "It's a lot of money," she says at last.

"Yeah," I say. "But maybe Ethan could ask his therapist?

About, like, therapists who donate their time? Or something?"

My mom bites at her lip again. "Yeah," she says, her voice cracking. "Maybe."

My mom shuts her eyes tight and pushes out a few more tears, then dabs at her eyes with a dishtowel. "I'm sorry, Caroline. For these past few months. They've been awful."

"Yeah, but it'll get better," I tell her, hesitation in my voice. I want to trust my own words. I want my mom to trust them, too.

"Okay," she says, and she smiles at me with her eyes, and I think maybe she does.

ETHAN—390 DAYS AFTERWARD

IN THE MIDDLE OF MAY, THE FLETCHERS MOVED AWAY, AND THEY TOOK Missy the Chihuahua with them. My mom told me they decided to move to a senior living facility in Austin so they could be near their daughter.

When my family walked over to say goodbye to them one Sunday afternoon before they got in their car to drive away, Mrs. Fletcher reached over and hugged me goodbye. Her hug was surprisingly tight and strong.

"We promised ourselves we'd stay until you came back," she whispered into my ear.

I wasn't sure what I was supposed to say back, but I remembered when I was little, how Mrs. Fletcher would hand me little peppermint candies over the fence that separated our yards.

"Thanks," I said, and she let me go, and I looked at my feet, a little embarrassed.

Their house has been vacant for over a month, but this morning when I walk outside to get the paper for my parents, I notice a big white moving van backing into the driveway. A man in khaki shorts and a yellow Polo and a woman in a green sundress are standing on the lawn watching the movers open the back of the van and begin to haul out boxes. The woman is holding a baby on one hip. She lifts her free hand up over her eyes to block out the sun.

"A family's moved in next door," I tell my mom. She's loading the dishwasher from breakfast.

"What did they look like?"

"Parents and at least one kid. A baby."

"I'll make them some banana bread to take over there tonight when we get back from Dr. Greenberg's."

"I'll help you make it," I say, and my mom smiles at me. A totally happy smile with no tears.

After my appointment we make the bread and wait for it to cool, and then my mom wraps it in tinfoil and ties a red ribbon around it, making sure to curl the ends with scissors. The two of us are about to leave our house when my mother's cell phone buzzes. She glances down.

"It's grandma," she tells me, sliding the banana bread into my hands. "You go on ahead. I'll meet you there in a second."

I blink, trying to believe what I've just heard. My mom is sending me into the world. Alone. It's pretty incredible.

I walk across the yard and when I get to the front door, I ring the doorbell.

The woman in the green sundress opens the door. She's still holding the baby. I think it's a girl. It's got dark curls and is wearing a diaper and a pink T-shirt that says "Little Stinker."

"Hi," the lady says, pushing some stray hairs back from her face. There are stacks of boxes in the entryway behind her.

"Hey," I say, searching for the right polite words. "Uh, I live next door? With my parents? We know you're new to the neighborhood, and we made you banana bread?" I hold it out awkwardly.

"Oh!" the lady says, and she smiles and takes the bread. "My name's Abigail," she tells me. Then she yells over her shoulder and up the stairs. "Miguel, come down and say hello to our new neighbors!"

A little boy, maybe seven or eight, gallops down toward us. His dark brown hair is messy, and there are faint traces of green and blue Magic Marker all over his arms.

"This is my son, Miguel. My husband's not here right now. He made a run to the grocery store to get us the bare necessities to be able to feed these kiddos and keep them alive." She laughs at her own joke. I smile back, and then I realize I haven't told her my name.

"I'm Ethan," I say. "My parents and I live next door, like I said, and my mom is coming over any sec." I glance toward our house, then shove my hands in my pockets. I'm not sure what else to say or do.

"Mama, I can't find my Transformers," Miguel says, tugging at his mother's dress. He looks at me warily.

"Oh, sweetie, I don't know where your Transformers are in this mess," she says. She shifts "Little Stinker" from one hip to the next.

"I'm seven," Miguel tells me suddenly.

I nod and give him a little smile. "I'm sixteen," I tell him. Then I add, "I used to play with Transformers. They're pretty cool." Miguel smiles, and I can see one of his top front teeth is missing.

I sense Abigail looking at me, and I wonder if she's putting it together. A few of the local stations tried to run pieces about me when we hit the one-year anniversary of me being found, but I decided I didn't want to do any more interviews, so there wasn't anything in the paper or on television. But maybe this woman recognizes me anyway. Maybe she knows she's just moved her family next door to a famous kidnapping victim.

Just then, fortunately, my mother calls out hello as she crosses the yard between us, and she and Abigail start talking in their high-pitched lady voices and I'm left sort of standing there. I grin at Miguel again and he grins back, but mostly he wiggles around, bored. Abigail tells my mom the baby's name is Isabella, and they just moved here from the Valley because her husband has been named assistant superintendent for the school district.

"Well, please let us know if there's anything we can do to help as you get settled in," my mother says.

Just then, Miguel tugs on his mother's dress again.

"Mama, I need my Transformers real bad," he pleads.

Abigail rolls her eyes at us and then looks at my mother and says, "Please tell me it gets easier?"

My mother glances at me and in a voice that I think only I can tell is a little bit sad, she tells Abigail with a soft smile, "Yes, it does."

We say goodbye and then head back home. My mom goes inside, and I practice my drums until my dad gets back from work. That night, after dinner, we're all hanging out watching television when my phone buzzes.

On my way—those lyrics you sent me this morning were your best yet

I smile so big my face hurts. I text back.

Shut up—stop making fun of me

Dude I am speaking the truth and you know it so shut up yourself

Whatever get over here

Well if you stop texting back I can get on my bike okay?

K

I thought I told you stop texting me back!!!

I laugh out loud.

"What's so funny?" my dad asks from the family room couch where he and my mom are trying to decide what to watch next.

"Caroline," I say, looking up from my phone.

"I like Caroline," says my dad. "She's full of beans." And my mom smiles because even though she's never come out and said it, I know she likes Caroline, too.

I head outside to the garage just as she is pulling up on her ten-speed. She slides her guitar case off and dumps the bike on the lawn like always. She sets the case down and undoes her messy ponytail, runs her fingers through her hair, then ties it back up again. Her face is slick with sweat.

"Damn, it's hot," she says.

"I know," I say. "You still want to play?"

"Seriously?" she asks me. "Artists have to suffer for their art, you know."

I roll my eyes at her, and she rolls hers back at me.

"So I wasn't lying about your lyrics," she says, opening her case. "They really are my favorite so far."

"Yeah?" I ask, trying to be casual about it.

"Yeah," she says, and she looks me in the eyes. "I'm already thinking up a song to go with them."

"Okay," I say. "So what are we waiting for? Let's go."

I sit down at my drums, and Caroline plugs in her Fender. She takes a minute to tune it and then nods at me, and I pick up my drumsticks to count off. And as I do, I catch her eye, and she grins because she knows. She knows we've got a million songs ahead of us, all of them waiting to be found, and we can't wait to play every single one of them together.

AUTHOR'S NOTE

CASES LIKE ETHAN'S AND DYLAN'S ARE, THANKFULLY, INCREDIBLY rare. But just as the tiny percentage of children taken in stereotypical kidnappings need our help, so do endangered runaways and children in family abduction cases. For more information, please visit the National Center for Missing & Exploited Children at www.missingkids.com. If you think you've seen a missing child, contact the center 24 hours a day, 7 days a week, at 1-800-THE-LOST (1-800-843-5678).

If you or someone you know needs information about sexual assault, please call the National Sexual Assault Hotline operated by RAINN (Rape, Abuse & Incest National Network) at 1-800-656-HOPE. You can also go to rainn.org for more information or to use the Online Hotline. Services are free, confidential, and available 24 hours a day, 7 days a week.

Please visit autismspeaks.org for more information on autism.

ACKNOWLEDGMENTS

AS A FORMER JOURNALIST, I TEND TO ENJOY THE RESEARCH
component of writing a novel almost as much as the writing
itself, a tendency I was particularly grateful for when crafting
this book. Ethan and Caroline's story would not exist without
the enormous help and guidance of numerous mental health
professionals who gave of their time and knowledge to help
me create what I hope is a realistic and compassionate por-
trayal of two teenagers who are healing from trauma.

Frank Ochberg, MD, a pioneer in the area of trauma science and an expert on post-traumatic stress disorder, was incredibly generous with his time and wisdom. The counting
technique used in this novel by Dr. Greenberg is based
on the actual Counting Method developed by Dr. Ochberg to
treat PTSD. Dr. Ochberg's assistance made this book a reality, and I am forever thankful.

Rebecca Bailey, PhD, of Transitioning Families also pro-
vided incredible insight into what the therapy process would
look like for a young man like Ethan, and she answered my
questions with warmth and with language a layperson like me
could readily grasp. Her book *Safe Kids, Smart Parents: What
Parents Need to Know to Keep Their Children Safe* is a valuable re-
source for any mom or dad. Dr. Bailey is to thank for the
character of Groovy the dog.

Other mental health professionals who must also be
thanked for their time and feedback include Laura Davie,
LICSW; Ellen Safier, LCSW; Suzanne Senn, MS, LPC; and
Nathalie Wolk, PhD.

I would like to thank Zachary Gilley and Elaine Cagle for
being so brave and willing to share their personal stories with
me. You both trusted a nervous, strange voice over the phone
who wanted to ask questions about difficult life experiences,
and you both shared so honestly and openly. I'm forever
grateful to you both and in awe of your resilience.

The lovely and amazing writer Christa Desir was willing
to take time out of her incredibly busy schedule to read an
early draft of this book, and she helped me trust that I was
telling Ethan's story with authenticity and compassion.
Christa, you are so giving of your spirit, and your work with
survivors of sexual assault is one of the many reasons I ad-
mire you so much. One day we will meet in person, and I'll
blush out of nervousness and happiness.

In developing the character of Dylan, I must thank the writer Cammie McGovern for her sensitivity and feedback, and for being willing to read a very rough first draft. Cammie, I'm so glad that through this process I not only gained terrific guidance in creating the character of Dylan, but also gained a friend.

I must also thank Jelisa Scott, MA, BCBA, for her willingness to read and critique the manuscript in regard to the character of Dylan.

Thank you to Lieutenant John McGalin, Homicide Division, Houston Police Department, for answering questions about police procedures surroundings cases like Ethan's.

Huge thanks to supporters and friends who are always there for me as I wrestle with title questions, plot questions, book business questions, and the like, including Liz Peterson, Kate Sowa, Julie Murphy, Jessica Taylor, Summer Heacock, Leigh Bardugo, Emmy Laybourne, Ava Dellaira, Tamarie Cooper, the YAHOUs, and all the great people at Blue Willow Bookshop, especially Cathy Berner and Valerie Koehler.

Thank you to Sarah LaPolla and the folks at Bradford Literary. Thank you to the staff, faculty, and students of The Awty International School and Bellaire High School.

Many thanks to my agent Kerry Sparks and everyone at Levine Greenberg Rostan. I'm so very lucky to have you on my side.

Katherine Jacobs, editor of my dreams and kindred spirit, I don't know how you manage to do it, but you take these words I send you and you turn them into a book I'm proud of, and you do it in a way that makes me trust myself and believe I can be a better writer with each book I tackle. Thank you so much, Kate.

A million thanks to everyone at Roaring Brook Press and Macmillan, especially Mary Van Akin, the hardest-working publicist in the business.

And as always, many thanks to my family for being so supportive. Enormous thanks to my dear and talented husband Kevin, who answered all of my music questions and made me sound like I actually knew something about playing drums and guitar. Texas-sized love to you and Elliott forever.